NIGHT
IS THE
HUNTER

NIGHT
IS THE
HUNTER

A HARLAN DONNALLY NOVEL

STEVEN
GORE

wm

WILLIAM MORROW

An Imprint of HarperCollins*Publishers*

NIGHT IS THE HUNTER. Copyright © 2015 by Steven Gore. All rights reserved. Printed in the United States of America. No part of this book may be used or reproduced in any manner whatsoever without written permission except in the case of brief quotations embodied in critical articles and reviews. For information address HarperCollins Publishers, 195 Broadway, New York, NY 10007.

HarperCollins books may be purchased for educational, business, or sales promotional use. For information please e-mail the Special Markets Department at SPsales@harpercollins.com.

FIRST EDITION

Designed by Diahann Sturge

Library of Congress Cataloging-in-Publication Data has been applied for.

ISBN 978-0-06-202509-8

15 16 17 18 19   OV/RRD   10 9 8 7 6 5 4 3 2 1

For my mother-in-law,
Alice Zlatka Litov,
from dawn to daylight

Twilight, a timid fawn, went glimmering by,
And Night, the dark-blue hunter, followed fast,
Ceaseless pursuit and flight were in the sky,
But the long chase had ceased for us at last.

—"THE REFUGE," GEORGE WILLIAM RUSSELL

NIGHT
IS THE
HUNTER

CHAPTER 1 ===========

Ray McMullin, standing waist deep in chest waders, leaning hard into the current, his rod bent against the steelhead's run, wasn't a fisherman.

It had been two days on the river and Harlan Donnally was still waiting for the aging judge to explain why he'd made the nine-hour drive up from San Francisco to the northwest corner of the state, had been willing to sleep on frozen ground and wake to sunless dawns and to stand shivering as he did now in a twisting breeze that whirled the drifting snow and swayed the redwoods lining the banks.

Donnally pointed at the rod. "Keep the tip up and the line taut."

McMullin reached toward the drag on the front of his reel.

"Don't. Better leave it light." Donnally spread his arms to encompass the wide riffle in front of them and the stretches of smooth water above and below. "He can run, but he can't hide."

Donnally watched McMullin's lined and windburned face, looking for a reaction, suspecting since the judge first arrived that while he might not be hiding, he was running.

The rod bucked with the steelhead's head shakes as it ended its flight downstream and turned back into the current. It held there, the line tight, vibrating in the wind at a timbre too high for human ears, snowflakes veining the top of the nine feet of brown graphite. Then another buck and the ridge of snow rose from the rod, seemed to hesitate in the air, then tumbled and dissolved in the rushing water.

"Raise your tip. A slow pull. Don't let him use the current to rest."

The steelhead drove into the flow, using muscles evolution had given it to fight upstream from the Pacific, through the mouth of the Smith River and then hundreds of miles under rising rapids and over waterfalls to its spawning grounds, and finally again to the sea.

A ten-second burst brought the fish even with them. It leaped, a flash of silver, twelve pounds of body and fin tail-walking the surface, then crashed back into the water. A second leap, another burst, and it was fifteen yards upstream. More head shakes and then the line went slack.

The judge lowered his rod. "He's gone."

Donnally levered it back up. "Reel. Hard. He's coming at you."

The judge worked the handle, his red knuckles whitening, his jaw clenched, his eyes tearing in the breeze. Twenty turns later, the line tightened, and the rod bucked again, then plunged down and held.

"Now try to pull him toward you."

McMullin braced the cork butt against his wader belt and raised the rod. It gave. He reeled again as he lowered it, then raised it and reeled, raised it and reeled.

Donnally reached into his Landing Hand, a mesh pocket designed to preserve the fish's protective membrane as he held it.

"We don't want to tire him out too much. Lead him to me and let's unhook him."

The steelhead glided toward them in a slow surrender, his lid-less cold eyes staring up at them.

McMullin eased it close to Donnally, already wrist deep in the near-frozen water. He cupped his palm under the fish's body and secured his fingers around the tail just above the fin and the judge unhooked the barbless hook from its jaw.

Donnally released his grip.

The fish hung there, its gill covers pulsing, inhaling oxygen from the water; then with a flick of its tail, it wheeled into the current and was gone.

Donnally straightened up and looked at McMullin as though into a mirror distorted by time. Brown eyes and hair to brown eyes and hair, his five eleven to the judge's six feet. Forty-eight to seventy-four. Donnally's shoulders a few inches wider and squared to the older man's slumped and rounded.

It had been the judge's fourth hookup during the two days they'd been on the river, and none of the times had McMullin smiled, and after each Donnally had to instruct him again in the craft of fighting steelhead.

"You going to tell me what's been on your mind or are we just going to keep beating up fish?"

The judge didn't respond. He just gazed out at the river, his face bearing the same intensity, his lips pressed together, his eyebrows narrowed, that Donnally had observed both from the witness box and in chambers during the seventeen years he'd been a San Francisco police officer. It was that expression that always represented to Donnally what McMullin was as a human being. Unlike so many other judges who ruled by whim and impulse, when confronted by an issue, McMullin would hesitate, pause in silent contemplation, working out the arguments and weighing the facts against the law, and then not merely announce his decision, but outline its logic. There were a few attorneys in the Hall of Justice who considered him pedantic, but even fewer who made more than a formality of challenging his rulings.

Donnally had visited the judge in San Francisco a few times since a gunshot wound in his hip forced his retirement from SFPD a decade earlier and he moved north to Mount Shasta to open a café. But on none of those occasions had he observed this kind of gravity and formality, this kind of distance from the moment. It was as though the judge had abstracted himself from this place and this time, from the wind and the cold and the rush of water, even from the pressure of Donnally's gaze, and had concentrated himself in some other place and in some other time.

Finally, the judge spoke.

"Murder is the unlawful killing of a human being with malice aforethought."

Donnally squinted over at McMullin, thrown by the judge quoting the first sentence of Penal Code section 187 instead of answering his question.

The judge stared forward, but his eyes were unseeing, or perhaps reading the text in his mind.

"All murder which is willful, deliberate, and premeditated is murder in the first degree. All other kinds of murders are of the second degree."

Donnally couldn't grasp why the judge was giving the lecture. It couldn't have been because McMullin didn't think Donnally knew the section. Cops memorized all the serious felonies before they'd graduated from the academy, and the gangster's slug that ended Donnally's career hadn't destroyed his memory.

"Malice may be express or implied."

McMullin had now quoted the beginning of section 188 as

though he was preparing to instruct a jury on its meaning, except he appeared to be a jury of one and it seemed to Donnally that he was reminding himself, not Donnally, of the elements of the crime or, perhaps, trying to attach facts in his mind to the scaffolding of law.

"Malice is express when there is manifested a deliberate intention to unlawfully take away the life of a fellow creature."

Cases of express malice were common, too common for Donnally to think it was the point of the judge's recitations. It was the stuff of newspaper headlines and compulsive cable news coverage. Death penalty cases, murders committed during robberies or rapes or kidnappings, serial killings, and gangland executions.

"Malice is implied when no considerable provocation appears or when the circumstances attending the killing show an abandoned and malignant heart."

Implied malice was more rare. Drunk driving resulting in the death of a passenger or setting off fireworks causing the death of an onlooker. While those killings were never willful, deliberate, and premeditated, in their recklessness and in their endangering others they revealed an abandoned and malignant heart, and that's what made them murders.

"When it is shown that the killing resulted from the intentional doing of an act with express or implied malice, no other mental state need be shown to establish the mental state of malice aforethought."

The judge now sounded to Donnally as though he wasn't preparing to match facts with the law, but to apply the law to himself, and he wondered whether the judge was about to confess to some reckless act that had led to the loss of another's life.

McMullin took in a long breath and exhaled a misty cloud that swirled in the wind and then vanished against the overcast sky.

"I just received a letter from a defendant I sentenced to death twenty years ago. Israel Dominguez. The jury found him guilty of murder with the special circumstance of lying in wait."

Another breath and exhale.

"It was a New Year's Eve shooting through the living room window of an apartment near the housing projects in Hunters Point."

The judge raised his arm to forty-five degrees, pointing as though they were standing on the sidewalk in front of the building instead of on sand and gravel in the wilderness.

"It happened at midnight." He lowered his hand and tapped his wristwatch. "Right to the second. At the height of the chaos. The D.A. argued it was an execution of a Norteño gangster by a Sureño with the date and time chosen to give the shooter cover."

The judge didn't need to explain who those gangs were. They were as central to San Francisco crime as the Crips and the Bloods had been in Los Angeles. The Norteños—Northerners—were the outside arm of the Nuestra Familia prison gang. It recruited members from Northern California. The Sureños were the outside arm of the Mexican Mafia, based in Southern California, and had always been trying to spread north.

The gangs fought their battles on Mission District streets and in barrio bars of San Francisco. It was on one of those streets that Donnally, just stepping out of his car, and a young man and woman planning their wedding at a sidewalk table, had been caught in a cross fire between a Norteño and a Sureño. Donnally had killed the two gangsters, but too late to save the couple.

The judge glanced over at Donnally.

"There were lots of other gunshots going off in Hunters Point that night and four or five accidental shootings. The defense admitted that Dominguez fired into the house, but denied he was aiming to kill anyone, just to give them a scare."

Donnally pointed toward the pebbled bank. "Let's . . ."

McMullin turned into the current. He lost his balance. Donnally reached over and steadied him, then kept a hand on his arm as they angled their way through the water.

Once on shore, Donnally said, "I take it under the defense theory, the worst Dominguez could've been convicted of was second-degree murder under an implied malice theory. No premeditation, just a reckless disregard for human life, and therefore no death penalty. A maximum of seventeen to life, plus a few more years on a gun enhancement."

The judge nodded. "And all the appeals since his conviction have focused on the jury instructions I gave at the time, particularly whether I should've offered a voluntary manslaughter instruction."

"Under a heat of passion theory? That the victim somehow provoked it, brought it on himself?"

"But I couldn't. His attorney hadn't put on any evidence the killing was the result of an argument or a fight, and he didn't even ask for the instruction. But that didn't stop his appeal lawyers from claiming ineffective assistance of counsel on his part and error on mine."

Donnally was surprised the accusation didn't inject anger into the judge's voice.

"It was just try-anything, do-everything desperation. There was no evidence of manslaughter on the record. None at all. And the appeals court recognized it."

McMullin stared down at the clear water lapping against the rocks.

"There were times during the trial when I felt like taking the defense attorney into chambers and making some suggestions to him about what he should do."

"I'm not sure what kind of defense you—"

McMullin now looked over at Donnally and his voice tensed. "Maybe mistaken self-defense. At least argued that Dominguez believed he was in danger—it was gang territory, after all—then the jury could only have convicted him of manslaughter because there's no malice involved, just fear, even if it's unjustified."

McMullin spread his arms, almost in a plea.

"I would've done anything within the law to help his attorney and I told him so. Given him all the money he needed from the county indigent defense fund to hire a psychiatrist to look into Dominguez's mental state at the time of the shooting, what in his personal history that might have led to that predisposition, and for investigative time to look for witnesses."

"Why didn't he accept the help?"

"Panic, I think. Desperate to keep his client off death row, convinced he had to let the jury have at least a second-degree murder conviction. Let them have implied malice and abandoned and malignant heart and all that, just not willful, deliberate, and premeditated."

An image of McMullin's courtroom came to Donnally and of the defense attorney facing the jury and pleading for his client, and the rest of the logic of the case came to him.

"You mean the attorney was afraid if he pushed too hard at lessening Dominguez's responsibility by claiming manslaughter— that the victim did something to bring it on himself—the jurors would get enraged and snap back with first-degree murder and special circumstances and a death sentence."

"Exactly."

"But they did anyway."

McMullin looked away for a moment, then back and nodded.

"They did anyway."

CHAPTER 2 ═══════════════════

Donnally collected kindling and firewood from his truck bed and piled them into a rock-circled pit fifty feet up the bank while McMullin poured leftover coffee from his thermos. After getting the fire lit, Donnally accepted his cup and sat down on a boulder opposite the judge. The snow had let up and the wind had died down, leaving behind a recumbent fog, hovering over the rustling river.

"Dominguez was looking up at me all during the trial. Nineteen years old. Thin face. Tattoo of the Virgin Mary running up his neck. Sunken eyes. Just staring and staring." McMullin sighed. "A Kafka character couldn't have looked more pathetic."

"But there was no question of his guilt."

"Not as far as the jury was concerned. Two eyewitnesses. One of whom had known him from the neighborhood. More witnesses to the bad blood between the victim—"

"Who was?"

"Edgar Rojo. A Norteño."

"Rojo . . . Rojo . . ."

Donnally's mind filled for a moment with the immensity of the twenty-thousand-member gang, then it focused down to a nickname and a crime. He looked back at the judge.

"An Edgar Rojo came through when I was in homicide. They called him Rojo Loco, Crazy Red. Hard to forget a label like that. And the crime. Mayhem. He beat the victim, pounded him and pounded him, then threw him into the street and a car ran over him. Chewed him up. Lost part of an ear and all of a thumb. We were able to ID Rojo because one of the witnesses recognized his nickname."

"That was Junior," McMullin said. "The son. He's come through my court a few times. He was nine years old when Dominguez killed Edgar Senior. He was in the house when it happened and testified during the penalty phase about how devastating the crime had been to him. Seeing his father bleed out from a head wound right in front of him." McMullin paused, and then shrugged. "That could be what made the kid decompensate later and turn so violent. Maybe it was some kind of posttraumatic stress."

"Did Dominguez testify on his own behalf?"

McMullin shook his head, then took a sip of his coffee and blinked against the steam rising into his eyes.

"I even suspended the trial for a day so he and his lawyer could talk through whether he should. Since the verdict would depend on what the jury believed his intent was, I thought they probably should've heard from Dominguez himself what was in his mind before he fired the gun."

McMullin's face scrunched up like he was watching something painful, a frozen wince.

"The problem was that Dominguez had some juvenile priors the D.A. could bring in to impeach him if he testified."

"As in, you had the intent to kill when you shot at Tom and Dick, but not when you shot Edgar Rojo Senior?"

"Dominguez's priors weren't quite that serious, at least in terms of the injuries, but all were unprovoked nighttime assaults, and they were the reason his attorney didn't put him on the stand. I later heard from the bailiff that Dominguez and his lawyer had knock-down, drag-out arguments, presumably over whether he'd testify. He even heard the kid crying just before the attorney came out to tell me he wouldn't."

McMullin shook his head, anticipating Donnally's next question.

"The bailiff didn't tell me how the argument went or exactly what it was that set the kid to crying. He knew I'm not supposed to consider anything other than what comes before me in court. But it was easy to guess. Dominguez wanting to testify and say he didn't do it and his lawyer telling him not to and Dominguez being terrified of getting executed, thinking he better try everything. The problem from his attorney's point of view was that Dominguez would've torpedoed the defense theory of implied malice by testifying he was innocent. It would've guaranteed a first-degree conviction if the jury didn't buy it."

McMullin took another sip from his cup, then stared into it. "He had a second chance to testify during the penalty phase, but didn't choose to take it."

"Or his attorney talked him out of it."

"Most likely. It was hopeless by then anyway. The prosecutor brought in witness after witness to testify about his character and Dominguez got crushed by the bad-guy reputation he'd built for himself. And all the Sureño gang evidence came in because it was central to that reputation. All of it together convinced the jury that Dominguez was exactly the dangerous and unrepentant murderer capital punishment was aimed at and they voted for death in an hour and a half."

Donnally's peripheral vision caught soundless motion among the ferns filling the spaces between the redwoods along the opposite bank. He turned his head. A doe locked her wide eyes on his and her ears cupped toward him. He looked back at McMullin.

"What about before sentencing?" Donnally asked. "Were they allowing defendants to make statements back then?"

McMullin nodded. "Allocution. And it was permitted by law at the time of the Dominguez trial. It still is, but hardly any defendants opt for it for fear of sabotaging their appeals because they'd have to express remorse for what they did and to do that they'd have to make admissions. It's hard for a defendant begging for mercy to be convincing if he refuses to admit he really was guilty of what the jury convicted him." The judge shook his head. "It never works anyway. Judges always follow a jury's death recommendation."

Donnally circled back to what now sounded like McMullin's lingering doubt.

"What do you mean there was no question of his guilt as far as the jury was concerned? What about you?"

McMullin paused for a moment, eyebrows furrowed. Another wince.

"I think I thought he was guilty of at least second-degree murder."

"You don't sound certain."

The judge gazed across the river at the doe, now drinking from the shallows, and then said, "I think I was sure he fired the gun, but I'm not sure I was convinced he had the intent to kill and . . ." The judge hesitated. "And I'm not even sure I believed, in a moral sense, that he had the abandoned and malignant heart a second-degree murder conviction requires."

Donnally stared at the judge. "You think? You're not sure? That doesn't sound like you. You don't talk that way. You don't think that way." His voice took on an edge. "Merely thinking something was true was never good enough for you, and it sure wasn't the standard you set for detectives bringing arrest warrants to you."

McMullin drew back as though Donnally's assault had been physical.

"I . . . I . . ."

"You what?" Donnally pushed himself to his feet and tossed the coffee from his half-empty cup into the pale dead grasses behind him.

"Spill it."

McMullin looked down, staring at the smoke rising from the fire and at the almost transparent flame. He seemed to Donnally like a little boy avoiding the eyes of his accusing parent, delaying an inevitable confession. McMullin took in a long breath, held it for a moment, then exhaled, surrendering.

"It was less than a year after I was appointed and I was still trying to prove myself, prove I could pull the trigger. But now . . . now . . ."

"Now?"

McMullin looked up. "Now I would've rejected the jury's death recommendation and sentenced him to life without parole."

"Have you ever done that?"

Donnally asked the question only as a provocation, to draw McMullin out, for he already knew the answer. No judge in California had ever done it. Somehow and sometime past, he didn't know when, but certainly long before he became a cop, the exercise of judgment and the act of judging—what judges really thought in contrast to what they said from the bench and wrote in their rulings—had become separated, ripped apart by their fear of facing the electorate or of a D.A.'s attacks or of cable channels terrorizing viewers in order to jack up ratings.

Until this moment, he'd always viewed McMullin as the exception.

"Dominguez was the only capital case I ever did. As soon as it was over, I asked the presiding judge to transfer me to the civil division. And when I went back into criminal a few years later it was only to hold preliminary hearings and rule on pretrial motions and to preside over the calendar court. Sometimes I'd assign trials to myself, even homicides, but never special circumstances cases unless the D.A. had already announced that they weren't seeking death, only life without parole."

Donnally knew the next words would hurt but said them anyway.

"You mean you've spent most of your time on the bench in hiding."

McMullin's face flushed, then he shrugged. "I guess you could say that." He paused, another long breath, and his next words came out as a sigh. "Helluva way to spend my career."

Donnally thought of the many hours he'd spent in McMullin's chambers when he was a homicide detective, sometimes bringing search warrants for his review and signature, sometimes to talk through some point of law before taking the risk of compromising an investigation.

He now realized there was a fragile man within the hard shell of his role, his robe a place of concealment or a form of defense. And he wondered how much the Dominguez case had informed, or perhaps distorted, the judge's rulings and his sense of himself over the years.

And there was something else. Donnally felt a twist in his chest as he thought about the judge burdened for twenty years by a decision made too soon in his career, like a rookie cop who panics and kills a kid holding a toy gun and knows for the rest of his life and despite passing the department's shooting review that it could've gone another way.

Donnally thought of his own father, who he now saw in the judge's tortured reflection, a man who'd chosen for most of his life to unburden himself of his sins by refusing to acknowledge them.

A log rolled from the fire and thudded against a rock lining the pit. Donnally grabbed a stick and worked it back into place.

"What did Dominguez say in his letter?"

"What they all say, that he didn't do it. His argument was more complex than usual, but that's the bottom line."

Donnally extended his hand. "Let me see."

McMullin shook his head. "I didn't bring it with me. I left it in my briefcase in your house."

"Then why—"

"I wasn't sure whether I was going to tell you about all this and I was afraid having it in my pocket while we were camping out here would put too much pressure on me. I thought maybe some distance from it would loosen the pull."

The judge fell silent, staring at the flame, his body as fixed and unmoving as the granite boulder on which he sat.

Donnally had an idea about what McMullin was thinking.

How much simpler life would be if humans were inert, subject to the laws of gravity, the predictable mechanisms of attraction and repulsion, rather than of feeling and morality.

"But it didn't," Donnally said. "It kept tugging at you."

McMullin nodded but didn't look up.

"I think I must've been deceiving myself."

CHAPTER 3

Janie Nguyen walked from the entrance to Donnally's Lone Mountain Café as he pulled his truck to a stop in the night-lit parking lot in central Mount Shasta. She'd driven up with Judge McMullin from San Francisco to relieve Donnally at the front counter so they could spend the previous days fishing together. She stood under the porch roof as Donnally and McMullin approached.

She gave Donnally a hug, then the judge and said, "I'll get you two something warm to drink."

Donnally pulled the door open and followed her and McMullin inside into the half-filled restaurant. A few regulars sitting at the counter waved at Donnally as he entered. The tables were a mix of young skiers about to head back south and old fishermen dragging out the weekend with long stories about big fish. Janie gestured them toward a booth by the front window, then went behind the counter, poured two cups of coffee, and brought them over.

"I got a call from your mother's gerontologist," Janie said, as she sat down next to Donnally.

"Is she okay?" Donnally felt himself tense, troubled by why the doctor hadn't telephoned him directly. He was used to getting updates from her about the progression of his mother's Parkinson's, if not by phone, by text. He turned toward her. "Why didn't you call me?"

Janie took his hand. "Your mother is fine. The doctor dropped by to see her today."

Donnally didn't attach any special meaning to the doctor's visit to his parents' home. She and his mother had become friends over the many years of his mother's illness and she lived in Hollywood Heights just down the hill from his parents' home.

"There's been no change. She was actually calling about your father. Nothing serious, but she wanted to run some thoughts by me before she talked to you."

Janie was Donnally's longtime girlfriend, but Donnally suspected this wasn't the reason why the doctor wanted to consult with her, but because she was a psychiatrist.

"Depression?"

It wasn't just that his father was aging, almost the judge's age, but he'd been recovering from a late-life crisis, delayed and then exacerbated by his recent acknowledgment of his role in misleading Donnally's brother to his death in Vietnam almost forty years earlier.

Janie glanced at Judge McMullin before answering.

"It's okay," Donnally said. "He can keep a secret."

McMullin glanced back and forth between Janie and Donnally. "Secret?"

"My father is Donald Harlan. The movie director."

McMullin cocked his head and his gaze angled away. "Donald Harlan . . . Harlan Donnally . . ." He looked back at Donnally. "You mean your father uses a stage name? I thought only actors did that."

Donnally shook his head. "I changed mine."

The judge pointed at Donnally. "You were always known around the Hall of Justice as a man without a past," he said, raising his eyebrows, "but it now sounds like you were a man with too much of one."

Donnally shrugged. "It's a long story."

"I've got time."

Janie glanced up and saw a customer walking toward the counter and went over to take his payment.

Donnally took a sip of his coffee. He wondered whether there was a lesson for McMullin in his father's history. They were of the same generation, maybe shared some of the same flaws.

"My father was a press officer working out of the U.S. embassy in Saigon during the war. He gave a briefing in which he claimed that the Viet Cong had massacred some Buddhist monks up in Hue."

Donnally watched the judge nod and his eyes go vacant for a moment. He knew McMullin was watching news footage in his mind. Everyone in the country had watched it on Walter Cronkite. It was one of a handful of images that had defined the war for people McMullin's age: the mangled body of assassinated South Vietnamese president Diem, the self-immolation of a monk in a Saigon intersection, the bullet-to-the-head street execution of a Viet Cong soldier by a South Vietnamese colonel, and Don Harlan's press conference.

"That was your father?" McMullin said, a question more in form than content.

"He had a nickname. The press corps always referred to him as Bucky Harlan."

"As I remember it, the story he told turned out not to be true."

Donnally nodded. "But my older brother believed it. He dropped out of UCLA and enlisted. Six months later he was killed during the Tet Offensive. Ambushed by North Vietnamese regulars. Set up by some villagers. But before he died, he met some monks along the Perfume River and learned the truth. It had been Korean mercenaries hired by the United States who committed the crime. He also found out my father knew it all along."

McMullin sighed. "That's a helluva thing to live with."

The way the judge said the words suggested he was also thinking of himself.

"My father's whole career, all those war movies, was nothing more than a lifelong flight from himself and what he'd done."

The judge and Donnally's conversation at the river became a soundless echo in the room.

"But you said he—"

Donnally nodded. "He used his last movie to come clean with himself."

"I've seen all your father's films. At least I thought so. I don't remember anything like that."

"It got almost no distribution. None of the theater chains would run it."

"Sounds like he would've been better off whispering it to a priest in a confessional."

Donnally thought, but didn't say, *Or to an ex-cop on the bank of the Smith River.*

Janie returned and sat down next to Donnally.

"What did the doctor want to talk about?"

"She's thinking it may be time to run some tests on him for Alzheimer's."

Donnally sensed more than saw McMullin stiffen and look

away. The judge's coffee cup rattled on the saucer as he set it down. He thought back on the judge's failure to execute the basics of fighting the steelhead and his confusion, perhaps bewilderment, in trying to reconstruct his thinking at the time of the Dominguez trial. Maybe the judge had his own secret, one about his own mental deterioration that had made his mission more urgent than just a letter from an inmate who was facing execution and desperate to save his life.

Donnally felt a sourness in his stomach, and not only from the lukewarm coffee. Maybe the judge had fantasized the whole thing or had mixed up cases together in his mind. He pushed the thought aside for the moment and asked, "What's the doctor seeing in him now that she hasn't seen before?"

"That's part of the problem. She's hardly seeing him at all, and neither is your mother. He spends days on end in the basement studio. He doesn't shower. Hardly eats. He fired his film editor and is making all the cuts himself. His producers are calling because some of his investors are nervous about where their millions of dollars have gone, and your father refuses to call them back."

"And I take it that he won't let anyone look at what he's doing."

Janie nodded. "Like always. Except . . ." She paused and looked over at McMullin. He held up his palms as though to say the secret would be safe. "Except when he went for a walk he left a DVD he'd made of some scenes from the film on the kitchen table. She only had a few minutes to look at it. And it was bizarre. Crazy. Not like *Shooting the Dawn* and more like the experimental stuff he did in film school. Four different men staring into the camera, none of them speaking the same lines, then turning and walking toward the same white door. But not like screen tests. These were all famous guys, ones he's worked with for years."

Donnally found he'd folded his hands, interlaced his fingers, and was rubbing his thumbs together. He stopped. He knew his father would be humiliated if word got out that the man who'd made what was considered the most important Vietnam war film in history had reduced tens or scores of millions of dollars of his investors' money into a few thousand dollars' worth of something not even worthy of a student film festival.

Even worse, it might reveal what should've been obvious to Hollywood forty years earlier—that his father's first films were less conscious acts of artistic creation than reflections of a psychotic break triggered by the death of Donnally's older brother and his refusal to accept responsibility for his role in it. Even *Shooting the Dawn*, an epic that was still studied in classrooms around the country, portrayed both sides in the Vietnam War as maniacal, the American soldiers as *Deer Hunter*–like killers and all the Vietnamese—South, North, and Viet Cong—as devious and evil.

The argument of the movie was that if the war wasn't rational, then no one fighting it could be either, and no one, not even Don Harlan speaking from the safety of the American embassy in Saigon, could be held responsible for what he'd said and done.

It was only in his father's last movie that he'd displayed to the world the truth of what he'd done, and accepted responsibility.

But by then few wanted to listen, for later self-deceptions, distortions, and deceits, ones that had led the country into the 2003 Iraq War, occupied the public debate and no one labored anymore about the lessons of Vietnam.

Donnally wondered what other confession was left for his father to make and how he was choosing to make it.

"She'll try to get another look at the DVD," Janie said, "and make a copy, then send it up here so you can see it for yourself."

"Has she tried to talk to him?"

"Not yet."

For a moment, Donnally felt protective of his father, who now appeared smaller and weaker in his mind, a yellow-haired old man shuffling in the shadows.

"Then I'm not sure she's in a position to determine what he's up to."

"That's exactly the problem. She can't determine whether he's up to something and is in control of himself or whether something has risen up and taken control of him."

CHAPTER 4

J anie glanced over from the passenger seat of his truck as they drove south from Mount Shasta toward San Francisco.

"By not approaching your father head-on, you're treating him like a suspect rather than as a possible victim of a disease. Like you're lying in wait."

Donnally glanced in his rearview mirror at Ray McMullin following them, his eyes concentrated on Donnally's tailgate as though being led through fog.

"I don't want to just stumble into things. He might react by thinking I'm trying to get him diagnosed with Alzheimer's as revenge for what he did to Donnie. He knows his public confession doesn't change what happened and he knows his feeling guilty doesn't mean I'm obligated to forgive him."

Janie shifted her body so she could face him. "But you have forgiven him, haven't you?"

"I'm not even sure I understand forgiveness. The forgive-but-not-forget idea. Seems to me it's only for saints."

A curve west left him squinting into the sunset fanning out against the sky. The next turn broke them free from the pine-lined highway and angled them toward the snow-tipped Castle Crags, the bright granite spires seeming more brutal, than beautiful.

"That's not right," he said. "It's more that I know people forgive terrible acts, but some acts are just too terrible."

Donnally felt Janie still looking at him.

"Is that how you feel about what he did?"

Donnally shrugged but didn't answer.

"You think Donnie would've forgiven him?"

Now he looked over. "Don't play that game. Dead people are just hand puppets and we're the ventriloquists. And thinking the words we put in their mouths reveal real insight into who they were and what they would've done is a delusion."

Janie's face reddened. "That's not what I meant, and you know it. Donnie had a personality, a way of looking at the world. It's not ventriloquism to imagine what his thoughts and feelings might be."

"Maybe that's the problem. Donnie probably would've forgiven not just my father, but the people who ambushed him."

Janie turned back in her seat and folded her arms across her chest. She stared ahead, her lips compressed.

They rode in silence except for the rumble of his tires on the ice-pitted pavement and the hum of tension in the cab. Donnally knew he'd started it and that it was on him to quiet it.

"Sorry. I went off course and didn't answer your question."

Janie blew out a quick breath through her nose. "All of our serious conversations these days seem to go off course."

"Not all of them. Just the ones that begin with my father."

"That doesn't make it any easier." Her voice was edged with resentment and impatience.

"I suspect Alzheimer's will. He'll be a different person and a lot easier to forgive."

She looked over. "So answer me. Why are you treating him like a suspect?"

"Because I don't know enough about Alzheimer's and dementia in general and his behavior in particular. Because his moment of insight into one thing hasn't made him less rigid in everything else. And because I'll only have one chance to get it right."

"I'm not sure it's true you'll have only one chance. It's not like you're playing the part of judge and jury."

"But it will seem that way to him, with you as a coconspiring expert witness."

Donnally thought back to his fireside conversation with McMullin, then realized the doubts the judge expressed about his handling of the Dominguez case were confusing his own thinking about how to deal with his father. The two men had merged in his mind as objects to be examined and, perhaps, manipulated for their own good.

He reached into his inside jacket pocket and handed Janie the copy of Dominguez's letter that McMullin had given him just before they headed south. She unfolded it.

Dear Judge McMullin:

I know you will be surprised to receive this letter after all these years, perhaps even surprised I am able to write to you. As you know from evidence presented during the penalty phase of my trial, I dropped out of school at twelve, but since I have been on death row, I have obtained a GED and then a B.A. from the Prison College Program, the only condemned inmate to have done so.

It has been over twenty years since my trial and soon the California State Supreme Court will take up my case, and soon after that I will be executed.

The irony of all this—the implied malice defense, the appeals based on your jury instructions, and the claims of ineffective assistance of counsel—is that I am factually innocent of the crime and all of these legal maneuvers were off the point.

The district attorney's theory of the case was just wrong. I had no malice toward Edgar Rojo Sr. I premeditated nothing. I did not form an intent to kill him. I did not fire a gun that night.

I told all of this to my attorney the first time I met with him and I never backed down.

Since I did not shoot Rojo, the manslaughter instruction would have allowed the jury to convict me of something for which I was, in fact and in law, innocent.

The same would have been true of the second-degree murder conviction my attorney sought, wrongly believing it was the only way to save my life.

The further irony of my situation is that even if the Supreme Court were to accept the fact of my innocence, I will be executed anyway. The court has adopted the view of former Justice Sandra Day O'Connor and Justice Antonin Scalia that the "Court has never held that the Constitution forbids the execution of a convicted defendant who has had a full and fair trial but is later able to convince a habeas court that he is 'actually' innocent."

Which is to say that I have already had my days in court and my innocence is no longer a legal defense.

Looking back, it seems beyond absurd that my trial and all my appeals have been based on a false premise, but so has your career as a judge. And you know that better than anyone.

I don't know whether you believed I was innocent when you sentenced me to death, but I know you doubted the first-degree, special circumstances verdict.

The truth is that the real killers needed to focus the police investigation on someone other than themselves and they picked me. Why, I don't know. Maybe because Rojo and I argued the day before. Maybe just because I was convenient or happened to be the same size or age or complexion as the real shooter. Maybe it was because I had the right reputation they needed so the police would believe I was the kind of person who would commit this kind of crime, that an argument over nothing would provoke me to commit murder.

I kept looking at you all during the trial waiting for you to stop it. But you never did. And that failure is the false premise of your career. You know it and I know it.

Since my fate is what it is, I've decided to fire my appeals lawyer and file the rest of the paperwork pro per. She's a well-meaning person just trying to make a living and she shouldn't have to bear the burden of my death for the rest of her life. By relieving her of her duties, at least she'll be able to say, "If only . . ." She would then be free to blame me when my application to the U.S. Supreme Court for a writ of certiorari asking it to review the California Supreme Court rulings is denied and my clemency request to the governor fails.

As you know, I've been blamed for worse.

Sincerely,
Israel Dominguez

Janie refolded the letter and stared ahead at the highway as it approached the bridge over the Pit River arm of Lake Shasta, the cobalt blue water polished by the sliver of sun, the windless surface seeming slate flat and rock hard. She glanced over at the distant Slaughterhouse Island, then back at Donnally.

"The guy's either completely innocent or a manipulating sociopathic son of a bitch."

CHAPTER 5

Homicide detective Ramon Navarro pulled his car to the curb near the two-story apartment building in Hunters Point in which Edgar Rojo Sr. had lived. To Donnally its faded pink stucco, its oxidized aluminum windows, and its patched gray cracks and spackle-filled bullet holes had the feel of predestined despair and of ruined dreams.

"Not much has changed in twenty years, has it?" Navarro said.

Drug dealers on the four corners half a block away alerted to the burgundy Crown Victoria. They held their places, but the ones sitting on the stoops of the row houses on either side of the storefront church across the street rose and slipped inside.

Donnally and Navarro both recognized them to be the runners who held the cocaine, but never the cash, who were employed to separate the drug handover from the money transaction.

"A lot has changed," Donnally said, as they stepped out. "In the old days, they all would've drifted away." He grinned as he looked over the hood at Navarro. "The kids don't know how to show respect anymore."

Navarro rolled his eyes. "Don't talk to me about respect. You know how hard all the old-timers in the department are going to be riding my ass if they find out I'm helping you with this?"

Donnally pointed at Navarro's decade-old herringbone sports

jacket. "If you cared about other people's opinions, you'd dress a whole lot better."

Navarro blew out a breath. "I wish this was just a fashion issue." He then looked up at the second-floor window where Rojo Sr. was killed. "Seems to me the Rojo murder was the worst declaration of war in the history of San Francisco. Worse than anything involving the black or Asian gangs. That killing proved the Sureños were a force to be contended with up here." He glanced up and down the street, then looked back at Donnally. "Can you think of a hit that cost so many lives in such a short period of time in such a few square blocks?"

Donnally shrugged. He'd never done the math. Navarro was probably right, but it was hard to tell. When he was in the department, the chief and the police commission exaggerated the number of gang murders as part of their annual budget pleas. In truth, many of those homicides arose less out of gang affiliation, and more out of personal animosity or a juvenile notion of dignity, jealousies over women, a dice game that transformed from a war by other means into just a war. Even when a killing was gang related, sometimes the gangs never knew who did it or why, whether it was the start of a new war or the taking of revenge for someone who fell in a past one.

"I went over to see Rojo Junior a couple of years ago at San Quentin," Navarro said. "It was just before he finished his sentence on the mayhem case. I figured I could leverage his being on parole into rolling him for information on a couple of homicides. His parole conditions would prohibit him from associating with felons." Navarro tilted his chin toward the red zone at the corner. "He and I both knew he'd be in violation as soon as he stepped off the bus."

"And?"

"He wouldn't go for it. Invited me to come out here and pick him up any time I wanted. Said he could do the time. He told me he became a Norteño the moment his father's head hit the floor and he wasn't gonna change." Navarro shook his head. "Nine years old and a Norteño junior gangster in training."

Navarro's meaning reached beyond the bare words he'd spoken and beyond the street on which he'd spoken them, for it had been a slug from a Norteño about Rojo Junior's present age, from this same neighborhood of pointless warfare, that had ended Donnally's career.

Donnally opened the folder Navarro had given him containing crime scene photos and the diagrams that had been drawn on the night Rojo Senior was killed.

To conceal his involvement in Donnally's investigation, Navarro had told his supervisor who'd spotted the file on his desk that he'd checked it out as part of a background investigation of a witness in a pending case. He'd been willing to take the risk because he knew Donnally would have done the same for him. Their careers at SFPD had done more than just overlap, they'd intertwined, both on the street and in the homicide unit. From the day in the early '90s when Navarro as a rookie patrol officer was assigned to an arrest team Donnally was leading, they had the silent understanding some cops have with each other.

Donnally pointed at the spot near the curb in front of the apartment building where a shell casing had been found. He and Navarro walked over and looked up at the living room window behind which Rojo Senior was standing at the moment he was been shot. Donnally then calculated the path the shell casing might have traveled after its ejection from the semiautomatic.

That put him in the driveway leading to the rear of the complex.

"How tall is Israel Dominguez?" Donnally asked.

"Five six."

Donnally raised his hand toward the window as though aiming a gun.

"That makes him five inches shorter than me." He glanced over at Navarro. "And Rojo Senior?"

"Five eight."

Keeping his arm extended, Donnally lowered himself to Dominguez's height.

"That's a real extreme angle. In order for Dominguez to deliver a headshot, Rojo Senior had to be standing right in front of the window. Even then it would be tough to hit him. A margin of two or three inches from thirty feet away."

The thudding of hard-soled shoes rumbled down the sidewalk.

Donnally and Navarro turned to see two lines of fifteen Muslim Nation members marching toward them. Young black men in black suits, black shoes, and black ties and white shirts. The columns spread on approach, one forming a barrier between Donnally and Navarro and the building, the other semicircled behind them. The men stopped, spread their feet to shoulder width, then locked their hands in front of their belts.

The leader of the Black Nationalist group, a slim six two with a close-shaved head and jewel-brown eyes, stepped toward them and said without raising his voice, "Get your white asses out of here. This Muslim Nation territory."

To Donnally, the last sentence sounded idiotic, just one of those Bay Area delusions, too often territorial, that he'd been happy to liberate himself from when he moved north. More dangerous in effect, but otherwise not all that different from the leather sub-culture in the Castro District, the purple-haired punks in the Haight, and the derivative demigods of the financial district. Just more and different gangs involved, like the dice players, at war by other means.

Navarro turned toward the men behind them in the street so he and Donnally could cover each other's backs.

Donnally pointed at Navarro's car outside of the semicircle and said to the leader, "I must've misread the map. I thought we were still in San Francisco."

Navarro reached for his radio and called in "406," officer needs emergency help, and gave their location.

The leader smiled at Donnally. "11-99 should've been enough." 11-99 was the code for an officer needing only nonemergency assistance.

"You guys scared?"

The rising wail of distant sirens sliced into the static of Navarro's radio.

Donnally shook his head. "You want to go one-on-one, let's do it."

Without the need of a command, the last three members at the ends of each line stomped once and pivoted toward the opposite street corners to face the soon-to-be-arriving patrol cars.

Donnally caught motion in the window of Rojo Senior's apartment. He looked up and spotted the frightened eyes of an elderly Hispanic woman. A large crucifix hung high on the wall next to her, the figure of Jesus gazing down at her in anguish. He was tempted to ask the leader whether the apartment these people lived in was part of his pseudo-Islamic state, but didn't. He'd be leaving the neighborhood—one way or the other—while the residents were condemned to live there, and there was no reason to make them part of this battle.

Two units approached from the east, one from the west. Their sirens died as they came to a stop. More rose up in the distance.

Donnally heard car doors open but kept his eyes on the leader, who locked his on Donnally's for a moment, then glared past him.

"Get back, old man."

Donnally glanced over his shoulder. The minister from the storefront church was crossing the pavement toward them. He was wearing a clerical collar and a burgundy suit and fedora. Donnally spotted his name, Reverend Julius Jones, written in hand-painted letters on the front of his building, just below the words *Burning Bush Church of God in Christ.*

"Take your slave religion back across the street," the leader said to him.

Reverend Jones kept coming. He slipped inside the semicircle behind the back of one of the members facing the police, then passed by Navarro and Donnally and stopped three feet from the leader. He pointed up into the man's face. "You don't live here anymore, George—"

"George is a slave name. My name is Aasim."

"Your name is George. Learn some history. It was the slaves who had names like Aasim. Go build your so-called nation in your own neighborhood. No one invited you to invade ours." The reverend pointed south. "Or is that frowned upon in San Bruno."

Donnally smiled at the leader over the reverend's shoulder. San Bruno was a white and Asian bedroom community on the peninsula. There were so few African Americans in the city that they were outnumbered by Native Americans.

"Fuck you."

Donnally stepped up next to Reverend Jones, then cut in front of him. He didn't like the feel of being rescued by someone old enough to be his father.

"Watch your mouth, George," Donnally said, making himself the target again. "What's Aasim mean in Arabic? Insulter of the Aged?"

"It means 'Protector.'"

Donnally heard movement behind him and looked back. The corner drug dealers were lined up behind the Nation members, hoping a fight would erupt and figuring this was their chance to draw blood and exact revenge. One of the few crimes the Nation disapproved of was drug dealing, and robbing drug dealers was therefore sanctioned. It permitted the Nation members to view themselves as Robin Hoods, though they never gave to the poor, except as bribes to convert them to their cult. Instead, they used the stolen money to support themselves and their women and children and, Donnally suspected, to pay the mortgage on their mosque in the next block.

Behind the dealers were patrol cars and uniformed officers, some holding batons, others cradling shotguns.

"Protector?" Donnally said. "You've got both the cops and the cons ganged up around you, so I'm not sure you'll be doing much protecting today." He looked hard in Aasim's eyes. "Do you?"

"Maybe not now." A compensating smirk. "But soon."

Aasim glanced left and right, then barked out a one-word command in Arabic and the members pivoted toward the west and marched away.

Donnally turned back toward Reverend Jones. "How long have you known this guy?"

"His whole distorted life. His father was a leader of Jam'iyyat Ul-Islam Is-Saheeh, the Assembly of Authentic Muslims, in prison."

He glanced at the receding backs of the Nation members as Navarro walked over to talk to a patrol sergeant.

"That's how the kid got recruited. A couple of years ago, the Mexican Mafia ordered his father's murder in Pelican Bay. George showed back up here right afterward on a mission from Allah to clear the Hispanics out of the neighborhood in the name of racial purity."

Jones nodded toward Navarro. "He's probably the reason the crew came hustling down here." Then toward the apartment house. "George has been trying to take over this building and kick the last of the Hispanics out so he can move all their women and kids in."

"Why's this particular place so important to them?"

"It's right in the middle of a redevelopment project. Ground zero. The city wants to raze four square blocks and build thousands of condos and low-income housing. Lots of white people and Asians and Hispanics will be moving in, and from then on they'll be running Hunters Point."

Donnally pointed at the church across the street. "That means that you'll be moving out too."

"Even when we're gone, God will still be here."

Donnally raised his gaze toward the second-floor apartment. "You know who lives up there?"

"The Rojos. They've been living in that same unit for twenty years, maybe longer." Jones shook his head as he stared up at the building. "I don't know why they stayed. Their oldest son was murdered standing right next to that crucifix."

CHAPTER 6

Donnally scanned the street as he drove his truck toward the Rojos' apartment just after sunset. He'd decided not to put the family in further jeopardy by trying to speak to them earlier in the day while he, or they, might still be under surveillance by the Muslim Nation.

The dope dealers were back on their corners, wearing hooded sweatshirts and puff jackets against the cold. The streetlights above them had been shot out, leaving them in shadow except when side lit by passing cars.

The day's trash littered the curbs and sidewalks. Malt liquor cans. Beer bottles. Taco Bell and McDonald's wrappers. Pages from *Auto Trader* and the *San Francisco Bay Guardian*.

The door to the corner A&B Market was caged with iron bars and bulletproof glass. Light emerged from a window and chute built into the door for sliding money in and purchases out.

A tricked-out 1980s ragtop Camaro with spinners on its wheels rolled by as Donnally pulled to the curb, the four occupants sitting low and staring over at him. He watched the car stop at the corner just long enough for the front passenger to hand a paper bag to one of the runners. The kid glanced inside, then tossed it to another who carried it toward the open front door of a duplex unit and passed it to a woman standing in the threshold.

Donnally checked the Velcro retention strap on his shoulder holster under his jacket. He then climbed out of his truck and headed up the driveway toward the concrete and wrought-iron stairs leading to the second floor of the apartment building. Two teenage girls were walking down as he headed up.

One of them stopped next to him on the second-floor landing. "Look at you, Five-Oh." She laughed. "All undercover and everything."

They were using 5-0 for police, as their parents had before them, the code having survived two iterations of the television show and a voyage halfway across the Pacific from Hawaii.

Donnally didn't mind them thinking he was still a cop and hoped they'd pass the mistake onto the dealers on the corner. It wasn't as protective as a body armor, but it would do.

"Maybe," Donnally said, "but I'm just visiting an old family friend. Somebody died."

The girl's smile faded. "Sorry. I didn't mean nothing."

Donnally noticed that the two were carrying textbooks and concluded that they'd just been playing a part they'd learned in the neighborhood.

"It's okay." He pointed at her books. "Good luck in school." He then headed toward the Rojos' apartment, three doors down.

Donnally knocked, waited, and watched the peephole go dark. Five seconds later, he heard the sound of a chain chinking as it was unhooked and then the click-thunk of a deadbolt sliding.

The elderly woman he'd seen in the window earlier opened the door. She had a wide Indian face and dark skin. He guessed she was Magdalena Rojo, Edgar Sr.'s mother and Junior's grandmother. She was drying her hands with a dishtowel. Five-year-old twins sat on the couch behind her watching television. They glanced up at him as they would at Junior's parole officer come to do a search for drugs and weapons, with a mix of familiarity and anxiety on their faces, then focused again on the screen.

Magdalena waited for him to speak.

"My name is Harlan Donnally and I wanted—"

"To start a riot?"

She didn't smile.

Donnally shook his head. "I haven't spent much time in San Francisco in the last ten years, so I didn't know about the Muslim Nation moving in here."

"They haven't moved in here yet, at least into this building, but they will." She glanced toward the direction from which the Nation members had marched that afternoon. "They've only gotten as far as the next block."

Magdalena backed away from the threshold and gestured with her free hand toward the interior, inviting him to enter. He stepped inside. She closed the door and pointed at the kids, and then down the hallway. Donnally wondered whether they were Junior's children, her great-grandchildren. Without giving Donnally another look, they turned off the television and walked down the hall and closed the bedroom door behind them.

Magdalena led him to the dining table and they sat down. The surface was still wet from wiping after dinner, and the apartment had the limey smell of corn tortillas mixed with the earthy aroma of pinto beans.

"You wanted?"

Donnally knew that question would be coming from whoever had answered the door, but other than knowing he wouldn't mention Judge McMullin, he hadn't decided on how he would answer it, until just then.

"I'm trying to understand why I was shot ten years ago when I was a cop."

Magdalena drew back a little, her body tensed.

"And not because I think your grandson was involved. The guy who shot me is dead."

"Did you kill him?"

Her words came across less as an accusation and more as an attempt to position herself in relation to him. Was she sitting across from a man who'd taken a life?

"Not because I wanted to. He was coming at me firing. I was caught in a cross fire between Norteños and Sureños over on Mission Street."

Magdalena's gaze shifted toward the television for a second, then back at Donnally.

"I saw it on the news. You were lying by the curb."

Donnally nodded.

"I think one was dead in the street and the other was on the sidewalk." She fell silent and bit her lip. "My grandson knew one of them."

"The Norteño?"

She nodded. "I don't know how he became involved with them."

"Yes, you do."

The words came out sharper than Donnally intended, but she didn't strike back. She just lowered her head and sighed.

"Why did you stay here after your son was killed?"

She looked up again. "For the same reason my ancestors buried their relatives on the family's *ranchito* in Mexico. You can't escape your history. It makes no sense to try. It just breaks you apart in your heart."

Donnally felt his hands clench under the table. Without knowing it, Magdalena had touched not only on the central preoccupation of his life, but also on the pressing problem that was fixed at the back of his mind even as he was talking with her: whether his father had begun a descent toward a day when he would have no memory at all, and therefore no way to place himself in the world. But at least in his father's case it might be a good thing as it might obliterate the break that divided his heart since his days in Vietnam.

"And I'm trying to understand my history," Donnally said. "I think the war between the Norteños and Sureños that was set off by the murder of your son led in one way or another to what happened on Mission Street."

Magdalena stared at him, again biting her lower lip, then she said, "My son was killed twenty years ago and you were shot, what? Eight, nine years ago?"

"Ten."

It was clear to him that Magdalena was thinking in terms of a chain of events and wondering whether the length of it could be followed back to the beginning.

Donnally, on the other hand, was thinking of roots or branches that radiated from a common trunk.

"Have you looked at the file about my son's murder?"

Donnally nodded. "But there are some things I didn't understand." He pointed toward the window overlooking the street and the low table below it. "The diagram showed there was a couch in front of that window on the night Edgar was killed."

She glanced at the one along the wall to the left. "A different one."

Donnally didn't ask why it was replaced, but wondered whether it had been too bloody to clean.

"So he had to make some effort to get close to the window?"

"Not really." Magdalena spread her hands two feet apart. "There was a space between the couch and the wall, so we could look to see who was pressing the buzzer downstairs."

She pointed down toward the front of the building.

"There used to be a sliding gate across the driveway and a door to let people in, but the speaker was always broken." She anticipated his next question. "But no one had buzzed before the shooting."

"What made him walk over there?"

"A phone call. My grandson was so upset and confused, even to this day he doesn't know what really happened during the call, just that his father hung up and walked to the window right afterwards."

Donnally had read about the telephone call in the police report and the inability of the police to discover who'd made it. He'd only asked the question about why her son had gone to the window in order to find out whether she'd learned something new over the years or was now prepared to add something that hadn't been contained in the file.

"You should talk to Israel Dominguez," Magdalena said. "He knows. But maybe he wants to take the name of the caller to his grave."

"Were you convinced that he shot—"

"There was no doubt it was him. The witnesses came to me, each of them, and swore it was him on their mothers' lives." She pointed at the couch. "Sitting right over there."

"Did they say why Dominguez did it?"

She shook her head.

"What about the D.A.'s theory that it wasn't just a prank gone wrong or a personal vendetta, but a contract killing of a Norteño by a Sureño?"

Magdalena sighed. "I wouldn't know about that. My son's friends knew not to bring their gang talk into this house."

If she didn't know, Donnally thought, it was nothing but willful blindness. Just like his father's about his own life. Except Magdalena's evasions, unlike his father's, didn't blossom into anger in his chest, only into sadness. She was living in the same place where, and trapped in the same moment when, her son was killed, but only acknowledging to herself half the truth about him and his life and therefore the reasons for his murder.

"How did you feel about Dominguez getting the death penalty?"

She hardened her voice, but it lacked a bitter edge. "He hasn't yet."

"I think you know that's not what I'm asking."

She looked down at the dishtowel in her hands, then back up. "That was for others to decide. We're little people. We were just barely up from the fields in Salinas, and back then we were here illegally. We went along and testified to what they told us to." Her eyes went vague. "And what they call justice was done."

"Do you think so now?"

Magdalena paused a few moments and fingered the cross hanging from a chain around her neck. Finally, with her voice devolving into a sigh, she said, "He's a mother's son. There's nothing more I can say."

CHAPTER 7

Buddy Cochran smiled when he looked up from his pastrami sandwich and spotted Donnally heading toward his centerline booth in the crowded Canter's Deli in Hollywood.

"Hey, kiddo. What brings you back down to Wonderland?"

Buddy held up his greasy fingers to display his reason for not shaking hands, then wiped his mouth with his napkin and pointed at the opposite bench.

Donnally slid in.

"This about your old man?"

"How'd you guess?"

"I guessed because if you hadn't shown up pretty soon, I would've called you myself."

A waitress walked toward the table with her order pad in one hand and a small plate of sliced kosher pickles in the other. Donnally ordered a coffee. Buddy told her to also bring Donnally a corned beef on rye and slid his check toward her so she could add them to his tab.

Donnally thought of waving it off, but he didn't want to deny the aging actor the pleasure he received from generosity.

After the waitress turned away, Buddy said, "Either your father has reached a new level of genius, or he's gone completely . . ."

Buddy looked down as though trying to duck the implications of the word that usually completed the phrase. "I mean . . ."

"Bonkers."

Buddy shrugged. "Yeah, that word will do just fine."

"Aren't you Buddy Cochran?" The middle-aged female voice cut into their conversation like a cleaver. Buddy's face stiffened as he stared across the table at Donnally, then he painted on a smile and looked up.

"Yes, I am."

"I knew it—I knew it—I knew it." Her voice soared to a squeal and her face flushed. "I just loved you in *Shooting the Dawn*."

The woman reached out with a take-out menu and a pen. Buddy signed on the front and handed it back. She touched it to her lips and held it against her chest, then thanked him and scurried toward the exit where her husband stood with his hand poised to push open the door, his face stiff and his jaws tight.

Donnally had often seen that expression on men whose wives had gone schoolgirl in the presence of Buddy. The husbands found themselves competing with the ghost of a square-jawed movie icon who lived on behind the sagging cheeks and between the overgrown ears and below the balding head of Buddy Cochran. They usually stared at Buddy with their fists clenched at their sides, straitjacketed by the knowledge that taking a swing at him now would be a form of elder abuse.

Donnally also knew, and was offended by the fact, that it sometimes was the husbands, not the wives, who stopped at his table. Men who'd fought in Korea or in Vietnam, who idolized actors like George C. Scott and John Wayne, who wore VFW or USS *Hornet* caps, and who confused Buddy the man with the roles he played early in his career. They sometimes even saluted him as though the uniforms he'd worn in the movies hadn't been just costumes and as though he'd once been their superior officer.

"Jesus Christ," Buddy said as he watched the woman follow her husband out of the restaurant. "I've gotten two Academy Awards since then and three other nominations, but all people remember is that damn thirty-five-year-old war movie."

Donnally wasn't going to say it, but Buddy had kept himself at the receiving end of those reminders by choosing to lunch every day at Canter's.

Same time. Same booth. In the sight line of every customer, even those who only got as far as the bakery and deli counters at the front.

Buddy's eyes went vacant for a moment, then he pursed his lips and shook his head.

"Sorry." He looked back at Donnally. "I shouldn't feel so ungrateful. If it weren't for that thing, your father would've wasted his life making commercials for Ivory soap"—he glanced around the restaurant—"and I'd be here faking a Yiddish accent and taking orders for knishes and chopped liver."

The waitress walked up with Donnally's coffee. She smiled first at Buddy, then at Donnally as she set it down.

"You got the sexy smile," Buddy said, after she walked away. "I got the one the girls reserve for old men. But I'm not really complaining. I am an old man and I think I'm finally coming to prefer to be treated like one."

"Unlike my father."

"For the first time in his life he's begun to rage against the dying of the light. Until about six months ago he seemed oblivious to the idea of his own death." Buddy grinned. "Maybe that's because he's always referred to as The Immortal Don Harlan."

His grin faded and he looked away, seemingly lost in thought or memory. Finally, he said, "There's an odd thing about getting old. It goes back to something I learned the first time I did my own car chase scene. You're racing toward something fixed, a climb or a turn, then all of a sudden there's this paralyzing moment when everything seems to be rising up or racing toward you." He looked back at Donnally. "The truth is I think he's coming to see he can't escape what now feels like the dark night of oblivion coming right at him."

"What makes you think that's it? I can't imagine him inviting you over for a beer to discuss his mortality."

"You're right. He wouldn't. It's more that he's showing the signs." Buddy paused in thought for a moment, then said, "He's always been an ambitious guy, in a hurry, but now he seems desperate. And I've seen enough people facing the end of their careers who've acted the same way."

Buddy took a sip of his iced tea. "Has he told you about the movie we just wrapped?"

Donnally shook his head. "He said he wanted it to be a surprise."

"And you haven't gotten over the surprise of the last one yet."

Don Harlan's previous film was a remake of all his Vietnam War movies from the early 1980s through the late 1990s. But this time no longer from the perspective of the American soldiers who he'd always portrayed as berserk *Deer Hunter* and *Apocalypse Now* monsters, but from the point of view of the kinds of villagers who'd set up the ambush by the North Vietnamese soldiers who killed Donnally's older brother. It had been an artistic success, but a commercial failure, playing first to a few near-empty art theaters, then at fund-raisers for wounded Afghanistan and Iraq War veterans.

"I'm afraid he's the one who hasn't gotten over it," Donnally said. "He went into a tailspin of depression, not because it didn't make any money, but because he'd spent his life hiding from the truth, then acknowledged it and put it out there where it could never be hidden from again. He only came out of the fog trailing behind it when a producer came to him with a bag of money to make something new."

Buddy looked away, seeming to gaze past Donnally toward the take-out counters. His face had flushed a little by the time his eyes returned to Donnally's. He looked to Donnally like a little boy trying to keep a secret.

"What?" Donnally asked, then glanced over his shoulder. He didn't recognize anyone in the booths behind him or placing orders and no fans were approaching. He thought back on what he had just told Buddy. "You have something to do with financing the new picture?"

Buddy rocked his head side to side. "Let's just say that some of us old-timers got together. We all have more money than we can ever spend and it only seems to serve to corrupt our children and grandchildren."

His granddaughter's drunken nights in New York clubs and screaming episodes with her parents were subjects of multimillion-hit Internet videos, and her tours through rehab were reported on afternoon entertainment news programs like box scores. Buddy had long since stopped giving interviews to the entertainment press because all the reporters wanted to talk about were her escapades.

And the last thing the girl needed was more money or the promise of it as an inheritance.

"We hoped . . . maybe . . ." Buddy ended the sentence with a shrug.

"How did you know he needed the lifeline?"

"He stopped talking to us. Wouldn't return our calls. We thought he was embarrassed because of what happened with his last movie, so we got somebody to front for us." Buddy half smiled. "If it happened to another director, he'd have appreciated the irony that some of the people he hired to act in the film were also investors. And we didn't realize going in that he'd have a lot of trouble finishing it."

Buddy looked down at his unfinished sandwich and pushed the plate away.

"He kept forgetting things, like what we'd shot the previous day, script changes, sometimes even who was playing what part."

Buddy fell silent, then he nodded as though he'd just gotten an insight into what had been going on.

"Looking back, I think some of it was structural. He was trying to tell the same story from four different points of view, like *Rashomon* and *The Outrage*. Except he was using different actors for each substory, and that made it hugely complicated. Four different guys playing different versions of what seemed like the same role."

Donnally thought of the DVD his mother's doctor had viewed showing the scenes of four men turning away and walking through the same door.

"Hell, none of us knows what the real truth of the tale is. It was like getting to the end of a mystery novel and discovering that somebody ripped out the last chapter."

"What's the movie about?"

Buddy shook his head. "Can't say. We all signed confidentiality agreements, even the caterers and prop guys and the uniforms who guarded the set."

"How about just a hint?"

Buddy raised his palms toward Donnally. "No can do."

Donnally looped back to his father's symptoms. "But not all of his problems had to do with the structure of the filming."

Buddy rocked his head side to side again, then spread his hands on the table.

"What do I know?"

"Enough so you were thinking about calling me."

Buddy held his nose. "He started to smell bad toward the end of filming. Body odor like an Amazonian stevedore in a Humphrey Bogart flick. That was the first thing we noticed that made us think the problem might be him and not the nature of the work." He tapped the Formica tabletop as though he was annoyed at a negligent child. "Everyone has time for a shower."

Buddy squinted at Donnally. "You haven't seen him since you came down?"

Donnally shook his head. "I wanted to get an idea of what to look for before I went up to the house. My mother's gerontologist hinted at a few things, but she doesn't know him like you do."

"I'm not a shrink, so don't look to me for a diagnosis. All I know is what I saw, not what it means. I'm not an expert in . . . in . . ."

Buddy's voice trailed off and he glanced away.

Donnally didn't force him to say the word *Alzheimer's*.

"And there was something else. He'd talk on and on, real excited and animated, about *Shooting the Dawn* and some of his older films. First I thought he was trying to make comparisons in order to give the actors guidance about what he wanted. Then I thought he was trying to use them as models to teach some lessons to the assistant director who was helping him. A smart young guy. A couple of years out of USC film school. Seemed really in tune with your father. I think he saw all this too."

Buddy shook his head, returning himself to the train of thought he had interrupted.

"But then it hit me. The old movies seemed more real to him than the scenes he was getting ready to shoot." He held his hand up close to his nose for few seconds. "I mean right there in his face."

After reading material Janie had given him, Donnally knew without Buddy saying it that short-term memory loss was one of the most common symptoms of Alzheimer's and was the way it often first showed itself. It was also the one most often ignored or excused merely as old age by friends and family. It was the oldest memories that seemed to the victim to be the most real and alive, but even those might be confused or conflated.

"Other times he would drift away in his own world, like a son . . . som . . ."

Buddy closed his eyes and held his arms out in front of him like a sleepwalker. He opened them again. "Like in the silent movies. I can't remember how to say it."

"Somnambulist?"

"Yeah, that's it. Somnambulist. Sometimes it was like we were talking to a zombie."

CHAPTER 8

W e're a long way from understanding the physiology of the brain," Dr. Katrina Pose said to Donnally. They were standing in the semicircular driveway of his parents' Hollywood Hills mansion. She had been walking to her car when he drove up. She smiled. "I'm sure you didn't need Janie to tell you that."

"But with respect to Alzheimer's, she's deferring to you." Donnally smiled back. "She still considers me to be in the normal range."

Donnally had first met Dr. Pose five years earlier at her office down the block from the Cedars-Sinai Medical Center. It was while his mother was undergoing tests for Parkinson's disease. He had expected the gerontologist to be Hollywood or Beverly Hills in her manner, wearing the intentional, calculated, and disinterested expression of those who were always, or hoped always to be, on camera. Instead, she looked like the tall, awkward, and smartest girl in high school who was now all grown up.

Standing there with her, Donnally felt the irony of his father having chosen her as his mother's doctor, but his now becoming her diagnostic subject.

He also knew that his father would someday view this discussion as a betrayal.

Donnally directed her away from the house and toward the native garden overlooking downtown Los Angeles in the hazy distance.

"It's not just his personal habits," Pose said, "or his sometimes seeming to live more in the past than the present. There are serious things happening that go beyond just memory impairment or some milder form of dementia, things that indicate Alzheimer's. And the fact that it seems to be developing quickly suggests it might be combined with some other neurological condition. Your mother said that with respect to recent events he gets confused about what happened, when it happened, and in what order. And there's his inability to think of words, common ones, even standard phrases in the industry. Falling silent halfway through thoughts and sentences, and then a burst of anger and withdrawal into himself."

Pose pointed down the hillside toward a new concrete retaining wall bisecting the shrubbed descent toward the cliff.

"One day I witnessed some of it. I was driving up and I heard him start to yell something to the contractor. Then he stopped midsentence, with his hand in the air, pointing and stammering. Finally, his face flushed and he gave up and went inside."

"And you're thinking this is physiological, not psychological? A brain issue and not just temporary depression?"

"There are lots of things that can contribute to the kinds of behaviors your father is exhibiting, even beyond the physiological. Worries about aging and loss of vitality. A first true recognition of the inevitability of death. The light of fame that has given meaning to his life fading into an empty darkness. Religious questioning after a lifetime of blind avoidance or acceptance. Sometimes it can begin with guilt, like your father's over your brother's death. Even things that were only partly in a person's control can cause the mind to suppress or rewrite the past, or distort the present or throw the victim into a vortex of confusion."

The doctor paused, then said, "In the old Freudian days we'd have called it the return of the repressed."

Pose was talking about his father, but Donnally was also thinking about Judge McMullin. He was beginning to wonder whether the source of the judge's doubts about the Dominguez case had the same sources as the peculiar behavior and distorted thinking his father had been exhibiting.

"Why did you start with guilt and not depression?" Donnally asked. "Because of his last movie?"

"More because of the way your mother has been framing it. I think they're combined in her mind as one thing or that it was guilt that led to depression."

Donnally glanced back at his mother's second-story window. He knew she was lying in bed, perhaps terrified by the thought that her advanced Parkinson's had left her helpless to care for her husband during his decline. He felt his heart wrench and his body lean toward the front door, moved by the urge to break off the conversation and go to her. But he fought it off. She needed clarity about his father as much as he did, but was less able to achieve it than he was.

"Are you sure that it isn't wishful thinking on her part?" Donnally asked. "Hoping it's something that can be talked through or medicated away, rather than Alzheimer's, which can't."

"Well, it's not that it can't be . . ." Pose's voice trailed off.

They both knew drugs could only delay the progression, and then only briefly, but not cure the underlying disease. That was irreversible.

Donnally glanced along the side of the house, past the parking apron and toward the garages in the back. The door to his father's was open and his car was missing.

"You know where he is now?"

Pose looked toward the empty garage and her brow furrowed. "He was supposed to be here this afternoon, and I saw him when I arrived; otherwise I wouldn't have called you to come down. He'd talked about some digital effects he wanted some help with from a company in San Diego, but I didn't think he was leaving town until tomorrow."

"Why San Diego? L.A. has the best people in the world for doing that kind of thing. Ones he's worked with for years."

"My guess? Secrecy. That's been one of his preoccupations."

Donnally felt a rush of anger, as though his father was evading him, even though he couldn't have been aware that Donnally was traveling down to see him.

"Any clue how long he'll be gone?"

Pose shook her head.

"I'm happy for the chance to visit my mother, but if he's already left, I'm not going to accomplish what I came down for. I was hoping to get a sense of him myself and try to figure out a way to get him in for some tests."

"Can't you stay for few days?"

Donnally shook his head. "I've got to get back up north. I've got someone else's memories to deal with until my father shows up again."

CHAPTER 9

The Paul Ordloff that Donnally found sitting at the bar in the Ocean View Lounge near Monterey along California's central coast matched the black-and-white photo in the San Francisco Bar Association Directory. Just add fifteen years, rosacea from nose to cheeks, skin jaundiced by the bar lights, and shoulders that Donnally guessed had been rounded by the gravity of his clients' crimes.

Donnally slid onto a stool next to him and made a show of glancing around the dark room with its walnut tables and shadowed booths packed with laughing and cackling attendees of the Annual Criminal Defense Death Penalty Conference.

"Where's the ocean view?" Donnally asked him. "Or is the sign out front false advertising?"

Ordloff held his highball glass up toward the neon Anchor Steam sign above the mirror behind the bar. "In here." Then he cocked his head toward Donnally, squinted at him, and smiled. "I know you. *People versus Bernard Bitsky.* Murder most foul." He took a sip and smacked his lips. "You were young and I was desperate."

Ordloff's direct examination of Donnally during a hearing on the defense motion to suppress Bitsky's confession still annoyed him, but he'd decided on the drive up from Los Angeles to Monterey that he wouldn't bring it up if Ordloff didn't.

But Ordloff did.

"You knew I wasn't lying," Donnally said. "Your client confessed before I could even read him his rights. Right after I put him in my car for the ride down to the Hall of Justice. That's the truth."

"Truth?" Ordloff turned toward him in a drunkard's lean and smirked, showing old smoker's teeth, long and yellowed with tar. "What did truth have to do with it? Lives were at stake."

"Like in the Israel Dominguez case?"

Ordloff pulled back and narrowed his eyebrows at Donnally. "The plot thickens as a new character suddenly enters the play from stage right." He glanced toward the door. "Sorry, stage left." Then back at Donnally. "The question is why. Are you with the attorney general's office now and trying to make sure Dominguez gets the needle?"

Donnally shook his head.

"Then gone private and working for his appellate lawyers?"

Donnally shook his head again and reached into his jacket pocket and handed Ordloff a copy of the letter Dominguez had sent Judge McMullin.

Ordloff read it over, holding it up and facing it toward the faint overhead lights, rocking his head side to side as he read it.

"I didn't realize you'd joined the great battle against death." Ordloff set the letter down, then reached over and shook Donnally's hand. "Welcome to the Monterey Death Festival." He pointed at the conference binder lying on the bar next to his glass. "I didn't see you listed as an attendee. I would've noticed your name for sure. I always look for familiar ones, especially ex-cops who've now gotten religion or people who might want to buy me a drink."

"I haven't and I will." Donnally glanced around. "I'm not sure why anyone opposed to the death penalty would even be here. Seems to me the best way to oppose it is not to participate. I'm not sure you can have it both ways."

"That's what lawyering is." Ordloff grinned. "Having it at least both ways and getting paid for it."

"I'm not sure that's an answer. As far as I can tell, ninety-nine percent of lawyers and judges won't have anything to do with capital cases."

Or, like Judge McMullin, would have nothing more to do with them.

Donnally gestured toward the tables behind them filled with attendees, their drinks, and their monogrammed conference binders.

"These people are the one percent that's left. They stop and the machine stops. I would've thought they'd have figured that out by now. You said it. Lives are at stake. If they don't want lives taken, they shouldn't be taking part in taking them."

Ordloff scrunched up an eye toward Donnally. "Do you always say everything that's on your mind?"

Donnally shrugged. "Not always." Then he caught the attention of the bartender, pointed at Ordloff's empty glass, and held up two fingers. The bartender nodded and reached behind him toward the scotch bottles lined up together in front of the mirror.

"But at least you end up asking every question that's on your mind."

Now it was Donnally's turn to smile. "I usually get around to them all."

The bartender poured and set their drinks down in front of them. Donnally slid a twenty to him. Given that the bar was located on the exclusive bay side of the city, he didn't expect to receive much in change.

Ordloff took a sip from his and said, "And your first question concerns why I put on the defense I did in the Dominguez case."

Donnally nodded. "In the letter he claims he's innocent and that he told you so from the moment you first interviewed him in the jail after Judge McMullin appointed you to represent him."

Ordloff leaned back and spread his hands as though speaking for all the attorneys around him in what he was about to say.

"Defendants all claim they're innocent."

Donnally knew that wasn't true. It was just the opposite. He'd gotten dozens of murder confessions when he was a detective. But he didn't challenge Ordloff. He suspected the man needed his fictions to shield his mind from the thoughts and images that probably attacked him after the alcohol wore off—like Israel Dominguez heading toward his execution.

"And Dominguez wasn't an exception," Ordloff said, "and no more believable than any other defendant facing two eyewitnesses who knew him so well that they knew which was his favorite jacket and the last girl he had sex with." He thumped the table with his forefinger. "They couldn't have been mistaken."

"Why not let him roll the dice? It was his life that was at—"

Ordloff interrupted him with a cutting motion and his words came in a rush. "It was my life too. Not just his." He caught himself and his face flushed. "Forget I said that. It came out wrong."

In Donnally's mind, it had come out exactly the way Ordloff was thinking it, maybe even the way he had been thinking it since the day he took on the case.

Donnally wondered how much scotch over the years had gone into filling a psychological moat to protect the man from too much of his own truth.

Apparently, not quite enough, for Donnally now had confirmation that at least part of Judge McMullin's theory and memory about what had happened was correct.

Donnally imagined McMullin's bailiff listening to Ordloff and Dominguez yelling at each other in the attorney interview room, the two talking past each other, Ordloff making arguments to the kid that masked his real fear and the kid crying in frustration and terror.

"Your life?" Donnally said. "You mean your professional reputation. Sounds to me like you didn't want to lose a death penalty trial and carry the loss on your record for the rest of your career, so you dummied up the kind of defense that might allow a jury to find its way to a noncapital conviction. And to do it, you had to disregard Dominguez's claim of innocence."

Ordloff's didn't respond. He just stared down at his scotch.

"It had nothing to do with my reputation," Ordloff finally said. "No one was paying attention. No one cared either about a dead Mexican gangster or the live Mexican gangster who murdered him, except the D.A. for whom a conviction in the Dominguez case was no more than a step toward promotion. You weren't going anywhere in the D.A.'s office back then unless you proved yourself by putting some crook on death row. Same thing for judges. They had to prove, in their far-too-revealing words, they could pull the trigger."

Donnally felt a reverberation from McMullin's riverside confession, the same phrase, the same fear of being seen as weak.

"Then if it wasn't your reputation, what was it?"

Ordloff looked over at Donnally. "You want to know the truth?"

They both recognized it was a rhetorical question, so Ordloff didn't wait for Donnally to answer.

"It was as simple as this. I wasn't prepared to spend my life living with the knowledge that Israel Dominguez was on death row waiting to be executed."

Donnally hadn't expected that much honesty from Ordloff, a lawyer who was more than willing to falsely accuse cops of perjury, and he wondered whether Ordloff was as divided a human being as McMullin, a tough court-self and a fragile private-self.

Donnally pointed his thumb over his shoulder. "I assumed everyone here was prepared to live with a client on death row, otherwise they wouldn't be at this conference. That's what I meant by participating in capital punishment. If you aren't willing to accept the result, you shouldn't play the game."

There had been a parallel in his own decision to become a police officer.

"It's no different than a cop deciding to strap on a gun. It's immoral to do it unless you're willing to take a life and live with it afterwards."

Ordloff shook his head and offered a half smile. "Very dramatic, but I think you're too much of a meat and potatoes guy—black-and-white-with-no-gray-in-between—to grasp the subtlety of what goes on here. The only way most of us can participate is because we lie to ourselves and each other about why we really do these cases."

Ordloff glanced behind him. "Sure, there are a couple of true believers out there, but everybody else is in it for the money." His forefinger thumped the bar. "Money—money—money. Whenever a D.A. charges a defendant with special circumstances, all of the capital defense lawyers hear a cash register ringing, if not for them, for somebody else."

"Then what do they come down here for?"

"See what's new in the law."

"They could do that on their computers. All the new cases are online."

"And people who go to church could just as well stay home and read the Bible all on their own, but they need the romance and the afterglow, or maybe the magic and mystery." Ordloff grinned. "Like transubstantiation." His grin soured. "And just like in religion, they spend a lot of time trying to explain away the anomalies, like when the good suffer evil or the evil lack nothing in the way of goods."

Ordloff tilted his head to his right.

"Look behind you, toward the far corner."

Donnally glanced over. He spotted four men sitting at a booth, a dim light shining down from above. Like Ordloff, they all had conference binders lying on the table in front of them.

"You see the guy in the gray rumpled sweats? A complete idiot. He couldn't tell you the difference between express and implied malice and he submits motions to the court covered with coffee splatters and jelly stains. And he got life verdicts in eight straight trials in a row. Eight. A world record. You can look it up."

Ordloff tilted his head again.

"The guy across from him? Skinny, with the specs. Yale undergrad. Harvard Law. Teaches evidence and criminal procedure part time at Boalt Hall at UC Berkeley. The smartest guy in the room—hell, the smartest guy in any room, any time. He did two capital trials and got two death sentences. And they were two

tion and at the same time give the jury something to latch onto, something they could convict Dominguez of that would keep him off death row."

Ordloff held up his conference binder.

"The first thing they teach you in these seminars, and I've been coming here for decades, is that if you claim innocence in the guilt phase of the trial, the jury will hammer you in the pen-ty phase. Hammer you. A defendant can't claim he didn't do it, en do a one-eighty and say he committed the crime because of use he suffered as a child and express remorse and expect the to believe him and show mercy."

That had been Judge McMullin's argument, but now there ed something wrong with it. Why couldn't the defendant laim innocence and ask the jury to let him live so he has ce to prove it? Jurors knew about convicts who were later by DNA evidence and by confessions from the real perpe-

ally pointed at the binder. "What about what they call doubt? When a jury isn't really positive about guilt and 's better to keep the defendant alive just in case."

still not listening to me. There . . . was . . . no . . . doubt ing."

threw up his arms.

as I supposed say to the jury? I know you found him d a reasonable doubt, but you were wrong, you really and you lied to the court in your verdict?"

od there, hands raised like a tent preacher or the cru-ntil the absurdity of the gesture was revealed to him gazes of a young couple walking on the path behind

of the weakest death cases that ever came through a California court."

Ordloff laughed.

"Harvard Law is the exception. The truth is that most of the lawyers who do capital cases aren't the best of the best, they're the best of the worst."

He swept his arm like a king gesturing toward his court.

"The reason we do death penalty cases—and all on the public dime—is because we weren't good enough to make the cut. Never made it to the big time and the big money cases. And we com-pensate for that failure by creating a mythology." Ordloff tapped his chest. "The myth of our great worth to humanity. That's one of the things we come down here to celebrate. Our great worth."

The words reminded Donnally of a discomfort he felt when he saw around the court building what Ordloff was calling the best of the worst. They handled the more exceptional cases that came through, but they, themselves, were so average, so unexceptional, mere day laborers in what was claimed to be the house of justice.

Their presence had always made the criminal justice process seem disjointed and irrational to Donnally. It sometimes left him with a feeling of having a kind of guilty knowledge—the same sort he was feeling now—like a quarterback who'd just watched the refs make a bad holding call against the other team and who didn't have the moral courage to refuse the penalty.

Maybe that was part of the reason he was happy in Mount Shasta. It didn't have its own courthouse, not even to handle traf-fic tickets, much less capital cases. Nothing to trigger his imagi-nation, putting him back in courtroom hallways, and giving him the queasy feeling that went along with it.

"In the end, of course," Ordloff said, "competence has no bearing on either the verdict or the penalty. In capital cases the outcome is completely arbitrary. Com . . . pletely. It isn't related to the seriousness of the crime or the strength of the evidence or the worth of the defendant. The consequence, again like a religion, is that a mythology has been built up around it."

The alcohol that Donnally thought had been used to build a moat now seemed like a flood that had burst a dam.

"Then why'd you get into it? I've seen you in action. You're not an idiot. Back then you were better than almost all the other lawyers who did these cases."

"I learned the lesson too late."

"Then why stay in it?"

"Because . . ."

Ordloff's voice trailed away as though he was contemplating the question, or had arrived at the heart of the matter and had to admit a truth to himself for the first time.

"I guess you could say it's the continuing punishment for having committed the original crime."

CHAPTER 10

You're not listening to me."

Paul Ordloff's voice rose above the win
crashing onto the breakwater along Monterey B
nally were standing on the shore trail, a half
Ocean View Lounge and the conference grou

Ten minutes earlier, Ordloff had stood up
bar, and then looked around at the lawyers
and tables and mumbled that he had to ge

Donnally hadn't been sure what Ordl
he hadn't objected to Donnally followi

"He was guilty. He was guilty. He
beat the air like a pounding gavel. "
in-wait murder. The Sureños wan
Israel Dominguez wanted the Sur
his ticket. That was the prosecut
was the testimony they produce
torpedoed Dominguez for sur

Ordloff turned toward Do

"Arguing second-degree
to attack their informant
jail or stay out of jail by

them. He lowered his arms, looked down at the binder, gripped it like a Frisbee, and tossed it toward the just-risen moon on the horizon. It spun in flight, disklike, then opened and dropped, flailing like a buckshot pheasant into the kelp-carpeted sea.

"That stuff is useless," Ordloff said, staring at it.

"Then why do you come down here?"

"Why do you think? The bar association makes us take continuing education courses. And this way I can stay drunk for three straight days and still get credit."

Ordloff pointed back toward the yellow lights of the conference grounds, now muted by a wispy fog skimming the water toward them. The stars above still shined bright and clear.

"The only thing . . . the only thing . . . you learn down here is how to protect yourself from your former clients and from the appeals and habeas corpus lawyers that sniff over the carcass of your work."

"You make it seem like all that moves these trial lawyers is money and fear."

"You got that right, pal. The twin sisters of human motivation."

"What about justice?"

Ordloff paused, staring at Donnally, then snorted. "I don't think you've understood a single thing I've said." He jabbed a forefinger at Donnally's chest. "You brain dead or something? It's not all that complicated."

Donnally took in a breath and felt his stomach tense. The flailing lawyer had nailed him in the gut with an inadvertent strike. There were few things Donnally knew about Alzheimer's, but one of them was that it was genetic. In his preoccupation with his father and McMullin, he now realized he might not have heard the starting pistol shot announcing the beginning of his own descent toward oblivion. For a moment, he felt an irrational sense of urgency. He recognized it and swallowed hard, suppressing it.

He also felt an urge to toss Ordloff into the bay.

"I heard you," Donnally said, "but I don't see life as that narrow and our motivations as that limited."

Ordloff stared out toward where his binder had fallen into the water. Finally, he said, "You know, Judge McMullin could've saved the kid if he wanted to. There were ways."

"You mean by not following the jury's recommendation?"

Ordloff shook his head. "No judge will ever do that. They'd get recalled in a heartbeat and the cable news channels would crucify them. But there are other methods judges use all the time."

"Like?"

"Like letting the D.A. use illegally obtained evidence so the conviction, or at least the penalty, gets reversed on appeal. Or make some bad rulings on motions. Judges who oppose the death penalty do it all the time. They know the defendant is going down anyway; they just want him to get a second chance to stay alive somewhere down the road."

"And you figure McMullin had those chances and didn't take them."

"He was new, but he'd been around long enough to figure out how the game was played." Ordloff squinted at Donnally as if trying to assess his reactions. "I know you've watched judges make bizarre rulings in these cases and never understood why. Well, I'm telling you now." He looked back the way they'd come. "There's a federal judge down in Texas that has been sitting on a habeas corpus case for over ten years, keeping the defendant alive by delaying his appointment of an attorney to represent him."

"Don't the relatives of the victim—"

"Nope. There aren't any left to complain. The defendant killed them all. That's what he was convicted of."

Donnally thought back on the trials he'd been involved with. It was the attorneys, far more than judges, who engaged in bizarre maneuvers, seeming to plant errors.

"Do attorneys sometimes do that, too? Not make the objections they're supposed to, don't seem to prepare the way they're supposed to?"

"All the time. Sometimes the appeals courts even catch them at it—or at least accuse them of intentionally sabotaging hopeless cases—and refuse to overturn convictions they should."

"Did you do that in the Dominguez case?"

Ordloff displayed a twisted grin. "Even if I did, I wouldn't admit it. I'd get disbarred." His grin faded and his mouth turned down. "But I didn't. Anyway, if I did try to build in some error, it didn't work. The U.S. Supreme Court is about to flush him down the judicial toilet."

Donnally watched Ordloff stare off toward the moon hanging above the horizon. The tide had gone slack and the fog separated and a shaft of moonlight shot toward them across the water. It lit up the dark patches that had formed under Ordloff's eyes. He looked to Donnally like he wanted to dive in and swim to where the light died and the night sky dissolved into the sea.

"You know the weirdest thing about American law, what makes it arbitrary, is that in a state like Texas we wouldn't even be having this conversation. Defendants convicted even of just second-degree murder are put to death all the time and governors down there make sure it happens. They'd get impeached if they didn't."

"This isn't Texas."

"Don't I know it."

"Then tell me something."

"If it'll keep Dominguez alive." Ordloff blinked against the moon's reflection and looked over. "I'll tell you anything. I'll sign anything. I'll testify to anything."

"I went to speak to Edgar Rojo's mother and to look over the scene. She lives in the same place."

"She talked to you?"

Donnally nodded.

"She sure as hell wouldn't talk to us."

There was an angry edge in Ordloff's voice, like the victim's family owed him something, not as an officer of the court with duties to his client to discharge, but to him personally. He stood there like a mirror image of the kind of cop Donnally had hated working with, the kind who wore his uniform not as a second skin, but all the way through to the bone.

"The wound was way too fresh," Donnally said, though he knew that fact couldn't have been news to Ordloff. "And I didn't approach it head-on."

"What did she say?"

"The important thing at the moment is that her son had received a call from an unknown person that caused him to walk behind the couch and look out the front window." Donnally angled his arm upward. "Unless Rojo was right up close to the glass, a guy as short as Dominguez couldn't have hit him. Even then it would've taken a sharpshooter."

Ordloff watched Donnally lower his arm, then said, "I knew about the call and about the police's inability to trace it. It was a dead end. And I'm not even sure it meant that much. Not on New

Year's Eve with lots of people on the street, coming and going. Lots of people looking to meet up and party."

"But you didn't think so at the time."

"No. Not at the time. It walked like a setup and talked like a setup, but we couldn't prove that's what it was or discover whether Dominguez had anything to do with it. And neither could the D.A. That's why McMullin limited the testimony about it. To keep the jury from speculating too much."

"What about the shooting itself? Dominguez have any experience firing a handgun?"

"What difference would it have made?" Ordloff smirked. "Was I supposed to argue to the jury that Dominguez was too unlucky a guy to have gotten off a lucky shot?"

Donnally shook his head. "That's not telling me anything."

"You've been to police seminars." Ordloff nodded toward the distant conference center as though law enforcement also used it. "You know as well as I do how those Sureños train their people. They're practically paramilitary. They have their own camps, just like terrorists."

He formed his hand into that shape of a gun. "When they decide to take somebody out, they take that somebody out. That's who they are and what they do."

Then he tilted his finger upward and pulled the trigger.

CHAPTER 11 ===

D onnally noticed the tail as he drove from his house far out in the avenues, a few blocks from Ocean Beach, that he'd bought when he was with the department and now shared with Janie. He was on his way to Fort Miley Veterans Medical Center to pick her up at the end of her shift. The trailing Chevy Impala focused his mind that had been divided all day as he sat in front of a computer at the court of appeals reading through the briefs in the Dominguez file. He hadn't anticipated that the consequence of his conversation with Ordloff was that he'd spend the next twenty-four hours feeling the Alzheimer's barrel pressed against his temple.

The car followed him as he made the three turns to get onto the commercial Clement Street and heading west toward the sunset. Donnally couldn't make out the face of the single occupant, but the front license plate was missing its frame, suggesting it might be a rental.

The problem for an ex-cop who laid his head in the town where he'd spent his career was that the past was never past. Chance sightings of the officers who'd sent them away remind crooks of wasted years, of dead time spent caged inside steel bars, pacing concrete. Animosities grind, sharpening thoughts of revenge, and then prison sentences end and the crooks return to the wide open streets with a narrowed sense of relevance. For them, there are cops and there are cons and nothing in between.

Donnally slowed, letting the driver catch up so he could get a glimpse through the windshield. Maybe the face would draw out a memory. But the more the gap narrowed, the more the descending sun's refection masked the glass. The driver seemed to catch on to what Donnally was doing and backed off again.

Veterans Drive into Fort Miley came up on his right, the broad entrance onto the grounds now seeming like an opening into a trap. There was no reason to let the guy—if it was a guy, for revenge knows no gender—start guessing at the connection between him and the hospital if he didn't know it already. Instead of turning into the property, Donnally cut left into a street of bungalows.

Donnally pulled to the curb midway down the block. He hoped the man following him would either park along the street behind him so he could catch a look at his face, no longer masked by the sun, or at least get the plate and call it into Ramon Navarro.

But the driver did neither. He pulled into the shadow extending across the pavement from the row houses lining the west side.

That the man had failed to disguise his surveillance, his incompetence at the craft, puzzled and annoyed Donnally rather than making him worried or fearful. He thought about walking up on him, but dismissed the idea for he'd likely spin a U-turn and flee before Donnally could close in.

Better to try to lead him into a trap.

Donnally scanned the street ahead to make sure he hadn't fallen into one himself, then popped his hood. He put a perplexed expression on his face as he climbed out of his truck, suggesting he'd noticed a troubling noise. A double, maybe even a triple, pretense. Donnally was pretending he wasn't under surveillance and the surveiller was pretending he wasn't surveilling, and neither's act was convincing the other.

As Donnally probed the engine compartment, jiggling wires and tugging at hoses, he called Janie, asking her to catch a cab home. He then drove to an auto supply shop and killed enough time inside for the sun to finish setting and for the distant clouds over the Pacific to smother the remaining daylight.

Donnally headed back toward Fort Miley through the gray evening, then wound his way between the wooded Lincoln and Sutro Heights parks to the coast. He pulled into a parallel parking space along the curving road north of the Cliff House, a two-story, modern museum-like restaurant overlooking the ocean.

The Chevy slowed, but there were no more spaces on Donnally's side and the hill across the road descended to the edge of the traffic lane. The car passed him. Donnally got enough of a glimpse of the turned-away head to confirm it was a man, but nothing more. He pulled into a spot in front of a low wall thirty yards south of the restaurant, facing the water. Its lights died, but the driver didn't get out.

Donnally walked into the street-level bar overlooking the downstairs dining room. He positioned himself by a window facing the street to make sure he could be observed, then ordered a beer. He drank half of it in the next five minutes, then made a show of getting the waitress's attention, pointing at the glass, and at the hallway toward the restroom to indicate that he'd be back and not to clear the table.

The route he chose kept him in view of the front of the building until just before he reached the turn toward the men's room. He broke off and cut down the steps to the dining room, then through swinging doors and past the kitchen to a back exit.

Rather than trying to sneak his way along the lighted parking area, Donnally lowered himself over the concrete retaining wall and climbed along the breakwater rocks. He reached a spot just below where the man had parked and peeked over the wall. He spotted a thirty-year-old Hispanic. Tall, thin, and pacing like a caged panther next to his car, his eyes fixed on the restaurant entrance. His oversized gangster-style sweatshirt hung loose on his body. The hood was lying back, revealing a narrow face and short hair under an Oakland Raiders knit cap.

Donnally watched him finger-flick his cigarette, shooting it down to the blacktop, the tobacco ember fragmenting and exploding upward, then walk around his car and open the trunk. The inside light glowed against an unfamiliar face. It revealed two prison tattoos, a heart pierced by a sword on one side of his neck and a spider web on the other. He ducked down for a moment, straightened up, looked around, then closed the lid and slipped something into his back pocket.

As Donnally reached for the semiautomatic in his shoulder holster, he recognized that a 911 call wouldn't help. The man knew where he lived and next time he'd lie in wait, not follow him. And if the man made a move and Donnally caught him and got him locked up, he could still reach out from jail to his crime partners on the street. Even worse, Donnally couldn't take a chance that, unable to get to him, the man would go after Janie as his proxy.

Whatever was going to happen between them had to happen now and be over with.

Donnally lowered himself and waited for a wave to crash onto the rocks behind him to cover the sound of ripping Velcro, then pulled back on the retention strap and drew his gun.

From the shadow cast by a lamppost, Donnally watched him light another cigarette, then walk to the wall and stare out at Seal Rock. Only then did Donnally notice the squawking and yelping seals and sea lions behind him and feel the chill wind against his neck.

The gangster looked again toward the restaurant entrance, then leaned back against the wall.

Donnally remained in his crouch until another wave crashed, then stood and pressed the barrel against the man's back.

The man's body stiffened.

"Stay cool," Donnally told him, locking his left hand on top of the man's shoulder to keep him from turning. "Move a fraction and I'll pull the trigger. I've got nothing to lose. You set it up this way by coming to where I lay my head."

The gangster dropped his cigarette and raised his hands head high.

"It ain't about that."

"Turn around, place your hands on the top of the wall, and spread your legs."

He complied.

Donnally spotted letters N O R T E Ñ O tattooed across his fingers on his splayed hands, just below his knuckles.

Donnally climbed over and patted him down.

A Mercedes roadster pulled into a space fifteen feet away. Two women got out. They paused by their doors after they spotted Donnally. He pulled out his retirement badge, flashed it toward them, then nodded toward the Norteño and uttered the word, "Fugitive."

The women squinted toward the tattooed man, then nodded at Donnally and walked toward the restaurant.

Donnally continued searching and removed a wallet and a pint bottle of brandy from the gangster's back pockets.

No gun. No weapon at all.

Donnally set them both on the top of the wall.

"If 'it ain't about that,' whatever 'that' is," Donnally said, "what's it about?"

"It's about why you bothered my grandmother."

Donnally reached over and flipped open the wallet. The driver's license bore the name Edgar Rojo Jr.

He knew only two things about Junior. At age nine he'd watched his father bleed out on the night he was murdered, and ten years later he beat a victim so badly that the man lost body parts.

Junior now seemed to him to be less like a panther, and more like a pit bull.

"Why'd you follow me?"

Junior shrugged. "I don't know. I went by your house and saw you driving away. I slid in behind, then didn't know what to do when I caught up with you."

Donnally had interpreted Junior's pacing as anticipation, like a lion getting ready to pounce. He now wondered whether it was indecision or anxiety.

"Turn around and sit back against the wall."

He slipped the gun into his jacket pocket so it wouldn't draw any more attention from restaurant patrons, but he kept it aimed at Junior.

Junior's eyes flicked back and forth as he turned around, looking for the gun. They fixed on Donnally's hidden hand and then he reached back and lowered himself to the wall.

Donnally tossed him his wallet. "You're still not telling me anything."

"I need you to leave my grandmother alone. You hear what I'm saying? She ain't part of nothing. She's suffered enough losing my father. No reason for you to bring it all back up again."

"You're a step ahead of me. I don't know whether I'll bring it all up again. I haven't discovered anything to prove it wasn't Israel Dominguez who killed your father or that the evidence didn't support the sentence he got."

Junior stared at Donnally as though they'd started the conversation a question too late.

"What's it to you, anyway?"

"It's coming up on his execution and somebody wanted to make sure the court got it right."

"That's them. Not you."

Donnally shook his head. "I've got no stake in this."

Junior flashed a grim smile. "Yeah, you do. You were ready to shoot me over it."

"And you were ready to do what?"

"If it was ten years ago"—Junior gestured with his thumb toward the ocean—"I'd have torn you into bite-sized chunks and fed you to the sharks."

"And now?"

Junior looked away, then back. "I don't know."

In Junior's manner and words, Donnally sensed doubts about things much older than what he intended to do to Donnally.

"Were you sure Dominguez killed your father?"

"I never heard nothing saying it wasn't him. But it was a war and in a war it don't make no difference who gets taken prisoner. You see what I'm saying?"

"You mean it didn't make a difference to you whether they got the right guy? The one who really pulled the trigger?"

"Course it did. But I was a kid. All I knew was what the police said and what my father's crime partners told me."

The approaching flash of strobing patrol car overheads drew their attention toward the restaurant. The unit rolled to a stop behind Junior's Chevy, against the traffic. The passenger officer looked back and forth between Donnally and Junior as he and the driver got out. He pointed toward the Cliff House.

"We got an officer needs assistance call from a woman in the restaurant, but I don't see an officer."

"There must have been some misunderstanding," Donnally said, then displayed his empty hands.

"Who are you?"

"Retired SFPD." Donnally pointed down with his forefinger. "I'm going reach into my back pocket and show you my retirement badge and ID."

The officer rested his hand on his gun and nodded. "But slowly."

Donnally eased his badge case out of his back pocket and flipped it open as the officer approached.

The officer took it from his hand.

"Donnally . . . Harlan Donnally." He glanced at his partner standing by his door, still using his car as cover. "This is the detective who got shot out there on Mission Street years ago." He looked back at Donnally. "That's you, right?"

Donnally nodded.

"They still teach what you did in the academy firearms train-

ing class. Got a little reenactment video and everything showing you in the cross fire." The officer emitted a breathy whistle.
"Scary as hell."

Donnally didn't respond.

The officer focused on Junior but continued speaking to
Donnally.

"Who's the gangbanger?"

Junior answered. "My name's Edgar Rojo and I ain't no gangbanger no more."

"Then why you wearing the tattooed advertisements all over
your face? Looks to me like you're banging hard-core."

Donnally felt a flush of annoyance at the cop's descent into
crook slang. By accommodating himself to the lawlessness it implied, it legitimized the criminal way of life. It made it seem that
the criminal world was the entire world, not just the badlands,
and that the police weren't representatives of law, but only of
power. Using the language of the gangsters made the police department into just another gang.

The officer didn't wait for a response. He walked Junior to the
back of the patrol car and spread-eagled him over the trunk. He
then told his partner to run a warrant check and read Junior's
name and date of birth off his driver's license. The partner eased
back into his seat and reached over toward the computer monitor
attached to the dashboard and ran the check.

A few seconds later, he climbed out again, "He's clear, but on
parole for mayhem."

"How long you been out?" the nearer officer asked Junior.

"Almost three years. My parole ends in a couple of months."

The officer smirked. "We'll see. Punks like you aren't off the
leash for long."

Donnally caught the motion of Junior's clenching fists.

"Stay cool," Donnally said, pointing at him, then he looked back and forth between the officers. "I got things under control. Thanks for stopping."

Both officers stared at Junior for a long moment, then got back into the patrol car, cut across the oncoming traffic, and accelerated away.

Junior shook his head as the car hit the first curve. "Fuck them assholes."

"Don't go down that road. You brought it on yourself by following me."

"Not the attitude, man. They brought that all on their own."

CHAPTER 12 ==

Donnally watched Junior fiddling with his spoon as they waited for the waitress to bring coffees to their table in Dudley's Place on Clement Street, a mile east of the Cliff House. Junior had tensed like a cat sneaking through a dog pound as they drove through the residential Sunset district toward the café. No dope dealers on the corners or hookers working the sidewalks or dice games in the shadows. The streets were quiet and clean and lined with the houses costing more than Junior would make in his lifetime.

As they walked toward Dudley's, Junior had stared up at the FISHEYE SUSHI BAR sign next door as though the words were written in Japanese and the neighborhood was the capital of a foreign and alien culture.

Junior looked over as a waitress walked by with what Donnally guessed from the menu to be a Carol Doda burger, named for the famous North Beach stripper. It was open-faced with two patties for breasts and olives and pickle rounds for nipples.

"It's just a hamburger," Junior said. "What's wrong with these people? Why they pretending it's more than it is? It's like making a burrito into a dick. Who needs that shit?"

Donnally was surprised by the anger and resentment in Junior's voice. It was as though he felt himself under assault and he was on the near edge of imagining himself opening fire on the waitress for carrying it, and the cook for making it, and the patrons for ordering it. But there was also resignation, suggesting that even in his fantasy he'd wait for the police to arrive and force them to kill him.

"These people haven't done anything to you."

"I told you. It's a war." Without raising his hand, Junior pointed his thumb toward the counter. "Look around. All white people." He rotated it in the direction of the kitchen behind him. "I'll bet you they keep all the Mexicans back there, soaked in sweat and dishwater."

Donnally surveyed the tables. "You mean except the one with the tattoos and gang clothes that everybody keeps glancing at."

Junior didn't smile. "Yeah, except him."

The waitress walked up with their coffees. She positioned herself as she set them down so that she wouldn't have to look at Junior.

"He'll order first," Donnally said, forcing her to turn toward Junior.

Her eyes fixed on the word *Norteño* running from hand to hand as she wrote down his order for a plain hamburger. She had started to ask him whether he meant the Famous Dudley's, then looked at his opaque eyes and stopped.

Donnally ordered the same, then she headed toward the pass-through to the kitchen.

Junior stared down at his coffee. Without looking up, he said, "I ain't no snitch."

"Why do you think I'm asking you to snitch on somebody? I haven't asked you to do anything. Or even to say anything."

Junior ignored him. "I've got to live in this town. You know what I'm saying. I got no place to go and no way to make money."

"What are you doing now?"

Junior finally looked up. "I work for La Raza Outreach. I try to get young gang members out in the Mission to give up the life. They'd cut my throat and torch my grandmother's place if anybody thought I was talking."

"I told you—"

"Eventually you will." Junior glared at Donnally. "That's how cops are."

Donnally knew Junior was right about that. Informants were the shortest way to get from the unknown to the known. But he still didn't know whether anything was truly unknown in the Dominguez case or whether Junior knew it, whatever it was.

"If you were a Sureño, instead of a Norteño, and had inside information about Dominguez and whether the Sureños sent him to kill your father, then maybe I'd push you to talk. But you're not."

Junior stared at him dead-eyed.

Donnally then realized they were talking past each other again. Junior was thinking about the Norteño and Sureño shootout in which Donnally had been shot and that he had used as a pretext in questioning his grandmother and that the cop had mentioned outside the Cliff House. Donnally was thinking about the Sureño conspiracy against Edgar Rojo Sr.

At the same time, Donnally didn't believe Junior was fooled by the cover story because his grandmother must have told him the questions Donnally had asked.

"I'm not looking to do anything about what happened to me," Donnally said. "It doesn't make any difference anymore."

That was a lie. It did. But Donnally wasn't going to tell that to Junior. He'd been working around the edges of the thing since it happened, but had never gotten a strong enough lead to run to the end.

When it happened, it appeared that it was just two gangsters walking toward each other and neither could back down, so they shot it out past Donnally and the young couple caught in the middle—until Donnally cut them both down—and he'd discovered nothing in the meantime to convince him that the appearance wasn't the reality.

"You believe in coincidence?" Junior asked.

"Like?"

"My father gets a call, goes to the window, and gets shot."

"Depends on who he got the call from and why they called."

Junior's face flushed. He lowered his voice and spoke between his teeth.

"Don't screw with me, man. If you been looking into this thing, you know who called."

"How would I know?"

"It was in the police report. Had to be."

Donnally shook his head. "The report just said you told the detectives there was a call, not who made it."

Junior's hands clenched into fists on the tabletop. "That *chingaso.*"

"Then who called?"

"It's none of your business." Junior pushed himself to his feet. "I've had enough of this. I'm gonna take care of him myself."

Donnally pointed at Junior, then at his chair. "Sit down."

Junior remained immobile. Donnally felt the eyes of the white patrons staring at Junior. Talk continued around them, but Donnally had the sense that the words, mixing in the hollow space around them, had somehow become disconnected from the speakers.

"Your grandmother told me you were confused that night and didn't remember what happened and who called."

"She's wrong. I remember. It's her that don't want to remember."

"And twenty years later, you're going to do something about it?"

"I'll do what I need to do."

"If you're doing outreach, that means you've come a long way. Why waste the trip?"

Junior stared ahead, toward the front door. His body moved side to side like he was boxing, as if preparing to dodge a punch, or preparing to throw one.

"I don't know what you have in mind," Donnally said, "but I know there's a better way to do it."

Junior blew out a harsh breath, then sat down. He stared at his coffee cup, his thumbs working against his fingertips.

Donnally expected him to get up again, and this time walk out.

Instead, Junior said, "I haven't come very far at all. I was ready, I'm still ready, to go blow that scumbag away."

"Not quite."

Junior shrugged.

"What changed for you?" Donnally asked. It was too soon to press him on who it was that called and why the detectives had hidden that fact by leaving it out of their reports.

Junior finally looked up. "You know why my father became a Norteño?"

Donnally shook his head.

"The drug cartel down in Michoacán, where the family *ranchito* is, forced a deal on our relatives. My father got caught in the middle. They was gonna suffer down there unless he did what they wanted up here."

"And that was . . ."

"Be on the receiving end of the cocaine they were shipping north."

Junior fell silent again. His eyes moved as though his mind was struggling over something, maybe weighing something, perhaps how much to say, or how much to admit.

"But it wasn't just force and threats. I know that. My father got something out of it too. You know what I'm saying. He'd been in the trade for ten years. It was a chance to move up and have soldiers and guns to protect his operation in the neighborhood. And a way to buy stuff for my grandmother and send money to the family in Mexico."

"And make himself look big."

Junior paused, and then nodded. "Yeah, he wanted that, too."

Since Junior's mother wasn't mentioned in the police reports and she hadn't testified against Dominguez in the penalty phase of the trial as Junior and his grandmother had done, she must have been out of their lives.

"I take it your mother wasn't around when all this happened."

"She got pregnant with me in Mexico and drove a load across the border to pay her way into the States. Got caught. I was born in the women's federal prison in Bryan, Texas."

"Where is she now?"

"Nowhere." He glanced away for a moment, then looked back at Donnally. "She never made it out."

Junior pulled out his wallet. He opened it and turned it toward Donnally, displaying a picture of a slim, long-haired woman dressed in prison blues, sitting at a picnic table next to a razor-wire fence.

"This is the only picture I have of her."

Donnally decided not to say anything about the woman's beauty. That wasn't something a son would want to hear from a stranger about his mother. Or to comment on her sadness. That was something Junior had lived with all his life.

There was nothing he could say, except, "Sorry."

Junior folded his wallet shut. "You didn't do nothing. That's just the way things are."

"I was a cop back then. Maybe . . ."

Donnally didn't know how to finish the sentence.

Junior narrowed his brows at Donnally. "You must be one of those guys who thinks everything is his fault. I had a shrink in the joint who talked about that. He said it was the flip side of paranoia." He lifted his chin toward Donnally. "You paranoid, too?"

Donnally shook his head. "No, just careful about what I do. I grew up with a father who wanted to be big, too. Huge. And he made it. He influenced how the whole country saw itself, but he ducked the responsibility that came with the power."

"He like a politician or something?"

"A movie director."

Donnally surprised himself. Talking to a stranger about his father. And he wasn't sure why. He wondered whether it was because Junior's father was missing for most of his life, while Donnally's father spent most of his life missing in another way, even lost to himself.

He also wondered whether he was prepared to disclose the

hidden truth about his father out of nothing more than a kind of fairness.

"What movies?"

"*Shooting the Dawn* and *Fallen.*"

Junior held out his arms like he was holding a machine gun, then jerked his arms in imitation recoils. "Bam. Bam-bam-bam." He lowered his hands. "I loved those flicks. Watched them over and over. Soldiers jumping up and spraying the jungle with them M16s."

He looked hard at Donnally. "And you been spending your life trying to make up for him?"

Donnally shrugged.

Junior smirked. "What a waste."

"Then what have you been doing?"

"Trying to get away."

Donnally stared at him. Junior had no insight into himself. None. The shrink in prison hadn't seemed to have done him much good. In Junior's language of double and triple negatives, he wasn't going nowhere.

"You were just about to go kill somebody. That's not getting away."

Junior smiled. "Only if I get caught."

"That's not what I meant."

Junior's smile died. "I'll never get away. I carry it all with me. All the questions and half the answers." He paused and bit his lower lip. "Why do you think the detectives didn't include the name of the guy who called my father just before he got shot? The guy that got him to walk to the window and look down."

Donnally thought back on the occasions when he'd left names out of reports.

"In my day, I'd leave out people I needed to protect. Maybe he was a witness in something else or maybe an informant for the police."

Junior shook his head. "You ain't even close, man. Ain't . . . even . . . close . . . He *was* the police."

J udge Ray McMullin gazed down at the police reports about the Edgar Rojo Sr. homicide. Detective Ramon Navarro had retrieved the file from storage again, but this time he made copies for Donnally to show to McMullin. All Navarro would say was that something was starting to smell bad, but he was still unwilling to be seen by other detectives in the department as sniffing along a trail related to Dominguez.

The judge turned each page, ran his finger down the text as he read, licked his fingertip, caught the top edge of the next, flipped it over, and continued.

Donnally wasn't surprised McMullin had no recollection of the issue of who'd made the call and why the name hadn't been disclosed. Not only had twenty years passed since the trial, but as a matter of law, judges don't read the police reports for fear of being influenced by untested allegations. They were allowed to consider only the evidence that had been placed before them in pleadings and in hearings, and no evidence relating to the identity of the caller had been submitted to him.

After fifteen minutes, McMullin closed the folder. "The name isn't here."

He shut his eyes and rubbed his forehead.

Donnally watched his skin stretch and whiten under the pressure, then redden. He had a sense the judge's thoughts had moved on, beyond the words on the page.

McMullin opened his eyes again. He stared at Donnally for a moment, then said, "And you believe Junior that it was a police officer who called?"

"It's possible. I made those kinds of warning calls myself. If I got intelligence a contract was out on someone, I'd contact the target to tell him, even if it compromised an investigation. Like with Emanuel Jones. You remember him?"

McMullin nodded. "His is still the longest sentence ever handed out by a judge in this county. Life plus three hundred years."

"Jones was only alive to get sentenced because I warned him he was about to get hit. And it cost me an informant. I came too close to burning him because only a couple of people were in on it and they were real close to being about to figure out who was in a position to know what was supposed to happen. That informant never gave me anything again."

"Then maybe that's all this was. A cop warning Edgar Senior. And since he got killed anyway, there wasn't any need to put a continuing investigation at risk by giving the defense access to that kind of information."

"Except Junior claims it wasn't just a warning. The cop told him to check the street. That's how he put himself in Dominguez's sights."

"How would Junior know what the caller said?"

"Because his father asked something like 'You mean the front window?' and then walked over and looked down."

"Is Junior claiming the officer was working for the Sureños?"

Donnally shook his head. "He didn't go that far. He might have been thinking it, but he didn't say it."

McMullin leaned back in his chair. It gave Donnally the feeling that he was withdrawing from the issue or preparing to minimize it.

"Maybe the whole thing was just a child's fantasy," McMullin said. "A way to look for someone big to blame for the death of his father. The bigger the conspiracy, the more important his father would be in the kid's mind."

"That's possible. It could be that the cop meant for him just to peek out through some curtains, locate where the killer was lying in wait, then sneak out the back."

"But that begs the question of why Senior wouldn't have just stayed inside and out of harm's way?"

"That depends on what the cop knew or believed at the time and what he'd said to Senior. Suppose the cop hadn't known how the killer was going to do it." Donnally gestured toward Mc-Mullin with an open hand. "Would you risk bringing violence to your mother's home? The plan could've been to firebomb the apartment or make it a home invasion. Maybe Senior makes a show of getting away or sends someone back with a message, 'Too late. You missed your chance.'"

"But the issue remains," the judge said. "Did the information the officer received bear on who killed Senior and why the killer did it?"

"Or just the why of it. Wasn't that the fundamental issue in the trial? What Dominguez was thinking. First-degree premeditation or second-degree reckless disregard?"

McMullin tilted his head back and stared at the wood-paneled ceiling. Donnally had seen that move in court as the judge listened to oral arguments on motions. It seemed to Donnally back then that McMullin wanted to use the blank screen above to focus his mind on the words alone, follow the logic of the arguments, uninfluenced by attorneys' gestures and facial expressions, the pleas behind the pleadings.

"Let's try to think through how it could've played out in court." The judge leaned forward again and folded his arms on the desk. "The D.A. interviews the officer. The officer says he's got an ongoing investigation. The D.A. asks him whether his informant told him ahead of time who would be doing the shooting or where or when."

Donnally provided the answer. "And the cop says no because he doesn't want to have to give up his informant to the defense and compromise an ongoing investigation. Or maybe the cop says the information is second or third hand."

"On that basis, the D.A. decides he doesn't have to disclose it to the defense. The informant only has inadmissible hearsay and isn't a percipient witness to the crime and has no direct knowledge regarding the shooter or his motive."

Donnally thought it through, not liking what he found. "If that's the most positive spin that could've been put on what happened, it's not good enough."

The reason was obvious, and the judge should've seen it. It was the court's decision whether or not the informant had information bearing on the identity of the shooter and the type and level of his culpability, whether it was first- or second-degree murder or voluntary or involuntary manslaughter.

In addition, there were exceptions to the hearsay rule: statements by coconspirators or statements against penal interest or excited utterances. And all were matters of admissibility that, under the law, fell to the judge to decide.

McMullin squinted as though his mind's eye was looking ahead along the path of Donnally's thinking.

"But what if the officer never told the D.A. about any informant?"

"Or the D.A. was careful to make sure he didn't ask. I've seen that game played in dozens of cases."

"In any case the D.A. is clean, even if the officer isn't. Since the D.A. doesn't know anything, there's nothing for him to turn over to the defense or disclose to the court. Whatever it is, it's not prosecutorial misconduct and not a basis to set aside the conviction."

Donnally was now getting frustrated. The judge still didn't get it, didn't see where Donnally was headed.

"Again, not good enough. The D.A. had an obligation to disclose to the defense the name of the cop who called Senior. He deprived the defense of the opportunity to file a discovery motion to determine what the cop knew or what police department records would show. Then it would've been up to you whether or not to have a hearing in chambers with the cop and D.A. so you could decide what needed to be disclosed to the defense."

"If anything."

To Donnally, the words sounded like a dodge, as if the judge was implying that there wouldn't have been anything, so no harm was likely done.

"But that's something we don't know," Donnally said. "It seems to me the D.A. didn't want to risk putting it in your hands to decide. And it wouldn't have been the first time a D.A. substituted his own judgment for the court's."

Neither had to say it aloud, but the most disturbing trend in the court system in the last thirty years was exactly that. The D.A. had been grabbing more and more of the court's authority. Prosecutors didn't even bother to make motions to dismiss all or parts of cases any more; they'd simply announce, "I'll dismiss count one if the defendant pleads to count two," as if the power was theirs.

The truth of the law, on the other hand, was that once a case was filed, the D.A. didn't have that authority. Only the judge did.

The practice had become such that if a judge ordered an informant to be disclosed and the D.A. refused, the D.A. would "dismiss the case" and the judge would go along.

Actually, it wasn't even that. The clerk would just make a note in the docket and the case would evaporate.

But a dismissal wasn't possible in a homicide case. Neither the judge nor the D.A. would want to face the public outrage and media assaults. Either the judge would back down and contrive a reason to deny the defense discovery motion or the D.A. would lie to the court about the underlying facts so no legal basis for the disclosure of the informant would exist. The corollary to "hard cases on appeal make bad law" was "hard cases in trial make cowards of judges and prosecutors."

"Maybe I should go talk to the D.A.," Donnally said. "Is he still with the office?"

"You don't know?"

"Know what? I don't pay attention to the comings and goings of San Francisco attorneys. I barely pay attention up in Mount Shasta."

"He's not a D.A. anymore. He's a judge." McMullin's gaze lowered toward the file on his desk and his brows furrowed. "No, that's not right." He looked up again. "Harvey Madding is what he's always been. Judge, jury, and executioner."

It was true. It was how not only the defense bar, but officers in the department, had always described Madding. Donnally was surprised the judge would repeat it aloud and wondered why he had.

"But we're getting ahead of ourselves," Donnally said, rising to his feet. "The prior question is what the cop knew. And I think we better find out."

As the door to the judge's chambers closed behind him, Donnally realized how disjointed and jumpy their conversation had been, as though the topics had morphed or migrated or changed direction midcourse. And he wondered whether it reflected a symptom of disease or depression, or only a desire on McMullin's part to find a legal basis to prevent the execution, or maybe the hope he could find someone other than himself to blame. Or maybe the wish he'd never come to see Donnally in the first place.

But underlying it all, and most troubling, was that Donnally feared their roles might reverse, just as they might with his own father.

Why open up that can of worms?" retired SFPD lieutenant Jimmie Chen asked Donnally, sitting in the knotty-pine den of his foothills home outside Red Bluff.

Donnally suspected that if he'd done his thirty years in the department as Chen had, he might've made the same career-end migration from the southern suburbs of San Francisco to the narrowing and rising north end of the Central Valley along the Sacramento River.

Donnally wasn't surprised where he found Chen because he and the other cops who preceded him north were at heart West Coast boys. They settled in towns like Paradise, Jackson, and Red Bluff. They wanted warm summers and mild winters and built their retirement houses far below the snow line and usually no higher elevation than Chen's three hundred feet above sea level.

Driving through town and then west on the winding roads climbing out of the valley, Donnally had spotted Bay Area dealership license plate frames on dozens of cars parked in home driveways. Next to them stood trucks with frames from the Chevy, Ford, and GMC dealers in the nearby towns of Redding and Anderson. They were evidence both of the officers' origins and their adaptation to a rural lifestyle that included hauling firewood to their homes and Jet Skis to Lake Shasta fifty minutes farther up the highway.

Chen had chosen to sit on a couch below plaques and awards that memorialized his career. Narcotics Detective of the Year. Certificates of appreciation from the Drug Enforcement Administration, the California Bureau of Narcotics Enforcement, and the Federal Bureau of Investigation. Centered among them was a framed gavel from his years as president of the San Francisco Police Officers Association.

"There wasn't any informant in the Rojo murder," Chen said, hiking one cowboy-booted leg over the other.

Donnally noticed that there were no stirrup indentations on the soles. They were boots that had never ridden a horse. Nothing more than a costume or a prop.

"There were just rumors on the street the Sureños wanted to be on the receiving end of the cartel cocaine from Michoacán. And the way to make that happen was to break the supply chain so they could grab onto the near end."

"Then what made the threat specific to Rojo Senior? He couldn't have been the only one the cartel was shipping to."

"Somebody overheard a conversation in a taqueria over on Mission Street."

"Which somebody was that?"

Chen shrugged. "I don't know. I could never trace it down. I just called Senior and told him some kind of hit on him was going down that night."

Donnally caught that Chen was trying to skip a step and wanted to push past it by prompting Donnally to ask what he meant by "some kind of hit." Instead, Donnally looped back. "How did the message get from that somebody to you?"

Chen's eyes went dead for a moment, then he smiled. "A patrol cop, Javier Morales. The somebody went looking for him after they overheard what was going down."

Donnally never considered himself a human lie detector, but he was certain Chen wasn't telling the truth. First the dead eyes, then the smile just before mentioning the name of a young motor-cycle cop who'd been executed by a Sureño under an overpass two blocks from the police station four years after Rojo was murdered.

But knowing Chen was lying was different from knowing what he was lying about, and why.

And there was something else, an implication that Senior might have been an informant, or leaning to become one hard enough that Chen would want to reach out to him and warn him and thereby create a debt.

Donnally tilted his chin up toward the certificates on the wall. "Weren't you in narcotics back then?"

Chen nodded, now with the pursed lips of a soldier who'd been to war.

The retired officer had been among the most productive drug cops in the department's history. Part of Chen's success in inves-tigating Hispanic narcotics trafficking derived from his Chinese-Filipino ancestry that made the dealers mistake him for Mexican or Central American. Another part was that he spoke good street Spanish. But most important, in Donnally's mind, was that Chen was a cowboy long before he owned the boots he was now wear-ing. Whatever block he was on he always acted like he was the new sheriff in a lawless frontier town. He viewed himself not as just a cop, but as The Law, as the western hero, the gunslinger. Even when he covered for Donnally in the homicide unit after he was shot, he still played the part, just in a three-piece suit. It had only been for a few months, but Chen had gotten a lifetime's worth of war stories out of it.

"And Morales contacted you because he knew you were involved in an investigation of Senior?"

Chen's eyes went dead again. "We were working up toward him. The cartel was driving the dope across the border at Mexicali and Tecate and then up Highway 101 through Salinas. They dropped off the cars at body shops in South City, near the San Francisco Airport, where they'd blowtorch open the secret compartments. They'd distribute the product from there."

"That means you probably either rolled somebody at one of the body shops or somebody who picked up the drugs and made the deliveries."

"Yeah . . . something like that. We knew the whole operation was managed from Mexico, but ICE and the DEA weren't getting anywhere on that end. We figured once we got a case on Senior, we'd lean on him to get his connection to come up here and introduce us. That way we could get an agent buying directly."

"Was he big enough to do that?"

"When he died, he was a Norteño captain with a big future. We were told he was originally recruited right from the top, by the key generals in *La Mesa* in the Special Housing Unit at Pelican Bay. But that's not how he got hooked up with the cartel. We think that was orchestrated from Mexico. It was drug money he kicked up to the Norteño leadership that moved him up in rank. And he was making a huge amount. The street dealers were all lining up at his door."

If Junior was right that his father accepted orders from the cartel in Mexico at least partly to protect his family at the ranch, there's no way he would've have cooperated with law enforcement. It would've been a death sentence for his relatives back home. Even if Chen had been able to make a case, Senior would have kept his mouth shut and done his time.

"We were even ready to pitch a deal to the feds to get Rojo's wife out of prison if he agreed to work with us."

Donnally didn't believe Chen was "ready to pitch a deal," for he couldn't imagine Senior changing trajectories, swerving from Norteño captain to government informant. If his wife ever did walk out of prison, it would be into crosshairs.

Now Donnally wondered whether the warning was for another reason, a purely self-serving one. Maybe it was simply that Senior was a known link in a drug distribution chain and losing him would mean starting over, delaying Chen's ascent from officer to sergeant to lieutenant.

But Donnally didn't offer his speculations. It struck him that whatever Chen was hiding would more likely be revealed by the contradictions in his story than by arguments with him.

"How certain were you that he'd cooperate?"

"Completely. Would've been a slam dunk. Federal mandatory minimum sentencing had been instituted a couple of years earlier."

The change in the law meant that drug dealers who would've done three or four years under the old law were being sentenced to twenty and thirty under the new one, and they'd have to serve at least eighty-five percent of their time before they could get released.

"If we were able to make the case we wanted," Chen said, "Senior would've faced life plus. He'd never get out." Chen grinned. "All these guys took one look at spending their whole lives behind the razor-wire fence of a maximum-security federal pen and cooperated."

That wasn't true. The drug world in those days had a term for those who didn't cooperate. They were known as stand-up guys, and the geriatric units in the federal prison system were now crammed with them.

The words *some kind of hit* came back to Donnally.

"Any idea why Senior walked over to the front window?"

"I wanted him to check the area, but stay away from his door because I figured the shooter would be kicking it in and I didn't want him to show himself in the windows on either side of it. That would be like setting himself up."

"Was he still on the phone when he was shot?"

"Nope. He said something about going to the front window and hung up."

Donnally glanced around the den as he tried to span the twenty-year, 250-mile gap between Senior's murder in San Francisco and Chen's retirement in the foothills. He spotted a Smith and Wesson .357 sitting alone in a glass-fronted and locked display box. It was one of the service revolvers some officers still carried in the 1980s, before the department as whole switched to semiautomatics.

Its polymer grip was shattered.

Chen had framed the evidence of the only shooting he'd been in like it was a certificate of courage—except Donnally's recollection was that Chen had never gotten the gun out of its holster.

It had saved Chen's life by deflecting a slug, not by firing one.

Nonetheless, Chen had somehow worked it around in his mind so that it was a sign of his heroism, even though it was just something that happened to him that he had no control over.

Donnally scanned the certificates. His eyes settled on one

from the U.S. Attorney's Office and then realized Chen had referred to federal sentencing guidelines, not state.

"Was it some kind of joint investigation?"

Chen looked away, then back. "Everything we were doing in those days was coordinated in some way, you know that."

"I mean formally. Did the investigation have a code name, did you have meetings, did you share informants with the DEA or ICE or the FBI?"

Chen stiffened. Donnally recognized his voice had taken on the tone and force of a cross-examination. He backed off with a shrug and let his voice trail off into, "That kind of thing."

Chen stared at him for a moment, then relaxed. "It was heading that way. We were talking mostly with ICE because we were trying to work toward the border and the source in Mexico."

"And what happened?"

"We pulled the plug after Senior was murdered."

Donnally didn't believe him, but he did believe that talking to him longer wasn't going to get him anywhere. He'd done enough interviews and interrogations in his career to recognize when the lines of information, straight or meandering, had run out and only circles were left. He declined the offer of a beer and the inevitable trading of war stories that would be expected, and after a little small talk about Chen's ex-wife marrying another officer and his now-grown kids moving out of state, he left.

During the drive out of the foothills toward Highway 5, as he thought about Chen's cold eyes and averted gaze and his dude ranch cowboy boots, Donnally got feeling he was missing something.

Even worse, he felt like he wasn't getting any closer to the problems that were burdening Judge McMullin.

He'd planned to head north to Mount Shasta to check in at the café as a way of letting his mind sort things out in the background, but when he hit the interstate, he found himself taking the on-ramp south toward San Francisco.

And the reason came to him only after he'd made the long loop and accelerated into traffic. It was time to sit down with Israel Dominguez.

CHAPTER 15 ═══════════════

"What do you think you're doing, talking to people about me behind my back?"

The voice on the other end of Donnally's cell phone was his father's. That fact that it was already a couple hours past midnight meant nothing special. His father had always been impulsive and inconsiderate.

Donnally wasn't prepared for the challenge and didn't know how to answer.

"You think I'm some kind of criminal you need to sneak up on?"

"Hold on. Janie's asleep."

The words silenced his father, but Donnally could feel the pressure of the unanswered questions as he swung his legs to the floor and walked into the hallway and down the stairs to the kitchen.

"I was trying to avoid the conversation we're about to have," Donnally said, "until I figured out whether we needed to have it at all. And if we had to have it, I wanted to do it in person."

"I'm not a child."

Donnally sat down at the table. He noticed that Janie had printed out some scholarly articles about Alzheimer's for him to read. She'd highlighted a few sentences on the one on top of the stack. His eyes settled on the title. "Senile Dementia of the Alz-heimer Type."

"If you're not a child, then stop acting like one."

"You're right. It's acting."

Donnally felt his hand tighten around the phone, a mixture of incomprehension and annoyance.

"It's what?"

"Just acting. You know me. You know my stunts. I was trying to get into the experience, get into the role and see how people reacted to me, and then make the actors respond the same way. And I'm trying to create a buzz in the industry to set up the movie."

Donnally took in a long breath and exhaled. "How could dis-playing the symptoms of"—he didn't trust that his father was telling the truth so he didn't want to use the word *Alzheimer's* yet—"of cognitive impairment or clinical depression help sell a movie?"

His father laughed, a schoolboy, snickering laugh. "That's why it's so great. It's counterintuitive. Nothing anybody would've thought of."

"You lost me."

"The film is about Ronald Reagan and his suffering from Alz-heimer's during his second term."

Typical Don Harlan.

"So you're thinking you'd make it seem like the movie was made by a director suffering—"

"Who might be suffering—"

"From Alzheimer's who then makes a heroic effort to explore his disease in film?"

"Something like that." His father laughed. "And Buddy and all the rest of them have already got the buzz going. There was an article in *Variety* today."

In his burning face, Donnally could feel a familiar fury; his father was once again sacrificing fact for the sake of fiction and employing a cheap manipulation of emotion instead of facing a tragedy head-on.

Just like he did with *Shooting the Dawn* and almost all his other films, telling the big lie in the service of what he considered to be the greater truth.

Except it was clear to Donnally this wasn't a greater truth, any more than *Shooting the Dawn* was; it was just a deeper lie, first about his older brother and now about himself.

But this time his father had made himself not just the director, but part of the show itself.

It wasn't Alzheimer's; it was insanity, or selfish childishness.

"Isn't this unfair to the people who really have Alzheimer's? Creating expectations that despite the disease, they should be able to carry on as if they didn't have it?"

His father didn't answer.

"Making them feel guilty as though their loss of ability was a personal failure instead of the result of a disease?"

Finally, his father responded. "Hell, if they really have Alzheimer's, they'll forget about it soon enough." Then he disconnected.

Donnally stared at the phone as the screen went dark. He heard Janie's approaching footsteps. She stopped next to him and put her hand on his shoulder.

"Was that your father?"

Donnally nodded.

"What did he say?"

"He denied it. He said it was all an act."

She sat down in the chair to his right. "You really didn't expect him to admit it, did you?"

Donnally pulled back and looked at her. "What?"

"At the beginning, they almost never do."

CHAPTER 16

Donnally slipped his gun and badge case into the glove compartment as he turned inland from the Marin Rod and Gun Club along San Rafael Bay and down Main Street toward San Quentin Prison. He couldn't take a chance one of the trustees collecting trash in the parking lot or sweeping the sidewalks might spot him and make a move to grab them after he entered the building.

The badge and ID: a prisoner's ticket to walk out.

The gun: a correctional officer's way out in a body bag.

Donnally cut down to the waterside lot just before the main gate across from the post office, then walked up to the hallway outside the visitor processing office. He filled out the visitor's form and sat down on the bench along with relatives of death row inmates waiting to get buzzed in and processed through security.

The best Ramon Navarro could do for him was get him scheduled to meet Israel Dominguez in the family visiting room, the interviewing cages being reserved for attorneys, their paralegals, private investigators, and psychologists. Navarro also reviewed the list of inmates scheduled to have visitors to make sure none had been sentenced out of San Francisco and might have grudges hard enough toward Donnally that they'd fight through the guards to get at him and get even.

Death row inmates could only be executed once, so taking out Donnally in revenge for putting them on the row wouldn't make their punishment any worse.

Donnally noticed he was the only male over the age of seven waiting. The rest were wives, mothers, and children, all weary eyed from long drives from their faraway homes to the only prison in the state housing condemned men. All the women carried clear plastic purses with their cash and ID inside. Some of the younger ones wore tattoos, none wore jewelry, and the older women's breasts sagged in the absence of the support from underwire bras that would've set off the metal detector and barred their entry. Donnally had noticed them closing their jackets or sweaters and folding their arms over their chests when he entered.

A guard came to the window and pointed at Donnally. He rose. The door lock was already buzzing by the time he reached it. He felt the eyes of the women needling his back, asking how come he got to go in first since they'd all arrived before him. Because he had no expectation of accomplishing anything in the meeting with Dominguez, he had no explanation he felt he could offer them to justify his moving to the head of the line.

The door closing behind him felt like an escape.

It only took a few minutes to process him through. Displaying his ID, emptying his pockets, removing his shoes and belt, pushing them toward the scanner and stepping through the metal detector.

A correctional officer put him through the same search a second time a hundred yards further in, along a concrete walkway just before the inner prison gate.

The officer then directed him along a curving paved road toward death row.

Another door buzz, but no search this time, and he stepped into a cafeteria-sized room with a forest scene painted on the wall at the far end and vending machines along the near. In between were rows of metal tables and plastic chairs. Most were empty. Inmates dressed in blue sat at the others with one to four visitors.

One correctional officer perched in a booth overlooking the scene. Two others walked the floor monitoring contact between inmates and their visitors, watching for drug and weapons smuggling.

A door at the rear opened. A short Hispanic inmate carrying a brown accordion file stepped into the room and looked around. His eyes finally settled on the table at the opposite corner near the vending machines with one visitor sitting alone. The inmate nodded toward Donnally and then headed down the aisle.

None of the other prisoners looked at him as he walked between the tables.

Donnally wasn't sure whether it was because whatever inmates had to say to one another they could say back in the cell block, or because Dominguez was getting close to his execution date, or maybe because the other inmates had already made Donnally out to be a cop.

Donnally rose as Dominguez approached and extended his hand. Dominguez braced the file under his right arm and shook hands with his left, and then sat down. Donnally spotted Dominguez's withered right hand just before he slid it onto his lap under the table.

Donnally couldn't remember anything about it in the police

report and there was no issue raised about whether Dominguez had fired at Edgar Rojo Sr. using his right or left hand.

"Did your counselor tell you why I'm here?" Donnally asked.

"Only that you wanted to talk about my case."

"And just to make sure we can, you're not represented by counsel anymore?"

Dominguez shook his head.

"I'm not an attorney and I'm not a private investigator, I'm an ex—"

Dominguez raised his hand. "I know who you are. It was after my time, but I heard about you and the shoot-out on Mission Street."

Dominguez looked Donnally over like he was expecting to see bullet scars.

"And to make sure we understand each other," Donnally said, "my loyalty isn't to you. I don't know you. Judge McMullin asked me—"

Dominguez's eyes widened and he leaned in.

Donnally nodded. "That's right. Judge McMullin. He asked me to look into what happened during the investigation and the trial and help him figure out whether he'd made mistakes it isn't too late to correct."

Dominguez's face reddened. "You know the law as well as I do. Innocence is no defense this late in the appeals. That's the law."

Donnally fixed his eyes on Dominguez's. "And I have no reason to think that innocence is the issue."

He expected Dominguez to rise and march back toward the door leading to the cells, but he didn't. He just stared back.

"As far as I can tell at this point," Donnally said, "the issues don't go beyond what's bothering Judge McMullin. And that's whether the D.A. was correct that it was a first-degree murder, or whether your attorney was right to argue it was a second-degree under a recklessness theory, or whether there was ineffective assistance of counsel because your lawyer didn't put on manslaughter evidence and ask for a manslaughter instruction."

Dominguez hunched over, staring down at the worn tabletop, his body expressing bone-deadening weariness. Finally, he took in a long breath and exhaled, shaking his head, and spoke without looking up.

"I . . . just . . . don't . . . want . . . to die."

Donnally hadn't anticipated that Dominguez would come out and say it. It was a whole lot more truth than he'd expected.

"And that's all that this is about, isn't it? And everything in your letter was a lie."

Dominguez didn't answer right away. After a few moments, he rotated his face toward Donnally.

"It's not that simple."

Donnally watched the fingers of Dominguez's left hand flexing on the table.

"Everything in the letter was true. It's my life that's been the lie." Dominguez sat up again. "But not one I created. I've been living someone else's lie." He peered over at Donnally. "You know what I mean?"

Donnally knew exactly what he meant. He'd grown up with his father's mythologies about the death of his older brother and with his father's evasion of his own responsibility for it. But that wasn't something Donnally was willing to share with a death row inmate. His gut told him it was a mistake to have divulged to Edgar Rojo Jr. who his father was and the damage his father had done directly to his family and indirectly through his movies to American's self-understanding. And Donnally still couldn't figure out why he'd told him.

"I know what you mean," Donnally said. "But I'm not sure what the lie is. Just like you said. It's way too late in the process to start claiming innocence."

Dominguez's face flushed. "I didn't just start saying I was innocent. It's what I said from the beginning. I told the cops. I told my lawyer." He slapped the table. "But no one would listen to me."

A correctional officer looked over but didn't make a move to come toward them.

"My whole trial was about life or death, my life or death, not my guilt or innocence. I could tell by looking at Judge McMullin's face all during the guilt part of the case that he was already thinking about the penalty phase and how everything would play out. Just like my lawyer was doing."

"I heard you had an argument with your lawyer. What was it about?"

"Which argument? There were lots of them."

"Take your pick. Start with when the judge stopped the trial and sent you and him out to an interview room to talk."

Dominguez paused as though trying to picture the scene. "I wanted to tell the jury I was innocent. My lawyer wanted me to testify I did it, that it was just a prank that went bad."

"And use your testimony to support his argument that it was a second-degree murder."

Dominguez nodded.

"What about manslaughter under a mistaken self-defense theory? You two argue about that, too?"

Dominguez's face flushed. "You're not listening to me. Just like he didn't listen to me. I . . . didn't . . . do it."

Donnally caught the motion of a couple walking behind him toward the vending machines. He glanced over. A woman was putting change into one dispensing coffee ten feet away. The inmate standing next to her was staring at Donnally, bulldog-like, shoulder muscles tensed, as though he was trying to decide whether Donnally was a threat.

Donnally didn't recognize him, but recognized the meaning of the shamrock tattoo on his forearm: Aryan Brotherhood.

The inmate strode toward Donnally.

Donnally saw the correctional officer across the room alert to the drive in the inmate's steps and push off against the wall.

Donnally rose.

The inmate stopped two feet away, his fists tight by his sides.

Donnally glanced down at them, looking for a sharpened pencil or piece of plastic the prisoner could stab him with.

"You don't recognize me, do you?" the inmate said.

The correctional officer walked up behind the inmate, hand on his baton.

Donnally shook his head and fixed his eyes on the inmate's. If he was about to make a move, it would show there first. A clenched jaw or a turned head, then a swing.

"George Foster."

Donnally didn't recall the name or the face. "I don't remember you."

"Fifteen years ago. A rumble between the Aryan Brotherhood and the Hell's Angels at a motorcycle show at the Cow Palace."

Donnally could picture the fight, but not the man.

"You broke my brother's arm."

Then it all connected.

"He swung," Donnally said, his tone flat, like he was reading from an offense report. "I blocked him with my baton."

The inmate snorted. "So you say."

A second correctional officer walked up, forming the third side of a triangle, shoulders back.

"There a problem?" the officer asked.

Foster shook his head, still staring at Donnally. "You've got nothing to worry about, man." He winked. "I'm a cold-blooded murderer, not a heat-of-passion kind of guy." He turned toward the correctional officer and said in a lower voice as he walked by him, "If you believe what they say in the press."

Donnally sat down again.

Moments after Foster returned to his table, a correctional officer pointed at him, then at the door leading to cells. Foster gave Donnally a hard look, then hugged his female visitor and left the room.

"Is this going to be a problem for you?" Donnally asked.

Dominguez shook his head. "That's between you and him, not him and me. Anyway, this is our home, it's like a small town, and we usually don't mess with each other."

"Usually?"

Dominguez removed his right hand from under the table and showed Donnally his palm. A scar ran across it.

"A Norteño put a contract out on me ten years ago. April fifteenth. They can reach in anywhere and they got me when the guards were taking me to the dentist in the main part of the prison. I saved my life by deflecting the shank with my hand."

"You ever put a name to the contract?"

Dominguez nodded. "That wasn't hard at all. It was Edgar Rojo Junior."

By noon, the visitors had bought picnic lunches at the vending machines. Fried chicken, potato salad, chips, and sodas lay on all the tables, including the one between Donnally and Dominguez.

Inmates and their wives strolled up and down the aisles as though they were couples walking the tree-lined paths of Golden Gate Park. Whispering. Holding hands. Children trailing behind.

Donnally now understood the reason for the forest scene painted on the far wall. Prisoners and visitors were posing for photos in front of it.

Officers operated the camera, alert for the inmates' flash of hand signs just before the shutter click. Gang photos wouldn't leave the institution.

Also, by noon, Donnally had heard Dominguez's story.

Dominguez had admitted lying to the police about not being in the area of the Rojo apartment on the night of the murder.

Admitted to having been recruited into the Sureños by an uncle in L.A., but claimed to have been trying to get out in the months before the shooting.

Admitted knowing the Southern California Sureños wanted to

become the connection between the cartel in Michoacán and the Northern California street corners.

Admitted he knew Edgar Sr. was the link in the chain the Sureños wanted to take out and replace.

And the reason he thought he'd been IDed by witnesses as the shooter?

It was just as Rojo Jr. had said. It was a war and it didn't make any difference to the Norteños or the Sureños who fell on the other side, as long as somebody did.

Dominguez also told Donnally the Sureño leadership hadn't ordered any particular soldier to kill Rojo Sr. and didn't care how it got set up and how it got executed. Anybody could do it and rewards would follow.

It wasn't until years after the trial that word got around to Dominguez about who might have pulled the trigger, and by that time he, too, was dead and there was no proof that he'd done it, just rumors.

But Donnally wasn't ready to believe any of it.

Despite Dominguez having had twenty years to come up with an exculpatory story, there remained a contradiction, not in the story itself, but in his life.

On the one hand, Dominguez had teams of lawyers handling his state and federal appeals not only to help him create the story, but to translate it into legal arguments relating to actual innocence.

On the other hand, over two decades, they hadn't done that translation, made the claim of factual innocence.

"Why take that route now?" Donnally asked. "If you're right about the law, it's too late. Sounds like you'd be better off pursuing some kind of legal gimmick. Cruel and unusual punishment, an angle like that. Maybe you bring the whole machine to a stop."

Dominguez shook his head. "Six hundred guys are on the row. They all got lawyers and paralegals. If they haven't been able to come up with something to jam the gears, I won't."

"The question remains, why'd you wait?"

Dominguez didn't answer right away. He looked down at the table and flicked aside a chunk of batter that had fallen from his fried chicken.

"I've been thinking about that, a lot. Seems stupid to have waited, except it didn't feel like I was waiting." He looked up again. "It was something else."

Donnally didn't respond, didn't ask the obvious question. The burden was on Dominguez to explain himself, not on Donnally to draw it out of him. He hadn't come to death row to play therapist.

"It's like this," Dominguez said. "It comes out of my childhood." He took in a long breath and exhaled. "I guess you could say I grew up wanting to be invisible."

Donnally felt tension in his legs, ready to rise. He wasn't in the mood to listen to self-serving psychological insights aimed not at fact, but at sympathy. It was bad enough that these guys had lawyers helping them construct false stories to disguise their guilt, it was worse that they had shrinks to fudge up a psychiatric diagnosis to excuse it.

Donnally guessed his thoughts must've shown on his face when Dominguez raised a palm toward him.

"Just hear me out. There's a point to this."

Donnally didn't answer. He just stared back.

"I was pretty good at sports when I was in elementary school, but during recess when we were choosing sides, and all the other kids were yelling 'Pick me, pick me,' I was always wishing I could just disappear into the ground."

Dominguez's eyes went blank, as though blinded by the image of the sunlit schoolyard in his mind, then nodded.

"That's really why I dropped out. It wasn't about brains or grades."

He glanced over at the other inmates.

"Lot of guys here are like that. Just wanted to be left alone. The difference is this. When somebody edged into my space, I wanted to disappear. Evaporate. The rest of these guys wanted to strike back, hurt someone. When somebody came into their space, that somebody was gonna get hurt, maybe die. They were all just murders waiting to happen."

Donnally wondered whether Dominguez was taking a maze-like route toward excusing his actions, implying that if these killers had no control over their actions, then he didn't either and he couldn't be held responsible for murdering Edgar Rojo Sr.

Donnally knew from both Judge McMullin and Navarro that Dominguez had a history of violence that predated the homicide, so it was clear he hadn't done much evaporating when he'd been threatened in the past.

"You ever read Rumpelstiltskin when you were a kid?" Dominguez asked.

Donnally was surprised. That wasn't a name he expected to hear at San Quentin. And he wasn't sure how a German fairy tale could be relevant to a Hispanic on death row.

"Or it was read to me," Donnally said. "I know the story."

"I didn't get a look at it until I got in here."

Dominguez gestured toward the other tables. And in that gesture, a cloudy thought that had been forming in Donnally's mind crystallized into words. The prison had become Dominguez's entire world and the condemned really were a village within it, and Dominguez had come to define himself by those he shared it with.

"A lot of us come in here reading at about a fifth-grade level. Simplified classics and kids' stories are all there is for us to read. Short words and big letters." Dominguez shook his head. "None of us understand much of what the lawyers were writing about us at the beginning, even during our trials. The lawyer says, we're gonna file a *Brady* motion." He smiled. "And we're thinking, what's a *Brady* motion?"

It was a motion that required the prosecutor to turn over all the evidence that might help the defense. And that included anything that indicated innocence or suggested mitigation or that might show a prosecution witness was lying or the detective had a history of dishonesty—and Donnally didn't believe Dominguez had chosen *Brady* as an example by chance.

"It's weird how all the court pleadings read. 'Defendant claims' or 'Defendant asserts.'" Dominguez's face flushed again and he thumped the table with his forefinger. "We don't assert anything. It's the lawyers doing all the asserting. And if it ain't them, it's some penalty phase psychologists talking a shrink language we don't understand."

"And you somehow learned more from a Grimm's fairy tale than from what the lawyers and shrinks put together about you?"

"All the shrinks did was give the jury all kinds of reasons why I killed somebody I didn't kill."

"And Rumpelstiltskin?"

"Explained everything to me."

Dominguez laid his forearms on the table, exposing his damaged hand as though he was now ready to reveal an inner truth about himself.

"It's like this. Rumpelstiltskin was a little guy like me, and a criminal. He was an extortionist running a protection racket. He tells the girl, you give me your jewelry and your first baby and I'll make sure you stay alive. Don't give me what I want and I'll let the king kill you."

Dominguez raised his eyebrows, waiting for Donnally to indicate he was following the story so far.

Donnally nodded.

"Rumpelstiltskin spent his whole life hiding his identity, nobody knowing his name or, if they knew it, they didn't know he was an extortionist."

Donnally remembered a phrase from the story.

How good that neither man nor dame knows Rumpelstiltskin is my name.

And he was surprised by an image of Dominguez as a child that came into his mind.

Dominguez paused and his eyes went bright for a second, as though he'd just thought of an implication of the story he hadn't considered before. Finally, he shrugged and said, "Maybe that's why he became a criminal, because he didn't fit in." Dominguez blinked. "Anyway, it all came crashing down on Rumpelstiltskin when somebody matched him with his name."

Donnally shook his head. "It was because he couldn't keep his mouth shut. It all came crashing down when someone heard him dancing around and bragging about what he did and saying his secret name out loud."

"Except it wasn't me. It was just my name."

"It wasn't just your name. You were IDed by guys who knew you."

"They lied. I didn't do it. Anyway, I don't mean that. I mean name like in reputation, like when your name stands for something. And back then if you're going to survive on the street, your name better mean something bad. That's what all my fights were about."

Donnally thought back on Dominguez's letter. His claim that he was accused because he had a reputation as the kind of guy who'd commit this kind of crime. Now he was admitting it was a reputation he wanted, even made for himself as a kind of armor, and was claiming he then got imprisoned in it.

But Donnally didn't have a clue how any of this answered the question in his mind. Why hadn't Dominguez made the innocence claim before?

Then it started to come to him. It was the isolation of death row, the unreality of the place, and the disconnection from life outside, even from his own lawyers and the courts that would judge him.

"And when you got here you tried to go invisible again."

"It was like nothing about my case had anything to do with me." Dominguez tapped his chest with his withered hand. "With me."

CHAPTER 18

like I said after I read his letter," Janie told Donnally as they walked on the beach that evening a few blocks from their house in San Francisco, "Dominguez is either innocent or a sociopath." They stopped and gazed out at the rising moon streaking the water and at the star-speckled sky. "Or both."

They remained silent for a few moments, then Janie looked over at Donnally.

"Sociopaths can be very convincing. They have a kind of superhuman verbal fluency. They're masters of word play, not just because the truth means nothing to them, but because they see language as paint and brushes, as a way to make persuasive pictures."

Walking from death row back along the sidewalk toward his car and thinking the same thoughts in different words, Donnally had been struck by nothing so much as by what Janie was calling Dominguez's verbal fluency. Even though he'd slipped into gonnas and ain'ts as he spoke, Dominguez knew how to manipulate complicated concepts and deliver them to his listeners' minds with emotional impact.

But none of that meant what Dominguez had said about himself and about his trial and the later appeals wasn't true.

"And that fluency is often combined with a sense of entitlement, a belief that they aren't bound by the same rules as everyone else. So they feel neither responsibility nor guilt."

Donnally watched a seagull wheel above the water, wings flashing in the moonlight reflecting off the ruffled white surf.

"I'm not sure that's it. He seemed more resigned than anything else, like he had spent his life living in the shadows."

"Maybe, but pulling the trigger sure yanked him into the daylight. If his Rumpelstiltskin analogy is accurate and if my theory is correct, it's not at all surprising to me that he would cocoon himself again right after the shooting and try to hide there."

Donnally closed his eyes and interlaced his fingers on top of his head. "That means there's no way he could ever admit to anything having to do with the murder, even if it costs him his life in the end." He held up one hand to his left. "On one side, he couldn't bring himself to claim it was second degree, testify to it, and maybe get a life sentence." He held up the other hand to his right. "And the logic of the case was that a claim of innocence would guarantee his execution."

"That's the way it works out psychologically."

Donnally lowered his arms and opened his eyes. He now recalled that he'd heard two different endings to the Rumpelstiltskin story and described them to Janie. In one, Rumpelstiltskin stamped his foot so hard after he was discovered and identified that he sank into the ground, consumed by the earth. In the other, Rumpelstiltskin plunged his foot so deep into the earth that his whole leg went in and in a rage he pulled at it so hard he tore himself in two.

"You want me to go see him," Janie asked, "and try to find out which it is?"

Donnally thought for a moment. He worried that if it was the former, Dominguez would take her visit as an invasion.

"Not yet. Let me talk to some witnesses and try to find out more about what happened."

Even as he spoke the words, Donnally wasn't sure what he really meant. He was starting to think the pieces of the puzzle were somehow already before him, but that his mind wasn't putting them together into a picture that made sense.

Maybe because Dominguez had just painted a new one.

A young man and woman passed by behind them. Their shoes made crushing and shooshing sounds in the sand as they walked. Then they giggled and ran off.

Donnally felt a rush of annoyance at the normalcy of the couple, and at himself. He was only entangled in the Dominguez case because he'd become reacquainted with Judge McMullin after a lawyer Donnally knew had been murdered in San Francisco. And he'd only become reacquainted with that lawyer because a dying friend had asked him to locate his sister who he'd abandoned at a Berkeley commune in the 1960s. None of it was anything he would've chosen to do. He turned to face them, nothing more.

As he stood there, shoes settling into the sand, feeling the weight of Dominguez's life pressing down on him, Donnally felt an urgency, a need to break his connection to San Francisco. He felt like sweeping the unfinished puzzle into the trash, walking back to the house, getting into his truck, and heading north. The problem was that Janie was his anchor and pulling free from San Francisco meant breaking up with her, or asking her to come north. Maybe that's what he should do, ask her to go with him. Get himself away from San Francisco and from a past that kept ensnaring him in other people's problems and ensnaring her in his stumbling efforts to try to solve what seemed like the unsolvable.

Even more than that, he had his own father to deal with and he no longer wanted to bear the burden of McMullin's doubts or of Dominguez's confusions and evasions—

Evasions.

The word emerged from the whirlwind of his thoughts and hung there before him.

He looked down at Janie.

"Dominguez wanted to testify at his trial," Donnally said. "His attorney talked him out of it. Doesn't that suggest something? That he was willing to come out of hiding to proclaim his innocence, regardless of the risk, regardless of whether it torpedoed the penalty phase?"

Janie squinted up toward the stars for a moment, then looked over at Donnally. "I have two answers for you. First, in the end he didn't testify. And second, guilty sociopaths often get on the stand and lie. They figure that they can convince anyone of anything at any time."

"You mean his crying about his lawyer making him back down was just an act?"

"Why not? You told me his life was based on a fictional character anyway."

Donnally shook his head. "Not *based* on a fictional character, *explained* by one. Those are two different things."

G et out of my shop." Oscar Benaga gripped a torque wrench in both hands, braced across his body. "It's ancient history."

Donnally stood his ground in the doorway between the office and the garage of Benaga's Elite Auto Repair in Hunters Point, a few blocks from where Benaga had claimed to have witnessed Israel Dominguez murder Edgar Rojo Sr.

Even though there were three lifts with cars raised on them, Benaga was the only mechanic working and no one had been in the office Donnally had passed through.

"Only as ancient as Israel Dominguez getting the needle in a week."

Benaga, now twenty years older than the twenty-four-year-old who testified in Dominguez's trial, secured the wrench under his armpit and wiped his hands on a red cloth, seeming to spread the axle grease around his palms and fingers rather than removing it. His brown pants and shirt were soiled with oil and transmission fluid.

Of the two witnesses who'd identified Dominguez as the killer, only Benaga was still alive.

"That's his problem, not mine."

Donnally spotted the number 14 tattooed on Benaga's thick

forearm, representing the fourteenth letter of the alphabet. *N* for Norteño.

It made sense that Benaga was using a red cloth and wearing brown clothing, rather than the standard auto shop blue. Blue was the gang color of the Sureños and the Mexican Mafia, enemies of the Norteños.

When Benaga turned to toss the rag into a barrel, Donnally caught a glimpse of the letters of N-O-R-T-E tattooed on the back of his bald scalp.

"You have those tattoos when you testified against Dominguez?"

Benaga's eyes hardened into a stare. "Look, man, I didn't testify against nobody. I just said what I saw." He jabbed a finger at Donnally. "And don't call him Dominguez, like he was a human being. His gang name was El Búho, the Owl, always coming out of the shadows, backstabbing, never fighting straight up, man to man, in the light of day."

Rumpelstiltskin.

Then it hit Donnally that it was the El Búho nickname, what Dominguez referred to as his "name," his reputation on the street, that had lent credibility to Benaga's identification of him as the killer.

"That's not the question. The question is whether you had those gang tattoos when you testified."

Benaga shrugged. "Lots of people got tattoos. Don't mean nothing."

Donnally spotted another tattoo on his neck with the words *El Lobo* written in fine script under it.

The Wolf.

Another gang-named, maybe even self-described, predator

whose ends were just as deadly and which were always explained as nature's means to nature's ends.

Edgar Jr.'s words came back to him. It was a war, as though that was a natural state of the world, and because of that fact, anything, everything, was justified.

The tattoos and membership may not have gone directly to the issue of guilt, Donnally thought, but it certainly went to Benaga's bias as a witness and should have been brought out at trial by his attorney.

Benaga's testimony had been that he knew Israel Dominguez only as a kid in the neighborhood, rather than as an opposing gang member, and that even though the streetlights had been shot out, the moon was high, and the muzzle flash lit up Dominguez's face.

"Did Dominguez's attorney ask you if you were a member of the Norteños?"

"Of course he did."

"And you said?"

"No, but that I'd do what I needed to do to live in the neighborhood. If that meant joining a side, I'd join a side. I didn't officially hook up with them until I went to the joint a couple of months later. So I wasn't lying."

The rumble of a car slowing and then idling drew their attention toward the street. It vibrated with the thumping of its subwoofers, thundering behind the music of a group Donnally recognized, *Intocables*, Untouchables. The red-bandannaed passenger riding low in the restored 1980s Caprice Classic rotated his head toward Benaga, then back toward Donnally. Benaga waved them on and the driver gunned the engine and the car lurched and sped off.

"Did you know Edgar Senior?" Donnally asked.

Benaga blocked the question by raising his hands in front of his chest. "I'm done answering questions, man. You want to know something, read the transcript. It's all in there. I've had lawyers showing up at my door for twenty years asking me the same questions, and the answers never change. Never will."

They stared at each other for a few moments, then Donnally said, "One more. You can decide whether to answer it or not."

Benaga didn't respond.

"Do you believe that Dominguez intended to kill Senior?"

Benaga smirked. "Nobody would try to just scare a guy like Edgar, especially shoot into his house. He wasn't scareable and he'd do anything to protect his family, especially his boy. Anybody do something like that to Edgar and miss, he might as well have put the gun to his own head."

CHAPTER 20

Donnally's cell phone rang just before he turned into his driveway and just after he spotted Junior's car parked down the block, mostly hidden behind a panel van. It was forty minutes after he'd left Benaga's. He didn't have time to say hello before the caller yelled, "Why didn't you tell me you were going to see Benaga?"

As Donnally expected, it was Junior.

"And why didn't you tell me you had my house staked out?"

Junior took in a breath, surprised to have been spotted, then he said, "I'm not staking out your house. I just wanted to see you in person."

The phone disconnected.

Donnally walked to the sidewalk at the opening to his driveway wondering why Junior had such an indirect way of approaching him, first following him and now waiting for him down the block and calling instead of just parking in front of the house. It was something he was certain Janie would understand, but all that came to him was an image of Junior as kind of a lost, nowhere man.

An older immigrant Chinese woman weeding in her yard across the street held her trowel like a knife as she watched Junior roll up and get out of his car. Donnally raised a hand toward her, half a wave, half a signal that everything was okay.

Junior stopped just a foot and a half away. "Don't you know who he is."

He'd said the words not as a question, but as an accusation.

"He was a witness to your father's murder. I don't care what else he is besides that. I'm not writing his biography, or his obituary."

"Fuck you."

"Then who is he?"

"He's the guy who keeps the Muslim Nation from driving my grandmother out of her place and keeps all the other Mexicans safe in the neighborhood."

"That's a job for the police."

"Fuck the police." Junior pointed at Donnally as though he was still one of them. "Cops don't do shit. One of them Muslims beats up a Mexican and runs into the mosque, nothing happens. Cops just knock on the door and beg Aasim to send the guy out, but he never does and they never go in after him. They're afraid. They just walk away. That's why the neighborhood needs Benaga."

Donnally had read that the police had a hands-off policy toward the Black Muslim sect in Oakland, but he hadn't realized San Francisco had also adopted it.

"Aasim calls his group a nation," Junior said, "and the police treat him that way. Ask anybody. The politicians are afraid of him, too."

"I don't see what that has to do with me talking to Benaga."

Junior looked past Donnally and down the block, like he was trying to see whether they were being watched, then back at Donnally.

"You know how hard it is to get some distance from the Norte-ños? To get them to leave you alone?"

"You got away."

Junior shook his head. "It's blood in, blood out, man. Not just snitches, everyone. Even the generals who just want to retire in peace go out that way. They get hit even in super max."

"Then how . . ."

"Me and Benaga have a kind of a truce because my father died in the cause. But if he goes to war against the Sureños or even if Norteño factions go after each other again, I've got to take his side and go get a gun."

"The cause? Your father died for a cause?"

Donnally felt like he was talking to one of Janie's delusional patients. Even as a cop he never understood the kinds of things these guys killed each other over.

"Gangbanging is a cause? Wake up. It's an evasion of causes, or at least an evasion of any decent ones."

Junior emitted a sharp, bitter laugh. "Spoken like a man who ran away."

Donnally had regretted telling Junior about his father even while they were still at the café, and now he regretted it even more.

"At least I never put a contract out on anybody."

Junior drew back as though Donnally had cocked his arm to throw a punch, then glanced around and leaned in and said in a hard whisper, "Benaga tell you that?"

Donnally shook his head. "It's not important who told me."

Junior shrugged. "What difference does it make? Nobody died."

"It makes a difference because it's about you. Who you are."

"You don't know nothing about me."

"You set up the attack on Dominguez, and that tells me a lot."

"What you going to do about it?"

"Probably nothing. You're right. Nobody died. But tell me *why* you did it."

"It was time he paid for his crime. We waited long enough."

"We, not the cause again?"

"Okay, so it wasn't about the cause, at least directly. It was about us waiting too long."

"Why then, after ten years?"

Junior shrugged again. "Things kinda came to a head."

"That's not an answer."

Junior glanced down the block again, then over his shoulder. "Let's just say we had a meeting. Call it old business that needed to be taken care of."

"That's still not an answer."

"You wearing a wire?"

Donnally shook his head.

"Spread your arms."

Donnally pulled his gun from his holster so Junior couldn't take it from him, and let Junior pat him down.

Then Junior said, "We were at Benaga's house, over there by his garage, watching the Giants playing the Dodgers one night. He takes out a piece of paper and starts writing down all the hits that went down after my father was killed. The ones by us and Nuestra Familia and the ones by the Mexican Mafia and the Sureños. He shows it to us and tells us it's unbalanced—that's the word he used, *unbalanced*—because we never got to anybody in the Sureños as high up as my father was. A street captain."

"What did that have to do with Israel Dominguez? If the issue was rank, he was a nobody. No rank at all."

Junior stiffened. "Hold on, man. I'll get to it."

"Then get to it."

Junior stared at him for a moment.

Donnally feared that he'd pushed him too hard, and he'd turn and walk away.

Finally, Junior said, "Benaga started talking about guys we could whack and we toss the names back and forth. He settles on a Sureño captain down in Bakersfield, right near the border between them and us. Then somebody says, that'll start another war and he says, then let's take out Dominguez, make a kind of a statement, like we never forget our own."

Donnally remembered the Norteño oath from years ago. He'd seen it spray painted on the sides of buildings and on walls and fences in the gang neighborhoods.

Revenge is a promise all the time.

"That's how the decision got made," Junior said.

"There was nothing personal in it? It had nothing to do with Dominguez being the guy who killed your father?"

"Course it did. That's why I carried the message into San Quentin."

"But why then? What was going on ten years ago that made it so important to do something right at that moment?"

Junior paused in thought as though it was a question he'd never asked either Benaga or himself, then he shook his head.

"I have no idea. I was just a nineteen-year-old kid. I didn't think about the big picture, only about getting by."

"Like now?"

Junior shrugged. "Like now, like always. Nothing changes for guys like me."

CHAPTER 21

Donnally watched Junior drive away, then walked inside the house thinking back over the years, but not so much about him getting shot as about what had gone on before he'd stepped into the cross fire. The killing he was investigating when he got out of his car to walk into the Mission Street taqueria wasn't gang related in any way. It had nothing to do with the Norteños or Sureños. Neither the shooter nor the victim were gangsters. It had just been a stickup robbery in front of the restaurant.

He'd driven there ready to cut a deal with the owner. Donnally would get the D.A. to dismiss an unrelated narcotics case in exchange for information about the identity of the killer. He wasn't even looking for testimony, just for a name, one he could use to obtain a mug shot and put together a photo lineup to show to the witnesses who'd already agreed to testify.

But a gap still existed in his mind between his reason for going to the restaurant and what had happened to him on the street before he could get inside, and he still didn't know whether he'd failed over the years to discover the link that connected them or whether there had never been one. He was certain he understood the mechanics, but wasn't convinced he'd ever understood the meaning, and Benaga's ordering Junior to set up the attack on Dominguez around the time he'd gotten shot added a new fact, a new event, but nothing more.

As Donnally stood at the kitchen counter making a sandwich, he wondered what else was going on ten years earlier that might have made it urgent for the Norteños to get rid of Dominguez.

Was it really about gang honor, or had that just been the cover for the real reason?

And if doing it was so important, why hadn't they tried again after they'd failed?

Then he wondered whether Benaga later decided that mangling Dominguez's shooting hand was good enough revenge or worked as a living symbol even better than death.

But he didn't think so. Revenge required parity, in this case a matching killing, or it wasn't a promise kept.

Donnally sat down at the table, the first piece of furniture he'd bought on his own after he moved out of his parents' house. Maybe because he'd spent the last few days investigating a homicide, he felt a renewed connection to it, its oak surface and its scrapes and scratches, the wearing of life on wood. It was the same one that was there all the years he was at SFPD, the same table at which he studied for the sergeant's exam, studied for his master's degree in criminal justice at San Francisco State, and where he wrote out search warrant affidavits after he made detective.

It was also the place where he sat reviewing the medical reports and the retirement forms, when he signed his name declining disability benefits, figuring that since he could walk and talk, he could still find some kind of work he wanted to do. He didn't need the taxpayers of San Francisco paying his way. He'd do that himself.

Being conscious of his sitting there also made him notice that it was where he and Janie did most of their arguing.

He remembered Janie wondering one day years ago why they didn't argue in bed like her parents always had. Then Janie saying her folks were always trying to hide their conflicts from the kids . . . then he and Janie both realizing again that despite her being ten years younger than him, they'd met too late to have kids together . . . no way he could see himself as the sixty-year-old father of a teenager . . . and she getting that look on her face that said she was asking herself why didn't she just move on and move out before the clock ticked all the way down and go find somebody else to have children with . . . but instead of talking about that, which would've led to an argument that would've made a real difference in their lives, maybe even led to them breaking up, they argued about why Donnally had forgotten to tell her that her mother had called a day earlier.

Donnally found he was holding his breath and let it out.

In recent years that had changed. Fewer arguments, no forgotten messages, more intimacy, but still there remained Janie's regrets about children. He felt like he'd let her down, that if they hadn't met her life would've been different, there would've been a husband waiting for her at home and kids sitting around a table doing their homework.

The sandwich now didn't look very appetizing, the bread looking drier than he knew it really was and the turkey more bland.

He pulled a Coke out of the refrigerator and took a sip.

Except the decision, or maybe there were lots of decisions, to turn the two of them into an us had been mutual. They both carried a key that would unlock the life into which they'd placed themselves, but neither had ever chosen to use it. And it wasn't accommodation or settling. Not every relationship needed kids, a dog, and an SUV. And theirs didn't. Love and trust were enough.

The sandwich looked a little better. He grabbed it and headed toward the first-floor bedroom where they had a desk and a laptop.

The walk down the hallway felt like a migration from the known into the unknown. He felt his mind make a jump as he reached around the threshold and turned on the light.

And he was back into the Rojo Sr. murder.

There was too much he didn't know about what had happened in San Francisco since he'd put police work behind him. He'd even stopped reading the newspapers and watching the local news when he came down from Mount Shasta to visit Janie and work on the house. More than anything, it was because he didn't like being reminded of all the dead people he'd known. Every murder reminded him of another he'd investigated, every sidewalk crime scene reminded him of another body that had bled out, every son reminded him of a father who died, every daughter, a mother. Children he'd once interviewed as witnesses were now becoming victims, and killers.

Donnally sat down and ran an Internet news search on "Norteños" and "San Francisco," and focused on the period between eight and twelve years earlier, the two years on either side of the attempted hit on Dominguez and the Mission Street shoot-out.

The coverage centered on gang fights between the Norteños and Sureños in San Quentin, scattered homicides around the Bay Area, mostly unsolved, and three federal racketeering indictments.

He knew little about the gang fights. And the two Norteño-related homicides he'd worked were connected neither with internal prison conflicts nor with the federal cases. They were straight-up disputes over control over a couple of blocks in the Mission District.

Because he'd never been assigned to the narcotics unit and never needed the overtime, he hadn't worked the wire rooms in the joint SFPD-FBI and SFPD-DEA investigations or performed surveillances of drug transactions.

He also hadn't spent much time with street drug task force officers or narcotics detectives. Some he'd suspected of planting drugs on suspects and of filing false police reports and of lying in search warrant affidavits and in court testimony. Too many were cowboys like Chen or true believers. Just like Junior, both state and federal drug enforcement agents saw themselves as engaged in a war, and all was fair, even if not legal, and they figured that if the guy they grabbed wasn't guilty today, he was guilty yesterday or, if left on the street, would be guilty tomorrow.

And everyone in the department knew it.

Most cops in SFPD refused assignments on the drug task force or in the narcotics division, didn't want to deal with the pressure to make their numbers and to help other officers make theirs. Narcotics officers who didn't deliver enough bodies to the jail soon found themselves with their long hair shorn, their beards shaved, their uniforms back on, and their shoe soles pressing a patrol car accelerator or walking them down a sidewalk beat.

Donnally sat back and drank from his Coke. He realized it bothered him that Junior hadn't attacked him for trying to reopen the factual issues relating to the guilt, or the level of guilt, of Israel Dominguez, only for bothering his grandmother and talking to Oscar Benaga.

He had the feeling that he'd missed something in their conversations, either at the café or in front of the house. Maybe because he was moved or diverted by Junior's confusion, his disorientation, his disconnectedness, his struggle to find a place for himself in the world.

Twenty-nine years old and Junior still had no clue about who he was, not even a clue about who he didn't want to be.

Even more, Junior was prepared to murder, or at least felt the urge to murder, a homicide detective for failing to disclose in his offense report that it had been Chen who'd called his father just before he walked up to the window where he was shot.

And that only made sense if Junior now feared that some truth, something beyond the mere fact of the call, had also been suppressed.

The logic brought Donnally back to the reason he'd done the Internet search. What was going on ten years ago when he was shot and Israel Dominguez was stabbed in San Quentin and even twenty years earlier when Rojo Sr. was murdered?

And the only way to find out was to enter a corrupt world he'd avoided throughout his career and he thought he'd left behind altogether a decade earlier.

CHAPTER 22 ═══════════════════

Fifty-six-year-old Chuck Grassner, working security just inside the entrance to the 44 Double D Club in North Beach, looked to Donnally like a man who'd work for free just to see the shows. Dressed in a stretched-out blue sport coat, unpressed shirt, creaseless pants with shiny knees and steel-toed work shoes, he wore a watery-eyed, flushed-skinned alcoholic's face.

Seeing him stationed by the open door, trading back slaps and hellos and "How many hookers does it take . . ." jokes with entering customers, confirmed for Donnally that Grassner wasn't in it for the money.

Throughout his career at SFPD, from patrol officer, to narcotics detective, to joint designated state and federal agent, and back to patrol as a sergeant, Grassner's mantra had been, "Thirty and out. Thirty and out. Thirty and out." And at exactly thirty years to the day, including unused vacation and sick leave, he was out. He didn't even hang around long enough for a final end-of-shift drink or return for a retirement party.

He'd hit thirty and he was out.

Standing across Broadway, Donnally didn't know how Grassner now spent his days but knew that he spent his nights in the fifty-two weeks of San Francisco's version of Mardi Gras.

Donnally had decided to seek out Grassner because he was a talker, couldn't help himself, and the edgier the information, the more he thrilled in the telling. In the days before police departments had intelligence units and computer databases, officers like Grassner functioned like archives, some in homicides, some in fraud, some in sex crimes, and some in drugs. And Grassner had been pals with Chen during the height of the crack cocaine years, when careers were made not by how many black street dealers they caught, but how many Mexican suppliers they took down.

And the pair's rules of police practice were based on a narrow-focused street pragmatism unconstrained by courtroom legality. They viewed judicial rulings not as the application of law and precedent, but as mere judicial whim and compared bringing an affidavit to a judge to giving the judge a hand job, always gesturing with their hands in front of their crotches like they had twelve-inch penises.

At times it felt to Donnally that Grassner acted like a guilty adulterer trying to set himself up to get caught. And after Donnally left the department, Grassner did get caught, for what Donnally never learned, except the punishment was that he finished his career in uniform and on patrol.

In the locker room a couple of years before he left the department, Donnally overheard Grassner explaining to a young vice officer how he'd obtained evidence to convince a judge to issue a wiretap order by illegally listening in on the target's conversations. He used the information to identify members of the gang and to figure out when they made their runs and where they stored their drugs. He'd seize drugs during pretext traffic stops or by towing and searching cars he'd claim had been parked too long on the street, then roll the underlings on his original target and incorporate that illegally derived evidence into the affidavit in support of the wiretap application.

Other times officers like Grassner took information obtained from illegal wiretaps and used it in affidavits to obtain search warrants, just pretending that the source was an informant or an anonymous caller, and then walked over to the courthouse to find a judge who needed a metaphorical hand job.

Grassner thought, and proclaimed to everyone at every opportunity, "It was a hoot."

That was the other phrase he used as often as "Thirty and out."

"It was a hoot."

Sometime, probably early in his career, and somewhere, probably with his knee on a suspect's back or his boot exploding a door, Grassner had bartered his integrity for an adrenaline rush.

Looking at Grassner now, joking and laughing at the titillating center of San Francisco, Donnally wondered whether it had ever been about integrity. Grassner seemed to just like the adventure. He didn't care as much about stopping crime as about having a good time. And the more reckless he became, the greater the thrill, and like a junkie it took more and more to thrill him.

Donnally had never met a street narcotics officer who believed the drug war could be won. They were merely addicted to the job and Grassner had the worst addiction he'd ever seen.

When Donnally confronted him about what he'd overheard in the locker room, Grassner's story had been that it was just a hypothetical he was using for training purposes, explaining what an officer should never do.

Donnally didn't believe him and Grassner knew it.

Donnally failed in his attempts to identify the case. There

were too many wiretaps in those years, too many dealers, and too many drug seizures.

He hadn't spoken to Grassner for five years. He'd last seen him in a roofing supply store where Donnally had stopped in to pick up some shingles. Since Donnally hadn't heard from Grassner after he was shot, it was like encountering an old friend who'd failed to send condolences after a parent died, and it framed an obligation Donnally thought he might now be able to exploit.

Donnally worked his way up the crowded North Beach sidewalk past a frat boy vomiting in the gutter, a middle-aged, midwestern couple giggling at vibrators in a sex shop window, finally passing a group of men in starched shirts and loose collars ducking into a club.

Grassner reached out his hand as Donnally approached, ready to greet another customer, then looked up, faked a double take, and rubbed his eyes.

"Well, come at me with a gold-plated dildo," Grassner said. "Look who's here. Never thought I'd see the day when Harlan Donnally would show up in perv country."

Grassner glanced behind him at the bank of photos of naked women above the ticket counter, then pointed at the poster in the center announcing it was lesbian shower night.

"That the kind of thing you're into now?"

Donnally forced a smile and shook his head. "Word around the Hall of Justice is that you'd gone from being part of the solution to part of the problem. I had to see it for myself."

Grassner grinned back. "Just part of a different solution. I'm part of a secret crime suppression unit. Guys with boners don't be out doing stickups."

Donnally emitted the obligatory laugh, then asked, "You got a break coming up?"

Grassner nodded toward the entrance to the showroom.

"Wait in there until I can find somebody to handle the door."

Donnally could see the bar facing just inside, most of the stools occupied by men staring toward the stage.

Grassner waved at the ticket taker behind the counter, then pointed at Donnally, indicating that he should be allowed into the show without paying.

Donnally walked in and slid onto a stool and ordered a beer. He put down enough money to cover the cost and a tip. He didn't want to put into his pocket whatever residue his change might have scraped up.

The sign had been accurate. It really was lesbian shower night. Two women, who may or may not have been lesbians, were soaping and fondling each other within a three-sided glass enclosure set up the middle of a fake locker room. The fourth side, at the back, was formed out of gym lockers. Cheerleading outfits and pom-poms lay on wooden benches just out of splash range. The music was heavy on bass, but not so loud that the audience wouldn't be able to hear the women's practiced moans.

Donnally glanced around, classifying the men watching as tourists, after-work financial district partiers, and loners. He then divided them further into the cheerers, the starers, and the fantasizers who revealed themselves by their open mouths and wet lips. He was working on further subdivisions when Grassner walked up.

The bartender delivered a shot of bourbon to Grassner as he

sat down on the stool next to Donnally. The move was as smooth and practiced as an NBA outlet pass. Donnally guessed Grassner spent his breaks each night on one of these stools.

"So, what's on your mind?"

"Memory lane."

"Yours?"

"Yours."

Grassner raised his finger into the air, indicating that Donnally should wait, downed the shot, and then signaled the bartender for another. He smacked his lips and nodded at Donnally to continue.

"I'm trying to figure out what happened in a twenty-year-old murder case. Edgar Rojo Senior out in Hunters Point. He was shot when he was standing in his mother's living room."

Grassner stared toward the stage. The women were rinsing each other off, running and giggling. "Rojo . . . Rojo . . ." He finally blinked and looked back. "A Norteño guy?"

Donnally nodded.

"Yeah. I remember him, Rojo Loco."

Donnally shook his head. "That's the son. He's still alive."

Grassner scrunched up his face for a moment. "Now I remember. Blasted right through the front window. A big-time hit."

"By a kid named Israel Dominguez. He's been on death row since then."

Grassner pulled back like someone had pushed a rotten fish up to his nose. "You haven't gone private and become one of them bleeding hearts like those Innocence Project assholes."

"I haven't signed up with anybody. A friend of mine is puzzled about the trial and wanted me to look into it."

Grassner shrugged. "I don't know much about what took place either at the time of the homicide or the trial. All that happened when I was still on patrol. I heard a lot about it though after I started working with the feds. When they wrote out their affidavits to wiretap the Norteños, they'd do, like, a history of the organization. Who killed who, when, and why. Who had the drug connections in Mexico, how it got handed off over the years as people got taken out or sent to prison."

The bartender slid another drink in front of Grassner.

"What was important about Senior?"

"Since he was the link between the cartel in Mexico and street corners up here, he was the guy all the black Hunters Point dealers dreamed of hooking up with. You make a connection with him or somebody like him and a month later you're riding in an Escalade. Without him, it's ratty old hoopties until you die." Grassner rotated his stool toward Donnally. "You didn't hear about him back in the day?"

Donnally shook his head. "I never worked out of any of the southern substations."

Grassner took a sip of the second bourbon, making this one last. Donnally wondered whether Grassner had limited himself to two drinks during his break, or management had.

"Senior wasn't in place long enough to spread north into the Fillmore or the Tenderloin," Grassner said, "maybe four or five months altogether. Then bam."

"What about Israel Dominguez? The shooter. You ever hear about him?"

"Sure. A Sureño. El Búho. They all had nicknames like that. I remember him as a teenager when I worked the Mission but didn't have much contact with him because he spent a lot of time in juvenile hall for assaults. He was just the kind of sneaky back-stabber the Sureños always had a use for."

"What about Oscar Benaga?"

"El Lobo."

"So it says on his neck."

"He ain't no wolf, he's a snake." Grassner made a weaving motion with his hand. "Slithered out of one case after another." Then a chop. "I really wanted to lop his head off."

"What made it so hard?"

"Shrewd guy. We thought we had him once, got him indicted in a federal racketeering case. Not at the top with the other heavies, but down on the bottom. He was a big guy in the business, but the whole case against him rested on one call."

Grassner fell silent, then a half smile came to his face.

"Benaga and his guys were distributing cocaine out of a meat market a couple of blocks from where his shop is. Listening in on their calls over the months, we figured out their operation, from sources to code words. Finally we got a call with Benaga ordering a goat and saying where he wanted it delivered. Goat was always a code word for a kilo. Always. The DEA and FBI guys and us were doing high fives all around the wire room."

Grassner blew out a breath, like an expression of relief. It felt to Donnally like a setup for dramatic effect.

"All we needed was one overt act on his part to make him part of the conspiracy and make him liable with everyone else for the whole thing. He'd be 10-7 for twenty years."

That had been another of Grassner's expressions. He took the code meaning "out of service" from the police world and applied it to crooks as if both sides were somehow equal and opposite, somehow morally equivalent. Donnally wondered whether he'd applied it not only to Donnally, but also to the gangsters who shot him, both 10-7. Donnally out of the department and the gangsters dead.

Grassner laughed. "What did we find out in the end? The only time we intercepted him in half a year of wiretapping, the asshole was really ordering a goat. A real goat to roast at a real party." He shook his head. "You should've seen the look on Jimmie Chen's face when Harvey Madding—you know him, he was the prosecutor in the case—called us into his office."

Donnally felt a vibration pass through him. Madding was the D.A. who'd prosecuted Israel Dominguez.

"Why Madding?" Donnally asked. "He was never a U.S. attorney."

"On special assignment. They were thinking they would charge some of the gang-related homicides in federal court and they needed someone with both narcotics and death penalty experience. He was there to supervise some wiretaps and train the AUSA's in capital trial tactics."

"For how long?"

"A year, more or less. Anyway, Madding showed us all the photos taken at the party the defense attorney had brought him. A dozen pictures of the goat roasting over a big, backyard fire ring and Benaga standing there next to it drinking a Coors and turning the spit. And Madding was pissed, starting to wonder whether his fifty-page indictment was just the world's longest menu."

Grassner held up his hand, the tips of his thumb and forefinger an eighth of an inch apart.

"We had about this much credibility left with Madding. Him thinking that one attorney after another was gonna show up at his office with photos of chorizo and chickens and rib eyes on the grill and him having to go into court dismissing case after case until everybody in the indictment was back at the meat market and doing business again."

Grassner paused and looked out toward the stage. The women were drying themselves, spreading their legs and bending over, their butts toward the men in the crowd, who were now clapping and whistling and yelling.

Finally, Grassner looked back at Donnally. "I still don't get what all this has to do with you and why you're knocking on my door now."

"The California Supreme Court will be issuing its final decision in the Dominguez case. When exactly we don't know. They never announce in advance the day their decisions come out. But soon."

Grassner snorted. "Sounds like a real rush to judgment. It's only been twenty years."

Donnally ignored the crack.

"Judge McMullin is worried that he may have made some bad rulings in the case."

Grassner flopped his hand forward in a dismissive wave.

"Nothing new there. Judges all start to worry when the needle starts inching toward the vein. Especially now because people are finally getting executed. Back then nobody believed it would actually happen."

Donnally remembered those days. Death sentences didn't seem real, just symbolic notches on the prosecutor's belt. Prosecutors went into capital cases already pissed off, convinced they'd never be carried out because throughout their careers they'd watched state and federal appeals courts finding ways to set aside the penalty or inject delays until the defendant died of old age or disease. He now wondered whether that had played into McMullin's unwillingness to set aside the jury's recommendation and sentence Dominguez to life without parole. Maybe he believed Dominguez would never get executed.

"Madding had no confidence Dominguez would ever take the long walk to the green room. That's part of the reason he volunteered to work for the Justice Department. He wanted to see one of his death sentences actually get carried out. And the feds don't waste time. Timothy McVeigh got the needle less than four years after he got convicted."

"McMullin is wondering whether the right verdict might have been second-degree murder or even manslaughter."

Grassner drained the last of his bourbon, then blew out a breath through his teeth.

"Sounds just like McMullin. He should've been a law professor instead of a judge. Thinks too much." He glanced over at Donnally, his eyes cold, but his mouth smiling. "As I recall, that was your problem, too."

CHAPTER 23 ═══════

Driving south toward the National Archives in San Bruno on the peninsula where closed federal court files were stored, Donnally remembered what the narcotics team of Grassner and Chen had insisted everyone call them in the old days.

Chuck and Chink.

They even had business cards made up in the name of Chuck & Chink, Inc., with a drawing of a two-handled battering ram and a slogan:

Door Busters R Us

The chief suspended both of them for a month after an investigative reporter on special assignment discovered one of their cards while looking into an allegation that Grassner and Chen had kicked in the door to the wrong house, thrown an eighty-five-year-old woman to the kitchen floor, and jammed the barrel of a Glock into her ear.

The newspaper editor later demoted its regular crime reporter because Grassner had given him one of the cards a year earlier and he'd failed to write a story about it, justifying the failure with the claim that the card was neither newsworthy nor reflective of the officers' real attitudes.

Donnally had no doubt it was.

The journalist had gotten too close to them, had become too dependent on them for feeding him stories, not only about their cases, but about others, even about Donnally's shooting. And Donnally owed them a debt for their doing it for they directed the public focus away from him. Not enough to call them Chuck and Chink as they wanted, but he owed them nonetheless.

When the department was under attack from radical attorneys and the left-leaning police commissioners were speculating that somehow Donnally was at fault in his own shooting, Grassner and Chen had fed reporters incriminating story after incriminating story about the two dead gangsters, some real, some fictitious, some fantastical. One had them as secret members of a cartel-backed organization fighting to take over both the Sureños and Norteños. They even gave it a name absurd enough to lend credibility to the story: *Los Chingasos Locos*, The Crazy Pricks.

In a later story, Grassner and Chen had the two gangsters fighting over a woman they were both in love with. In the following one, the two were fighting over a man they were both in love with.

Donnally wasn't sure of their motives. He'd never noticed altruism to be among them and, while he was the beneficiary, he doubted they'd done it for his benefit.

For a couple of news cycles, they'd pushed the shoot-out as a ludicrous attempt to ambush Donnally in which the gangsters had mistakenly shot each other. They weren't bothered at all by the fact that the ballistics examination would soon disprove the tale. Donnally had found it more troubling than ironic when it struck him that his brother had died in a real ambush while he had survived one that was entirely fictional. But instead of receiving a silver star attached to a body bag like his brother, Donnally received a retirement badge.

Staring at the highway ahead as it wound through the hills south of San Francisco, Donnally wondered whether he'd made a mistake in talking to Grassner or Chen, or both, or in mentioning McMullin's name to Grassner. He hadn't forgotten about Grassner's connection to the reporter, but he hadn't worked out how it could come back to hurt the judge until too late.

Donnally thought of a private investigator who once was a detective in the department about whom it was said that he was always aware of what he was thinking, that his mind never idled or drifted unobserved. But Donnally knew he'd never be that man. His mind didn't work that way. Even worse, sometimes his own thoughts came back to him feeling like a déjà vu experience, something seen or felt in a dream that had now become real.

Donnally now realized he'd risked embarrassing McMullin with a news story that would expose the judge's doubts about a pending execution and, if the historical unwillingness of governors to commute death sentences held true, was unstoppable.

The public, especially in a city like San Francisco, enjoyed the sport of second-guessing judges but wouldn't accept a judge second-guessing himself. That would strip McMullin of the protection of his robe and subject all the decisions he'd made throughout his career to psychological analysis, maybe even expose to the world what Donnally had discovered on the banks of the Smith River, that there was a man behind the man, or perhaps, within the man, and this had imparted a double intent and a double meaning to everything the judge had done since the Dominguez trial.

Donnally buried his concern over the risks he'd taken with the hope that his trip to the archives would get him closer to what McMullin needed to know. And that wasn't just whether the Rojo shooting was a hit or a stunt gone wrong, but whether the judge was fair to himself in fearing his whole career had been a fraud. And despite the feeling he was navigating a maze through the lens of a kaleidoscope, Donnally understood the case and McMullin's sense of himself were linked not only in the judge's mind, but in fact.

One thing that remained certain in this anarchy of uncertainty was that the murder was part of a complex set of events that was meaningful only in a context Donnally still didn't understand, and that Grassner didn't fully remember, or had chosen not to disclose. And he hoped this context could be discovered in the Leo Ryan Federal Building, the concrete bunker housing the archives, that was coming into view.

The letters over the entrance to the campuslike facility reminded him that San Francisco was a city of too much context, and too much of it tragic. Congressman Ryan had been murdered by the city's Jim Jones and his People's Temple followers in Jonestown, Guyana, in the 1970s.

And being in San Bruno reminded Donnally that Aasim, the leader of another cult, the Muslim Nation, was probably sitting right now at his kitchen table a mile or two away drinking his coffee and plotting how to terrorize the Hispanics into moving out of Hunters Point.

Walking from his car to the building and looking up at Ryan's name and remembering the Nation members encaging him and

Navarro in front the Rojo apartment, Donnally wished more than ever that he was up in Mount Shasta serving breakfasts in the café. For he felt less like he was engaging in an investigation and more like he was suffering an immersion, as though the floor of the kaleidoscopic maze was made of quicksand.

At the same time, entering the building, getting out from under the Leo Ryan sign, felt to Donnally like an escape from confusion and speculation into the safety of a library and the quiet comfort of fact.

Donnally displayed his ID and the records request form he'd e-mailed over. The clerk walked down a long hallway and returned rolling a cart. On it were stacked the dockets for the federal indictments targeting Hispanic narcotics traffickers from the two years bracketing the murder of Edgar Rojo Sr. and bracketing the attempted murder of Israel Dominguez ten years later. There were only six cases, but at least fifteen, two-inch-thick volumes each.

That is, at least fifteen public volumes.

He knew there were more of them containing filings by the prosecution and the defense that had been made under seal: informant cooperation agreements and discovery motions that included information or allegations that one side or another didn't want disclosed to the public, even notes the judges may have taken for their own use during the case.

As Donnally took a chair in the reading room, he found himself wondering whether there existed a record of McMullin's thinking at the time of the Dominguez trial. And he realized that it would be wise to test the judge's memory to make sure nothing he had said to him had been distorted by anxiety or depression brought on by the oncoming execution or by an impaired mind.

He called McMullin. "Did you take notes during the trial?"

Not all judges did, preferring that the official transcript be the only record.

After a moment of silence, McMullin said, "Not likely. My practice was only to take notes in complex civil cases. I'll ask my clerk to check. I'll call you back if she finds any."

Donnally disconnected, plugged in Janie's laptop, and opened the first volume. It covered an investigation into the transportation of cocaine and heroin from Mexico, up through the Central Valley and then to middlemen in San Jose and San Francisco.

The affidavit in support of the wiretap application began with a listing of the targets and with an outline of the crimes of which they were suspected. Then it moved on to a genealogy of Hispanic drug trafficking, starting from the founding of the Nuestra Familia during the 1960s to protect Northern California Hispanics in prison and later the formation of its out-of-prison arm, the Norteños.

As Donnally read through the affidavits, he typed out lists of events and names as he went, looking for crossovers with the Rojo Sr. murder.

Oscar Benaga and Junior had both been targets of a couple of the wiretaps, but Junior had been taken out of the mix by a five-year prison sentence for mayhem and Benaga seemed to have found a way to insulate himself from the day-to-day operations of the gang, graduating from street captain to consigliore, adviser to senior members of the gang.

Donnally wondered what Benaga had done or what talent he had that had advanced him in the organization, in addition to his skill in concealing his crimes.

The calls involving Benaga reported in the affidavits had less to do with past crimes and future conspiracies and more to do with matters of loyalty and fidelity to the gang constitution and the supreme power structure. There were even some bizarre calls from Benaga to underlings displaying an amateur's knowledge of the Aztec culture and language the wire room agents had tried to interpret as code.

Eagles as heroin.

Cactus as cocaine.

The ruler Itzcoatl as the drug source.

Each affidavit described the murder of Edgar Rojo Sr. as a threshold moment, not just in the Sureños' attempt to insert themselves between the cartels in Mexico and the street dealers in San Francisco, but in the war between the Norteños and Sureños and the Sureños' attempt to move the north-south territorial dividing line up from Bakersfield in the Central Valley to Highway 80 running between San Francisco and Sacramento.

And each affidavit repeated that the Sureño given the job of eliminating Edgar Senior had been Israel Dominguez—El Búho, the owl, the night hunter—a young, aggressive gangster trying to shoot his way to the top.

Donnally felt his mind lose focus as he read through the fifth affidavit. The boilerplate paragraphs the agents had copied and pasted from one to the other over the years made it like a landscape that was so familiar parts of it became invisible. It wasn't a problem of not seeing the forest for the trees, it was a problem of seeing the same trees over and over again.

But he couldn't skip even a sentence. He didn't know whether the pattern might break and a new fact or allegation slipped in.

Even the gang's genealogy became repetitious. The same names. The same crimes. The same methods.

The list of informants had grown from Informant A through Informant C in the first affidavit to Informant A through Informant W in the one he was reading, the investigations building on each other as members were caught dirty and agreed to cooperate in exchange for lesser sentences.

And after the informants were identified by the gang and murdered and there was no further need to protect them, their names were revealed.

Informants A, C, D, H, and M left the gang as Junior had said everyone did. Blood out. Murdered on orders from the generals in Ad Seg in Pelican Bay State Prison. A, C, and H were killed because earlier affidavits had revealed enough about their criminal history and background that their identity became obvious to members of the gang, and D and M were killed because they were the only ones present in all the places and at all the times the affidavit had described.

The fifth affidavit brought Donnally to the year before he had been shot and Benaga had ordered the attack on Israel Dominguez on death row.

Donnally fought against assuming a connection between them, but he nonetheless read the affidavit with a dual agenda, half looking for clues that would illuminate the murder of Edgar Rojo Sr. and half looking for clues to why the shoot-out between the Norteño and Sureño happened just as he was walking in to meet the potential informant.

Then a thought. Donnally wondered whether the taqueria owner was one of the lettered informants in the racketeering affidavits and wondered whether this had been the reason he'd agreed to the meeting to discuss the terms under which he would identify the shooter in the case Donnally was investigating.

It would've just been a variation on a theme, not a new tune, and maybe he was hoping to get rewards from two different pockets, from SFPD and from the FBI, doubling his money for doing the same job.

Until this moment, Donnally's theories had been limited to only three possibilities.

That he'd walked into the middle of an attempted Sureño hit on a Norteño or a Norteño on a Sureño.

That he'd stepped in the path of the Norteño or the Sureño

on his way inside the restaurant to take out a fellow member, the taqueria owner, who the gang believed had turned snitch.

That he'd walked by chance in between a Norteño and a Sureño who'd both posted up on the same block, both obligated to try to take out the other for the sake of what they called respect.

Donnally leaned back in his chair and stared up at the high fluorescent-lit ceiling.

Then a moment of unease. The same narcotics cops he'd relied on in exploring what happened to him, including Grassner and Chen, were also working in those federal investigations. They would've known the identities of the lettered informants and would've known whether the taqueria owner he'd been on his way to meet was one of them.

Even more, some of those informants might have disclosed, if not to Donnally, at least to Grassner and Chen, the real background to the shooting.

But both Grassner and Chen had written it off as coincidence, to chance, to just an OK Corral shoot-out on Mission Street in San Francisco. But it had been crooks against crooks, not cops against robbers, except for the cop caught in the cross fire.

Donnally had accepted this explanation as it related to him since most of the street homicides he'd investigated arose out of chance and circumstance—gangsters and drug dealers bumping shoulders in the mall or at a concert or a car show—but he knew even as he lay in the hospital that the parents of the couple killed by the Norteño's and Sureño's wild shots would never be able to accept that kind of explanation.

For them, chance was an irrational moment, not the end event of a chain of causes and effects understandable, but not yet understood, that had led to their children slumped over a sidewalk table and bleeding out onto wedding magazines.

As soon as he learned to get around on crutches and was able to drive, he had visited both sets of parents.

At first, the solace Donnally had offered them had been met with suspicion.

Had it been Donnally's bullets that had gone astray and killed their children?

Why should they believe that the San Francisco crime lab and a police administration, terrified of potential parents' lawsuits, hadn't switched the slugs or mangled them to disguise the gun barrel that had rifled them.

Why should they believe that the internal affairs reconstruction of the event wasn't anything more than an attempt to deceive them and the lawyers who were soliciting them as plaintiffs in a suit against Donnally and the department?

Unlike the patrol officer who'd rolled up on Donnally and Junior outside of the Cliff House and mentioned the training video, Donnally knew the real reason for the reenactment. It had been created to assure the parents that Donnally hadn't killed their children.

The department had made a hero out of Donnally in order to defend him, to show that it all couldn't have happened any other way.

Except Donnally knew it could have.

As his father would say, inevitability was a fact of fiction, not a fact of life. In the real world, everything could have been otherwise.

What if he'd been more alert?

Looked first to the left, instead of the right?

Caught the motion of the Norteño reaching behind his back instead of the Sureño ducking toward the trash can?

If he had, he could have yelled a warning that might've saved the young couple.

Driving away from the home where they met, he knew that for the parents, chance—bad luck, being in the wrong place at the wrong time—wasn't an acceptable explanation for death. It was an evasion, and he'd felt it then and felt it now as he looked at the affidavits lined up on the cart next to him.

Coincidence and chance were, for survivors, like walking on a trampoline, the earth seeming to give beneath their feet as they tried to follow a path of cause and effect back to solid ground.

For cops, coincidence itself was the solid ground, but if and only if—like a high-wire walker ignoring the hundred-foot drop—they didn't think about it too much.

How many crimes had he solved because he'd once been assigned a similar case, or because he'd remembered the nickname of a victim he'd met years earlier when he was a patrol officer that later gave him a lead to a killer, or a building he remembered only because he'd run through it chasing a suspect a month before?

If it weren't for these kinds of coincidences, many crimes would've been left unsolved, perhaps been unsolvable.

Except cops called it experience or street knowledge, not coincidence.

That was another thing his father had said. Coincidence in fiction was merely a device. For Donnally, in real life, it was everything.

For his father, life was a series of if-onlys. If only Donnally's older brother hadn't seen the press conference in which his father lied about the Buddhist massacre. If only he had enlisted in the navy instead of the army and served on the sea instead of land. If only he hadn't been ordered up to Hue. If only he hadn't been sent to the village where the executions took place. If only he hadn't been able to find a survivor willing to tell him the truth.

The other name for all those if-onlys was regret, and maybe Alzheimer's would be his father's escape from the prison formed by them.

Donnally rubbed his eyes, gone dry as he stared into the what-might-have-been past and what-soon-might-be future, then moved on to the next affidavit.

In this one, the genealogy and history were compressed. It began after the death of Edgar Rojo Sr. and after the war between the Norteños and Sureños had broken out. It was as though a new generation had taken over the Norteños and Edgar Rojo Sr., long dead in body, was finally dead to the underworld.

Junior had been wrong. His father hadn't died for a cause. He'd died a pointless death and the gang that had sworn never to forget had forgotten.

An hour later, Donnally turned to a sixth affidavit. The attempted death row murder of Israel Dominguez didn't even warrant a footnote.

Where are you?" Donnally asked Judge McMullin over his cell phone, waiting in the foyer of McMullin's mansion in Pacific Heights.

"Shoot, I should've called you. I had to stay late in chambers to read and sign some search warrants."

"How long . . ."

"Twenty minutes."

Donnally knew McMullin was lying about why he hadn't shown up, but he didn't confront him, just disconnected the call. The housekeeper had already told him McMullin had come home early, planning to meet Donnally, but had left to go out for dinner. She'd assumed McMullin had either canceled or had moved the meeting to the restaurant or to another time altogether.

He wondered whether McMullin had been subconsciously avoiding him, maybe feeling silly he had involved Donnally in what Grassner had suspected. That the whole thing was about nothing more than a judge getting queasy when forced to face the mortal consequence of a decision.

But standing just inside the judge's door, Donnally wondered whether what he was really searching for was a way to relieve

McMullin of responsibility, find something the judge could use to excuse or justify himself.

Then a sudden, tense, sour, self-accusatory moment.

Why was he willing to do this for McMullin, but not for his own father?

The answer came to him just as fast.

While his father had always hidden from the truth and then finally revealed it only on his own terms, McMullin was not afraid to risk putting his career and reputation on the line for the sake of the truth, and on Donnally's terms, and at the risk of public exposure of his weaknesses and failings either at the time of the trial or now, or both.

Donnally heard a phone ring in the house. Thirty seconds later the housekeeper reappeared and directed him into the judge's first-floor study. As he entered, he found the room reminded him that McMullin had a heritage that extended back through generations in San Francisco. The Gold Rush, the Barbary Coast, the Great Earthquake, the 1936 World's Fair, the building of the cross-bay bridges. The city's history was his family's history.

Portraits on the wood-paneled walls showed his ancestors posing in this same mansion, or cutting ribbons at City Hall, or giving electioneering speeches in Union Square. Hanging between them were plaques and gavels from civic organizations, city councils, and state and federal courts displaying a history of civic duty.

Glancing around, Donnally guessed that the Georgian desk and block-front chests and hutches had probably been shipped around Cape Horn from Boston during the early part of the nineteenth century, back when his Irish relatives were indentured sailors, maybe even laboring on those same ships.

But despite the feeling of permanence and solidity and binding to the past, it reminded Donnally of something else. That McMullin was the last of his line. Widowed, no children, no brothers or sisters, and cousins probably too far removed to matter.

Donnally turned as McMullin entered the study. The judge tossed his overcoat onto the couch and walked over and shook Donnally's hand. The still-shiny grease stain on the judge's tie proved what his housekeeper had told him was true; he'd gone out to dinner, not worked in his chambers.

Donnally decided not to confront him. There was nothing to be gained, for nothing had been lost but a few minutes.

On the other hand, maybe something had been gained, some evidence of the deterioration of the judge's mind.

A half hour after they sat down, Donnally finished his report of what he'd learned and what he'd done.

As he watched the judge looking over the notes he'd taken of their conversation, Donnally thought back on something McMullin had said sitting by the Smith River.

I think I thought he was guilty of at least second-degree murder.
I think I thought.

It almost sounded like part of a child's nursery rhyme.

I think I thought. I think I thought. I think I thought.

Donnally watched the judge reading, adding words or phrases, underlining sentences. It was as though McMullin was alone in the room, his concentration isolating him from his surroundings.

His mind returned to a call he'd made to the judge from the federal archive.

"Did you check with the clerk about whether there are any sealed notes in the file?"

The judge gave him a blank look.

Donnally felt a rumble of frustration. The judge had forgotten to ask. There was no point in showing his annoyance and embarrassing the judge, so he said, "Let's check together tomorrow."

The judge nodded, then his brows furrowed. "I thought you were done with this. Isn't that the point of this meeting?"

"That's what I thought, too. But I'd like to see if there are any leads left to follow."

In fact, he only wanted to find out whether he'd wasted his time, time that would've been better spent trying to ascertain his father's actual mental state.

"The court clerk's office opens at 8:00 A.M. Why don't you come by my chambers at 8:15?"

Donnally arrived at the door to Judge McMullin's chambers in the Hall of Justice at 7:55.

McMullin stepped out of the elevator halfway down the hallway four minutes later.

"You're early," McMullin said, walking up.

The defensive edge in McMullin's voice made him sound as though he'd intercepted the judge on his way to commit a burglary.

Donnally handed him one of the two cups of coffee he'd purchased at the café across the street.

"There are some things I need to take care of in L.A. in the next few days, so I thought I'd get an early start here in case we find something today to go on."

McMullin gave him a narrow-eyed gaze as though he wasn't sure whether to believe Donnally, then turned away and unlocked the door.

And Donnally wasn't sure he believed himself.

Donnally had woken up with the suspicion, distant and faint, that the judge might want to destroy some of his notes, if there were any to be found, ones that might suggest he'd recognized even during the trial that a miscarriage of justice was occurring.

As he was driving over to the Hall of Justice, Donnally followed that hypothesis to its conclusion. For the judge, discovering through Donnally's work something that had become meaningful with the passage of time and succeeding events would be psychologically safer than the recognition that he'd known it all along and had been afraid to act on it when it would've made a difference.

It had been the judge himself who'd admitted that since he'd been new on the bench, he felt he needed to prove himself, to prove, in his words, that he could pull the trigger. But the question now, in the judge's mind and in Donnally's, was whether or not that trigger pulling—that sentence of death and the execution that followed—would be justifiable homicide.

Donnally followed McMullin inside.

The judge set his cup on the desk and called the clerk's office to have the file, including the sealed portions, delivered.

As they sat drinking their coffees and waiting, the judge said, "If you don't mind my asking, have you made any progress figuring out what's going on with your father?"

Donnally shook his head, wondering whether the judge was seeking a diagnosis by proxy.

"That's why I want to go down there. It's not urgent. He's still months away from his film's release date, so there's no danger yet of him embarrassing himself in theaters or the press."

"Is that what you're worried about?"

"No, but it's the kind of thing he'd worry about. It's his world."

"But he's not worried about it now?"

Donnally wasn't sure.

If Janie was right and his father was hiding the truth from himself, then no, his father wasn't worried. Or at least not consciously worried.

If Janie was wrong, then his father would be desperate to outrun the disease in getting the picture finished and into the theaters before he lost the last bit of control over himself and his life.

Maybe his father was even playing the role of Alzheimer's larger than it was, exaggerating the symptoms in order to engender forgiveness from his investors or sympathy from the public if the film turned out to be a disaster.

"He doesn't sound worried," Donnally said, keeping his thoughts to himself, even the ones he had about the judge and whether his sealed notes would be more dangerous to his sense of self-worth and self-confidence than just the test of his memory they might represent.

A knock drew their attention to the door. A clerk entered. She set the folders on his desk and handed him a file request form, already filled out, but for his signature. He signed it and handed it back.

The judge waited for the door to close behind her, then opened the one marked confidential. He looked inside, drew back as though surprised, and then removed a manila envelope that was taped shut, stamped "SEALED," and marked as "Judge's Notes."

He stared at it at length, breathing in and out, as though preparing to begin an ascent. Donnally wondered whether the delay arose from a fear of what might be contained in those notes, what they might reveal about his memory and judgment, his sense of himself, that had blocked him from checking about the notes when Donnally had asked him to.

McMullin finally reached for his letter opener and slit the envelope open along the top. He withdrew about twenty loose pages torn from a legal pad, then looked inside and pulled out three scraps of paper. He read one to himself and smiled.

"I remember this." The judge held it up. It was a restaurant receipt. "This is from Bucci's across the bay. It's on the day I ran away. Back then, it was a great spot to hide out."

Donnally knew the restaurant. A low-key place in what was once the industrial district of Emeryville near the western anchorage of the Bay Bridge. Red brick. Concrete floors. Italian food and local wines. Now all the surrounding warehouses, factories, and steel mills had been converted or torn down, replaced by high-tech offices, with severe shapes and huge windows, but back then, the judge was right, it was a place of escape.

The receipt offered more evidence to Donnally that he'd been right, that McMullin had spent his whole career in hiding, starting from that day.

The judge could have said it had a great wine selection or was an excellent place to eat. But he didn't. He'd said *hide*.

"That was when I suspended the trial so that Dominguez could talk to his lawyer." The judge pointed at a handwritten telephone number and a few words written on the back. "This must be Paul Ordloff's and this is the note I wrote to myself to call him and offer him a second day if he wanted. It was after the bailiff heard Dominguez crying."

"Did he take it?"

"You'd have to check the docket; I don't think so, but I'm not sure. I do remember that Ordloff was in a hurry to get it over with, and not because he had some other trial to start. Court-appointed capital cases were all that Ordloff and that crew did. Had them lined up like train cars, one after another, every six

months. The judges always accommodated their schedules in setting trial dates."

The judge paused. His vision seemed to turn inward.

"It was the psychological burden that finally got to all those
serial death penalty attorneys. The muck of cases like that. Lawyers get sucked down into it. Years preparing for trial. Three
months spent picking a jury. The evidence against their client
was usually overwhelming. The defendants almost all had hor-
rendous childhoods—abuse, neglect, early malnutrition—every
bit of which the lawyer had to pick through, and live with and
have nightmares about, trying to find mitigation for the crime."

McMullin bit the inside of his cheek, then shook his head.

"No wonder some of these lawyers begin thinking the defendant was more of a victim than the person he murdered. It's
crazy, but I can see how it happens and it clouds their judgment."

"Like Ordloff?"

McMullin nodded. "Some of them even cry during their closing arguments at the end of the penalty phase, real tears. And
the pressure during trial is enough to break anyone. Can't let
their attention waver. Can't fail to make a motion or fail to make
an objection or an appellate lawyer down the road will trash him
and make him look incompetent. And if the case does get over-
turned for ineffective assistance of counsel, even because of a
half second of inattention in a six-month trial, it would be reported in all the legal papers and he'd get referred to the state bar
for discipline. Humiliating."

Donnally had the feeling the judge was either seeking some
kind of reflected sympathy, for the attorneys were not alone in
getting sucked into the muck, or seeking a way to delay having to
read through his notes and confront what was there.

Then it struck him that not just Ordloff, but McMullin him-self had been on trial throughout the appeals. His evidentiary rulings, his jury instructions, his every comment, recorded by the stenographer, could, like the spontaneous admission of a criminal, be held against him.

Donnally wondered whether the judge appreciated the cour-age he was now displaying. Remaining silent about his doubts, not calling Donnally, letting Dominguez go to his death, would've put his own trials to an end.

Yet here the judge was, stepping into the crosshairs—almost.

Donnally pointed at the pages. "You want to go through those together?"

The judge looked down and exhaled as though fearing a diag-nosis he was about to receive from an oncologist, then looked up again.

"Maybe you should have your own copy."

The judge rose and turned to the printer-copier on the cre-denza behind him, fed in the pages and copied the loose scraps, and handed them to Donnally.

The judge looked at his watch, then pointed toward the hallway.

"I've got a settlement conference to take care of. I'll do it in the courtroom. You can stay here."

Donnally stood up. "Mind if I take them with me?"

The judge shook his head. "Just keep them close. And not just for the sake of what may be in there, but also for the sake of the confidentiality judges need so that the notes they leave to them-selves will be truthful and not calculated to protect their reputa-tions down the road."

Donnally followed McMullin partway down the private hallway running between the judge's chambers and the courtrooms, then cut away and out through a door leading to the elevators.

He thought about McMullin's last comment on the ride down, wondering whether the judge, perhaps having doubts about his rulings even during the trial, had used those notes to create a record that couldn't be used later to embarrass him.

Donnally stepped out of the elevator on the first floor and against the flow of lawyers and their clients trailing them.

Just like when he was sitting in the 44 Double D Club in North Beach, he separated them into categories as he passed by. Those swaggering in hoodies and low-hung jeans, those pale and dry-mouthed, and those who disguised their criminality in suits and skirts. All en route to the courtrooms above seeking . . .

What?

A Sureño with a tattooed number thirteen on his bicep bumped Donnally's shoulder, then mean-mugged him with a stare and a down-turned mouth. The thirteenth letter of the alphabet—M—meant Mexican Mafia. Donnally ignored him and moved toward the exit.

Donnally wasn't sure what it was they all wanted, but he was sure that for most of them, like that gangster, it wasn't justice.

CHAPTER 27

Donnally spotted a business card for Chuck & Chink, Inc. under his windshield after he climbed into his truck parked under the freeway behind the Hall of Justice. The print side was facing him, as if to ensure that only he received the intended message.

When he got back out to retrieve it, he heard footsteps come to a stop behind him.

He turned around.

It was Chen, challenging Donnally with a forefinger pointed at his chest.

"Why are you screwing with me?"

"With you? What does anything I'm doing have to do with you?"

"I knew McMullin was a wimp the first time I walked into his courtroom. And instead of manning up, he's orchestrating a stay of execution—and that means hanging me out as some kind of coconspirator in a wrongful conviction." This time Chen's finger punched against Donnally's jacket. "But . . . that . . . wasn't . . . a wrongful conviction. It was righteous all the way through."

Donnally pushed his hand away. "Do that again, and I'll break you in two."

Chen smirked and pointed at Donnally's hip, never looking more like the thug he'd pretended to be when he'd worked undercover.

"No cripple can do anything to me, especially you."

A car horn drew their attention to a patrol car pulling up next to them. The driver's window lowered and the grinning face of an officer from their generation in the department appeared in it.

"Somebody call an old-timers' convention and I missed it?"

Then the officer noticed the expressions on their faces and his grin faded.

Donnally forced a smile and walked over. "We were just talking about old times. Thankfully, they're all behind us."

The officer's grin came back. "Almost for me, too." He glanced in his rearview mirror at traffic backing up behind him. "Until then, it's same old, same old," and accelerated away.

Donnally turned back.

"The only way you can delay Dominguez's execution," Chen said, "is if you claim you've got new evidence and go to the governor. And the only way you can do that is if you say me and the D.A. held something back."

There were lots of other kinds of official misconduct, or even just plain errors, Chen could've offered as possibilities for getting a stay. It sounded to Donnally as though Chen was confessing to the fact of a concealment, but not the content of it, and implicating the D.A. along with himself.

"And it's got to be big enough to change the outcome of the trial. But there ain't nothing. All you can do is try to invent something to make it look that way."

Donnally stared at Chen, stunned by what seemed like desperation.

"Whatever you think is going on," Donnally said, "is all in your head. I'm not trying to do anything to anyone. I don't care what happens to Dominguez. He's not my problem."

"Then what's it about?"

"It's about McMullin being a good guy. He deserves to be able to sleep at night."

"Then he needs to grow up. If he didn't have it in him to be a judge and live with it"—Chen pointed past Donnally in the direction of downtown—"then he should've stayed in the financial district fiddling with contracts."

Chen stared at Donnally and raised his hand again, then lowered it and rested on his belt.

"You ain't gonna do to me what those assholes did to Manny Washington."

Now Donnally understood why Chen believed the accusation would be one of hiding evidence.

For six years, appeals lawyers had accused Washington of concealing exculpatory evidence in a capital murder case. Washington had failed to turn over to the D.A. statements and forensic reports in what he had considered at the time to have been an unrelated homicide, but which had a similar pattern. A kidnapping off the street, a rape, multiple stab wounds, and nothing stolen from the victim. In Washington's mind, the differences in time, location, and nature of approach and attack outweighed the similarities and he didn't want to compromise his investigation into the still-unsolved other case by making the details public.

One court after another had agreed that while Washington should have disclosed the information and that while failing to do so was a *Brady* violation, the error had been harmless since the evidence, no matter how the defense might have chosen to employ it, wouldn't have changed the outcome.

After the appeals ran out, the defendant's attorneys demanded DNA tests, claiming they would prove the defendant's innocence. Movie stars and musicians held a benefit concert in the Giants' ballpark to publicize the case and to attack Washington and the courts and to pressure the governor.

The early morning after the governor granted a stay of execution and celebratory parties were held in Beverly Hills and New York and hounded by the media, a humiliated and distraught Washington drove to the summit of the antenna-topped Mount Sutro overlooking the city and blew his brains out.

Six months later, the DNA tests confirmed that the defendant had, in fact, been the killer.

"You hear what I'm saying," Chen said, raising his hand again, this time fixing his forefinger inches away from Donnally's chest. "That ain't gonna happen to me."

CHAPTER 28 ══════════

From the moment he started walking from the house to his truck the next day, Donnally recognized the trip he was taking was, as Janie might have said in the psychoanalytic jargon of her trade, overdetermined.

And later, driving down toward Salinas in the Central Valley, past the ethereal high-tech world of San Jose, the garlic farms of Gilroy, and the dirt and dust of the lettuce and artichoke fields of Watsonville, Donnally still wasn't sure what he was doing.

Satisfying himself that he'd looked into everything?

Resisting being intimidated by Chen, even though he suspected he was probably wasting his time?

Or maybe just delaying the inevitable confrontation with his father?

The reason, or maybe the justification for the trip, Donnally wasn't sure which, was to find out whether the second witness in the case against Israel Dominguez, Chico Gallegos, had contradicted his testimony in anything he might have said to anyone after the trial and whether his murder a year after he testified was connected either with the murder of Edgar Rojo Sr. itself or with his testimony.

The judge's notes had revealed a great deal about what he'd

been thinking during the trial or, perhaps, what he wanted others later to believe he was thinking, but little about what had been troubling him then and what had troubled him since.

The scribblings mostly related to case law that he'd researched, to factual conclusions he reached based on the forensic evidence and the witnesses' testimony, and to notes regarding possible jury instructions.

Included among the notes were three charts.

One showed the elements of the crime of first-degree murder with special circumstances and check marks indicating that sufficient evidence had been presented to meet the legal standard for each: willfulness, deliberation, premeditation, express malice, and lying in wait.

The second showed the elements of the crime of the nonspecial circumstances, second-degree murder, implied malice and reckless disregard for human life, with no check marks, indicating, in Donnally's mind, that the defense had presented insufficient evidence to meet the legal standard.

The third showed the elements of manslaughter, including sudden quarrel and heat of passion, also with no check marks, indicating that the defense had presented insufficient evidence, or even no evidence at all, to meet the legal standard.

It had been a cryptic line among all these that had put Donnally on the road now.

Chico Gallegos. Sweating. Chen.

When Donnally had called him, Judge McMullin looked at his original notes and recalled that Gallegos had been perspiring more than any witness he'd ever seen, either as a judge or as a lawyer. Sweat had soaked through his collar, dampening his tie knot, and left his chest striped, zebralike, when his coat fell open.

At first, McMullin wasn't sure what the Chen reference was about, then he recalled that Chen was the detective who'd been responsible for Gallegos's security and had escorted him to court. He also recalled that both Oscar Benaga and Gallegos had been housed out of state between the time they were identified and interviewed as witnesses to the homicide and the time of their testimony for fear that the Sureños would kill them to prevent them from appearing.

Donnally was on his way to Salinas because it was where Gallegos had been murdered in a drive-by outside his parents' home.

What Donnally knew about crime in Salinas, or at least the way he pictured it in his mind as he descended from the Gabilan Mountain Range into the farmland encircling the city, he'd learned in gang seminars both in the department and at the police officer training center in Sacramento.

To think of Salinas now was to imagine it as the Norteño Mecca. It was the outside-of-prison headquarters of their parent gang, the Nuestra Familia, formed in the 1960s in a Central Valley prison to protect imprisoned northern Mexican immigrants.

Looking out his truck window at the men and women bent low over the rows of artichoke plants, thinking back to when the Nuestra Familia was founded, when farmers and grape growers smuggled workers across the border into indentured servitude, it wasn't hard to understand how the gang had come to see itself as the protector of farm workers, and later their descendants, from both the police and from the urban Mexican Mafia that had already established the Sureños.

Donnally remembered having some sympathy for the outcasts who needed to defend themselves in prison. The L.A.-based Mexicans considered themselves sophisticated and viewed the northerners, stooping with short-handled hoes, and handpicking artichokes and lettuce, as ignorant and stupid and weak. At the same time, the northerners were tired of being coerced into the subservient roles in the California state prison system and having their money and food and drugs extorted from them.

The first battle between the gangs was over shoes stolen by a southerner from a northerner in 1968.

Everyone but Donnally attending the gang seminar laughed when the instructor from the Orange County sheriff's department described the Norteño's surprise and shame when he spotted a Sureño wearing his shoes in the prison exercise yard.

Donnally had wondered at the time whether the reason he hadn't laughed with the others was that he'd learned growing up watching his father's movies to be suspicious of the appearance of early humor in a serious film, for it was usually a setup for later tragedy.

The officers stopped laughing when the instructor told them that the theft and the retaliation that followed set off the longest-running gang war in the history of California, one that left behind a thousand-body chain of revenge murders that ripped up and down the length of the state, tearing into every Hispanic neighborhood from Calexico in the south to Yreka in the north.

And one link in that chain was the bullet-ridden corpse of the Norteño Chico Gallegos, killed twelve months after he testified in the murder trial of Israel Dominguez, while he was posted up alone on his block in Salinas, guarding their territory while his partners made a run to resupply the weed they sold on the corner.

As Donnally pulled to a stop in front of the stucco bungalow where Chico's mother still lived, he glanced over at the spot in the driveway where Chico had been found, bled out from bullet wounds to his chest and back.

Donnally wondered whether the young Norteños now sitting on the porch across the street, leaning back in their chairs and drinking beer, even knew, or remembered, that one of their gang ancestors had fallen just fifty feet away.

CHAPTER 29 ═══════════════════

The sounds of dogs barking in the fenced front yards and chickens clucking in the back met Donnally as he got down out of his truck. The only thing that distinguished this block from any of those in the hundreds of small towns in northern Mexico were the license plates on the cars and the words *meat*, *fish*, and *vegetables* printed in English under the Spanish words *carne, pescado,* and *legumbre* painted on the wall of Mi Tierra Mercado, the corner grocery.

He didn't look over at the junior gangsters, and after the quick glances cast his way when he drove up, they'd stopped looking at him. There was nothing to see. Their war wasn't against a middle-aged white guy who could be a plumber or contractor or city inspector. It was against other young men, enemies who were nothing but reflected images of themselves, distorted in the mirror of their borderland lives.

Donnally was there, fifteen yards away, still existing in their space, but psychologically compartmentalized, an inert thing, not a living being.

The loose screen door rattled against its frame as Donnally knocked. He wasn't sure whether it struck loud enough to be heard on the inside. As he reached up again to rap on the wood siding of the house, the inner door opened and a woman appeared on the other side. Filtered by the dusty screen, she was more shape than matter, a five-foot three-inch figure backlit by dim inner light.

He guessed he also was a gray shape, the setting sun behind him presenting her with just his form.

She opened the screen door to get a better look at him. Heavy, in her sixties, and dressed in a brown Uptown Buffet uniform as though she'd just returned from work.

Donnally introduced himself only by his name and asked if she was Rosa Gallegos.

"Are you with parole?" she asked, then her voice hardened. "I told Juan he can't come back here again. You're wasting your time."

"I'm not with parole. I'm looking into the death of Edgar Rojo Senior in San Francisco a long time ago."

Rosa shook her head. "I wouldn't know anything about that."

"Your son testified in the case."

Donnally watched her stiffen but wasn't sure why. It was very old news. She'd had twenty years to get used to it, and whatever fallout there had been must have settled since then, perhaps even been washed away by time and by lives that went on.

"If you don't mind," Donnally said. "I'd like to talk to you for a few minutes. I promise I won't take long, but it's important to me."

He knew she did mind but guessed that an immigrant Hispanic mentality would cause her to let him in. He'd relied on that countless times in his police career to execute searches by consent that otherwise would've required search warrants, and he'd felt like a colonial master every time he'd done it.

Rosa backed away from the door in a motion that reminded

him of Edgar Sr.'s mother letting him into her apartment in San Francisco, resignation with an undercurrent of puzzlement regarding his aims.

They sat down on the couch in the living room. On the wall to Donnally's left was an unused fireplace, the logs inside dusty, and to the right, a small desk, neat with credit card, utility, and cell-phone bills in piles.

Rosa lit a cigarette. As she shook the flame from the match, she said, "Sorry for being so short with you. I was afraid my brother-in-law convinced the parole people that he could live here. I've told him over and over that he couldn't."

"When's he getting out?"

Rosa drew on her cigarette and smiled the smile of a woman who'd seen and lived through too much.

"You mean this time?" She didn't wait for an answer. "Next month."

Donnally looked over at the family photos standing in frames on the fireplace mantel and on the bookcase. He spotted a wedding photo. The bride in a traditional Mexican wedding dress, slim, white and with a bolero jacket, the groom in a bright double-knit, bell-bottomed tuxedo.

"You and your husband?" he asked, gesturing toward it.

Rosa nodded.

"He at work?"

"I assume so. It's dinnertime in Pelican Bay. He works in the prison kitchen." Another drag on her cigarette. "He's a lifer. A murder in L.A. Been in since before Chico passed."

Rosa glanced in the direction of the driveway, perhaps her stream of consciousness carrying her from a distant killing to a nearer one.

Donnally wondered what it was about these two mothers, Rosa Gallegos and Magdalena Rojo, both still living where their only children had been killed.

And he didn't think they remained in these homes because either one was trapped, at least in any physical sense.

The two of them still living in the shadow of their sons' deaths seemed to him to be a symptom of a disease he couldn't comprehend, that he didn't even have a name for.

He wondered whether Janie could even understand it. It seemed as much sociological or anthropological as psychological, a prison without bars, walls, and razor wire, but somehow too difficult, or too painful, to break out of.

But maybe he, looking through the lens of the past, was seeing more than was there.

Perhaps the Rojo apartment window and the Gallegos driveway had finally devolved from symbolic places anchoring living memories into lifeless things one simply looked through or drove over. After all, his own mother still lived in the last place she'd seen his older brother alive, standing at the threshold, wearing the dress uniform he was later buried in.

"Is his father how Chico got involved with the Norteños?"

"His uncle, Juan. My brother-in-law. My son got recruited on the street. His father joined in prison."

Rosa pointed toward a poster of Cesar Chavez marching along a rural road and carrying a flag bearing the *huelga* black Aztec eagle.

"My father marched with Cesar. Went to jail with him many times for *La Causa*."

Donnally felt a moment of uncertainty as he tried to follow the leap from gangsters in state prison who committed crimes against the weak to those Cesar Chavez had defended against the powerful.

Then he thought of Rojo Junior identifying himself with the cause and of the Aztec and the *águila* tattoos, the eagles covering Norteños' chests or backs he'd seen when he was in the police department.

And he grasped the connection she was trying to make and that had been the source of his sympathy. The cause in prison had been protecting the weak *farmeros* living in the north from the powerful Mexican Mafia in the south. And the cause in the fields had been protecting the poor *campesinos* laboring in the fields against the wealthy growers and the human traffickers.

"What was your son's cause?"

Rosa stared at him for a long moment, as though she hadn't expected such a blunt question, one that put her son's life on trial.

"He thought it was about dignity and respect. Solidarity." She shrugged. "But what do kids know."

"When you say 'he thought,' does that mean he came to have doubts?"

Donnally watched Rosa's eyes survey the living room, the curios and souvenirs from Mexico and Los Angeles and San Francisco, the photos of family members, the funeral brochures, even a photograph of a prison inmate taken in front of the forest scene on San Quentin's death row.

"After a friend was killed, of course he would have doubts, but it was mostly driven by anger." Rosa looked back at Donnally. "But, you see, they were all boys under the control of men."

She pointed upward. "They didn't understand that the orders issued from the Pelican Bay prison were not for any cause, but only for the benefit of *La Mesa*, the leadership."

Donnally thought of Rosa's husband in Pelican Bay.

"Is Chico's father part of the leadership?"

Rosa shook her head. "If he was, he'd be locked down with the rest instead of working in the kitchen. It's Chico's uncle Juan who's part of *La Mesa*. That's why I don't want him living here again."

Her eyes flicked toward the wall opposite the door. Donnally looked over. He could see nine or ten patched bullet holes in an angled path, climbing toward the ceiling, and imagined what had been their trajectory, probably fired from an automatic weapon into the house from the passenger seat of a car by someone aiming for her brother-in-law.

Rosa glanced at her watch.

Donnally realized that he'd caught her not returning from work, but getting ready to leave.

"I'm not sure what this has to do with why you came here," Rosa said.

Donnally shrugged. "I guess it doesn't." But he was sure it did. "Did your son talk about the shooting of Edgar Rojo Senior after the trial?"

"Not much. He got scared afterward and came back down here. He had doubts about staying in the gang, a lot of young people dying for nothing, and was terrified of being in the middle any longer."

"In the middle?"

Donnally didn't see how he could be in the middle of anything. He was on one side, the Norteños, and they'd protect him. And his face must have shown his ignorance.

"Between his uncle's side and Rojo's side."

Rosa first stared at him as though surprised he didn't understand the simplest fact about the Norteños during those years, then she swallowed hard and looked away, her hands now gripped together on her lap, as if trying to restrain herself after having revealed too much.

She seemed to be saying that the murder of Edgar Rojo Sr. wasn't a Sureño hit on a Norteño aimed at taking over a link in the drug trade, but part of a war among the leadership of the Norteños.

Donnally wondered whether she'd blurted it out because she was angry at her brother-in-law for trying to move back in with her.

There had been repeated references in the wiretap affidavits Donnally had read about internal power struggles among the Norteño leadership, but nothing—*nothing*—even hinting that the Rojo murder was part of it. It was described as a straight-up Sureño hit on a Norteño.

But what she was saying still didn't mean that Israel Dominguez hadn't pulled the trigger.

"Did your son ever express any doubts to you about whether Dominguez was the shooter?"

Rosa shook her head. "Never. Chico was there and saw his face and saw him fire the gun. It was more like he couldn't understand how Dominguez got himself into the middle of it."

Which meant that Rojo Sr.'s murder simply served ends that the Sureños hadn't anticipated when they had ordered it.

"Did he ever go back to San Francisco?"

"Later and only for a little while. A friend of his was killed at Twenty-Fourth and Mission, and he came down here again. He said he'd gone up for there for the last time. He wasn't going back."

From her tone, Donnally recognized it really had been for the last time and the reason had nothing to do with his long-term decision to make it so, but because he'd been murdered thirty feet from where they sat.

Rosa stood up and glanced again at her watch. "I need to get to work. My shift is from six until midnight."

Donnally also rose. He remembered there was no car in the driveway, and it gave him an idea about how to extend their conversation and give him time to find his feet again.

Once again, he felt like he was missing something in what she'd said to him, like when he was driving away from Chen's foothill home near Lake Shasta. Except this time he had the feeling Rosa also didn't understand the implications of her own words, like a witness to a homicide who hears a dying cry—a name or a phrase—and doesn't grasp the meaning.

"Can I give you a ride?"

Rosa looked at Donnally for a moment, then nodded. "I loaned my car to my niece. Let me get my purse."

After she walked down the hallway, Donnally surveyed the room, the curios, the paintings, the crosses on the walls, and the figures of Jesus and Mary. It felt like something was wrong, either there was too much of something or not enough.

Even more, and even if she didn't want it to be, her house was a Norteño hub. Her brother-in-law wouldn't have been expecting to stay with her unless he'd already made some kind of claim, maybe sending money to support her and the family after her husband had been imprisoned.

Or maybe she was his outside connection, willingly or not, for passing messages from *La Mesa* in the Special Housing Unit in Pelican Bay to the gang members on the streets.

Donnally stepped over to the desk and pulled out an envelope containing a credit card bill and another containing a cell-phone bill from the bottom of each stack, then folded them and slid them into his back pocket.

He heard a door close and walked over to the fireplace and was looking at her wedding photo as she entered the room.

Her footsteps came to a stop next to him and she said, "It now seems like someone else's life."

Donnally's gaze shifted toward a framed funeral brochure, her son's photo on the cover below the words *Iglesia de Nuestra Señora de Guadalupe, Obregon, Sonora.* Church of Our Lady of Guadalupe.

"You buried your son in Mexico."

Rosa nodded, staring at the photo. "He was born there. Here was only suffering, so it was only right."

Donnally turned toward her, and they walked to the door. It was now dusk. She paused at the screen and looked out at the young Norteños across the street, creeping along the sidewalk and pacing the shadowed porches like wharf rats.

"Maybe I better take the bus. There are already too many questions I'll have to answer when Chico's uncle shows up. There's really nothing I can do to stop him."

Donnally reached to open the door for her, then paused with his hand against it. "Why not get out of here?" He pointed at the words *Uptown Buffet* stitched on her uniform. "There are lots of those around the state to work at."

Rosa shrugged. "All my family is here and this kind of job doesn't pay enough to live on my own except in neighborhoods like this one." She fell silent, then said, "I don't have it in me anymore to start over on my own."

Donnally watched the freeway off-ramps sweep by as he drove north toward San Francisco. The chain restaurants and service stations glowed like lit oases in the slim sliding fog, and, in the distance, the faint lights of farmhouses and grain elevators blinked in the dark.

He let his mind try to orient itself, trying to merge what he had learned before he met Rosa with what she had told him. He had the sense Rosa and Chen had been talking about the same thing, one knowingly and one not.

Donnally called Judge McMullin and asked him whether there was any mention in pretrial discovery motions or during the trial of an internal Norteño power struggle that might have either motivated the Rojo murder or whose outcome had been affected by it.

"I don't recall any internal conflicts being part of the D.A.'s theory," McMullin said. "It's nothing any of the percipient witnesses were asked about or even could've been asked about. It would've been speculation on their part."

"Unless they were Norteños themselves and were involved in the struggle."

"I don't remember anything about that coming up in trial. And there's something else." Donnally heard paper shuffling. "I read over my notes and skimmed through the court file after you left. Paul Ordloff filed a pretrial motion to keep the D.A. from presenting evidence of gang membership and of Rojo's drug involvement in the trial. I thought at the time it was mostly a stunt, trying to set up an issue on appeal."

Donnally wasn't sure what kind of issue that would be, but guessed how it might work as a trial tactic.

"You mean Ordloff thought information about Rojo being a gangster would somehow prejudice the jury against Dominguez?"

"The logic was that the worse Rojo appeared to the jurors, the more likely he'd be the victim of a contract killing, rather than just the inadvertent victim of a stunt."

Donnally thought back on Benaga saying, *Anybody do something like that to Edgar and miss, he might as well have put a gun to his own head.*

"In any case," the judge said, "the jury had the right to know the context and meaning of the tattoos and the cocaine packaging material found in Rojo's house. And even though motive isn't an element of the crime, the jury needs to be able to draw some conclusions about it to determine intent."

"Who'd the D.A. use to explain the drug and gang stuff to them?"

"Jimmie Chen, since he was the department's gang expert and was in on the search of Rojo's house. He even came to me with a warrant so they could broaden the search from the immediate area around where Rojo's body was found to the rest of the house and to a storage area in the carport."

"Looking for . . ."

"He said drugs. He didn't want to be embarrassed later if they'd cleared the scene leaving kilos of cocaine behind."

But Donnally suspected that Chen, and probably Grassner with him, was looking for a lot more than just drugs. He imagined the detectives picking through the apartment, gathering intelligence not only about the cocaine distribution network, but also about the Norteño organization, how they communicated, what other body shops they were using to receive the drugs, who were the other captains in the Bay Area, like Rojo Sr. had been, and who might take over from him, and which black and Asian street drug dealing organizations they distributed to.

"I saw in my notes I suspected at the time that for Chen it was just a fishing expedition, but a murder is a murder and there was reason to believe that evidence relating to it could be found elsewhere in the house."

Donnally recalled the initials "JC," which he now understood meant Jimmie Chen, among the judge's scribblings in connection with a warrant and Ordloff's motion to exclude the evidence.

"You remember from the other day what was on the search warrant inventory of what they took out of the apartment?"

"No. I only skimmed it, but it's in the file. I still have it in my chambers." McMullin blew out a breath, almost a sigh. "In the end, and regardless of what was gathered up from the apartment, the gang identifications alone were probably enough to satisfy the jury that it was a first-degree, premeditated murder, even without the drug evidence."

Neither had to say why. With movies like *Goodfellas* in the theaters back then, and a history of *Godfather* films preceding it, none of the jurors would be able to imagine one gangster shooting at another without an intent to kill.

"Did you allow testimony about the cartel connection or only about the drugs?"

"I read over my ruling. It was that the D.A. could use the drug and gang evidence and expert testimony about it since all that showed up in the crime scene photos. But nothing about Mexico and cartels. That would've been too prejudicial."

The highway narrowed going through Gilroy. Donnally could smell the garlic in the air and see bits of light against the invisible foothills.

"And that must have included packaging material."

"A lot. And all labeled with a scorpion with a black body and red feet."

Donnally recognized the brand as a Cali Cartel product from those days.

"You think the jurors figured out the D.A.'s theory that the Sureños were trying to take over the distribution from the Norteños even though it wasn't directly presented to them?"

McMullin didn't answer right away. "That's an interesting question," he finally said. "Only if they'd read about the case in the newspaper or . . . Was there an Internet back then?"

"Barely."

"Then it would've had to mostly be in the newspapers. Reporters made a big deal about the Colombia and Mexico connection and used anonymous sources to speculate about it."

"You mean like Grassner and Chen."

Donnally had almost said, *Chuck and Chink.*

"I assume so. They always took it on as a personal mission to taint the jury pool in the cases they had an interest in."

CHAPTER 31

C hico Gallegos's mother was a liar.

All it took for Donnally to discover it was a skimming of her cell-phone and credit card records now spread out on his kitchen table.

Why Rosa was lying, he wasn't certain. That she was, he was positive.

She wasn't anyone's victim or trapped in her life or job or neighborhood.

Donnally didn't know what Rosa's hourly wage was, but the amount she spent during this month had to at least be double. Combine this with what she was probably paying in cash and by check, then she was spending at least three times what she was earning.

The credit card bills showed purchases at grocery, discount, and auto supply stores, the charges for the previous month paid in full and on time. There were no interest or late fees and the payments were automatic, transferred from a linked account at the bank.

Rosa had the means to get out at any time, unless she was part of what she had called "the cause" or was still getting payments from the organization. If so, Donnally suspected it was less because Chico had been important to the Norteños and more because his father was a member with a key job in the Pelican Bay kitchen and her brother-in-law served on *La Mesa*.

The cell-phone records for her number in the 831 area code showed call after call from and to a 408 number somewhere in or around San Jose. All brief. Most under a minute. Just long enough to issue or take an order.

Looking at the records spread out before him like an unfinished jigsaw puzzle, Donnally wished he'd waited until the next morning to look at them and instead had gone up to bed where Janie lay sleeping.

But now that he'd begun matching pieces together and a partial image was forming before him, he couldn't prevent his hands from reaching for ways to make that image whole.

Donnally carried the credit card statement into the first-floor bedroom, opened the calendar on the computer, and located the month it covered. The purchases were made on the second and fourth Wednesdays and Thursdays.

Donnally clicked the calendar forward, looking for where the pattern would show itself this month.

If Rosa kept to her schedule, she'd be in San Jose in two days.

He then checked the addresses of the stores where she'd used the card. They were all within a block of each other in the Little Saigon area. It was the home of the largest population of Vietnamese outside of Vietnam, about a hundred thousand people, at least one of whom drew Rosa to San Jose every two weeks.

A search of the telephone number Rosa called turned up nothing except that the prefix indicated it was a cell phone.

Donnally's own cell phone rang. He glanced at his watch. It was 1:00 A.M. Then at the lit screen. It was his mother.

"Is everything all right?" Donnally asked.

"I don't know."

"Then why . . ."

"Your father was just up here."

By here she meant her second-story bedroom where her advanced Parkinson's had now trapped her.

"He just stood in the doorway, not realizing I was still awake. When I pulled myself up a little, he came over and sat down on the edge of the bed. He was all fidgety and talking about how things would change tomorrow and that he was going to be okay and that everything would go back to the way it used to be."

Donnally could think of lots of what might be considered used-to-be's in his father's life, but he could think of none that were worth returning to and most still needed to be overcome.

"I wasn't sure what he was talking about, but he mumbled something and laughed and said, 'The Immortal Don Harlan returns.'"

Donnally flashed on Buddy Cochran's grin fading as he'd said the phrase in Canter's Deli and talked about his father's sudden confrontation with his own mortality and his suspicions about his father's mental state, not sure whether it was psychological depression or organic Alzheimer's.

"You want me to come down?"

"Please. It was a little scary."

CHAPTER 32

Twelve cars were parked in the circular driveway and lined up in front of the garage when Donnally pulled up to his parents' house a little after noon. It looked to him like the parking lot of the Beverly Wilshire Hotel. Convertible coupes for those of the Hollywood elite wanting to be seen in body and fashion and sedans with dark, tinted windows for those wanting to be seen only in the imagination.

Donnally wondered whether his father's bizarre behavior the night before had just been a stunt, a way of tricking his mother into calling and asking him to come down when he knew that the presence of others would prevent the confrontation both he and his father knew was coming.

His father was already walking down the front steps toward him when Donnally got out of his rental car. He held his palm up as he approached, fixing Donnally in place.

Donnally pointed at the other cars. "Nice stunt."

His father shook his head as he came to a stop. "Mother didn't know I had planned a showing of my new film."

"To who?"

"The actors who were in it. They have a right to know how I wove their work together before it goes into theaters."

Donnally remembered Buddy telling him, *None of us knows what the real truth of the story is. It was like getting to the end of a mystery novel and discovering that somebody ripped out the last chapter.*

"They'll be asked lots and lots of questions from the press about the story and their roles. I thought I'd give them something to work with."

"Very thoughtful, but off the point." Donnally pointed at his father. "And there's no soft way to say it. I'm not here to watch a movie. I'm here to find out whether you'll agree to get tested. I need to know whether you can still take care of Mom."

Donnally was at least as worried that his father would soon not be able to care for himself, but he feared putting it that way would be seen by his father as an attack on him, his personal dignity. He had been, and wanted again to be, The Immortal Don Harlan.

"I've been tested."

Instead of surprise, Donnally felt an upsurge of anger. "You what?"

"Just what I said. Every which way. Psych. Neurological. Blood. MRI. PET. At the University of Kentucky." He gestured toward the city below. "I couldn't take a chance anyone would recognize me so I went a long way away and used a fake name." His father grinned. "You can do that when you pay cash."

"That means you suspected you had it."

"Not at all. I just wanted to understand the Alzheimer's experience, from all perspectives. I even went to some family support group sessions back there."

"Then why'd you put Mother through this? Or did the counselor tell you it was right and fair to deceive the woman who loves you?"

His father winced as if Donnally had jabbed him. He lowered his gaze, shaking his head.

"Tell me, why'd you put her through it?"

"Because I'm a self-absorbed fool." He looked up again. "I didn't realize what I was really doing. I was . . ."

"You were what?" The words came out of Donnally's mouth like an uppercut.

His father drew back.

"I . . . I was too focused on today, everything coming together. This was supposed to be the last day of the act, or at least the day when I clued everyone in on it."

His father glanced up toward his mother's second-story window.

"In order to make the movie I wanted to make, I needed to live the life, like a method actor . . . but I wasn't thinking."

"It was worse than just not thinking. It was idiotic and mean."

"I've been so protective of your mother, isolating her from the chaos of my work, that I didn't realize how close she was watching, how worried she'd become until she told me she called you last night to come down."

Talking with his father was for Donnally like talking with a six-year-old.

"Have you explained everything to her now?"

Even as he spoke the words, Donnally understood that his father couldn't have explained everything. How could anyone explain what he had done? The most he could do was to try to explain it away.

His father nodded, then glanced toward the cars. "Everybody's waiting. Let's finish talking about this later."

Donnally wanted to finish it now, then go up and see his

mother, and head back to the Burbank airport. Instead, he succumbed and followed his father inside, feeling like he was trailing behind a mental patient into a facility's arts and crafts room.

Buddy Cochran and about a dozen other actors were seated in the basement screening room. They all glanced back as one and nodded or waved as Donnally and his father entered. Buddy fixed his eyes on Donnally, then looked heavenward as if to say, *God help us.*

The only person Donnally didn't recognize was a thirty-year-old man in rimless glasses leaning against the back wall. Donnally wondered whether he might be the assistant director Buddy had told him about.

As Donnally's father sat down at the control console, he pointed at the chair next to him. Donnally settled into it somehow feeling like a prisoner in an interrogation room, first to be confronted with evidence, then leaned on to confess to something, as if it was him on trial, not his father.

The lights dimmed and the screen brightened.

Buddy, made up to look like President Ronald Reagan, appeared sitting behind the desk in the Oval Office, staring into the camera and saying:

> *A few months ago I told the American people I did not trade arms for hostages. My heart and my best intentions still tell me that's true, but the facts and the evidence tell me it is not.*

"Everybody thought Reagan was lying," Donnally's father whispered to him. "But he wasn't. It was just undiagnosed Alzheimer's."

For the following hour and a half, Donnally watched Buddy, playing Ronald Reagan, struggling during the last years of his presidency trying to figure out what had happened during Iran-Contra and what had been his role.

One after another of his senior staff were brought into the Oval Office—

Donnally remembered Dr. Pose telling him that she'd seen four different actors on the DVD facing the camera, then turning and entering a room—

George Schultz, Casper Weinberger, Don Regan, and Oliver North each telling the president their version of the events that involved selling arms to Iran, a state sponsor of terrorism, in an effort to free the U.S. hostages being held in Lebanon, and using the profits to fund the terrorist Contras in El Salvador.

There were even scenes relating back to discussions in which the president had been a participant, but that he couldn't later recall.

His father used long flashbacks to events that took place in the Pentagon and in Tehran and in Central American jungles to display the stories on the screen.

Donnally thought back on Buddy telling him about his father trying to tell the story from four points of view, as was done in *Rashomon* and *The Outrage*, but using different actors for each version, each actor in the scene, like each government official, convinced his version was the true one.

In between were scenes of Reagan alone, at his desk, in his bed, staring out his window, struggling to remember what he had just been told by the four men, trying to coordinate and synchronize the accounts in his own mind, but each time his thoughts floating away, drifting back to scenes in the movies in which he'd appeared, those fictions seeming more real to him than the real war in Central America and the missiles in the Middle East poised to fire.

Midway through the film there were a series of jump cuts from one Reagan speech after another in which he talked about filming Holocaust victims in a concentration camp just after it was liberated, about a Medal of Honor winner going down with his plane during World War II, about a Christmas truce between American and Nazi troops, and finally a scene displaying his visit to a German SS cemetery in the 1980s where he'd said that no one was still alive in Germany who remembered the war.

Donnally heard his father chuckle, then lean over and say, "Most of the people in Germany who heard his speech were alive during the war, many of them were still in the government, some of them were standing behind him and in the audience as he spoke. Man, they must've thought he was an idiot."

Donnally didn't understand his father's laughter, didn't see the humor his father had seen. It was tragic and humiliating, not funny.

"And get this. The Christmas truce took place during World War I, not World War II. He only read about it in school. The Medal of Honor pilot going down with his plane wasn't a real soldier, it was Dana Andrews in *A Wing and a Prayer*, and Reagan never left Hollywood during the war, never visited a concentration camp, he only saw them in newsreels."

Donnally wondered whether his father understood the parallel with his own life, his delusion that the movies he had made for most of his career were for him more real than reality itself.

And Donnally found nothing humorous in Reagan's delusions. It was that same president, in that same distorted frame of mind, who'd sent soldiers to Lebanon to be massacred like Donnally's brother had been in Vietnam, who'd tried to provoke a war with Nicaragua, and who'd supported terrorists in Iran, Iraq, and El Salvador.

An actress playing the part of the president's daughter then appeared on the screen, sitting on a couch in the White House talking to Nancy Reagan, her face flushed with rage, saying, "He makes statements that are so far outside the parameters of logic that they leave you speechless."

Then Donnally realized that it had been his own mother who'd been speechless the night before, paralyzed by his father's irrational behavior.

And the first lady, looking down at her fidgeting hands, acknowledged that the only way she had been able to protect the president from himself was to isolate him both from his advisers and from the press.

And Donnally thought of his mother upstairs, lying in her bed, terrified for weeks or months about being unable to care for his father.

"Doesn't it all make sense, now?" Donnally's father whispered to him. "And think how the man must have suffered not knowing what his mind was doing to him and then coming to realize that it was his deteriorating brain, and not his rational, deliberative self, that was responsible for the thousands of lives that were lost in the Middle East and Latin America."

Reagan again:

> *First, let me say I take full responsibility for my own actions and for those of my administration. As angry as I may be about activities undertaken without my knowledge, I am*

still accountable for those activities. As disappointed as I
may be in some who served me, I'm still the one who must
answer to the American people for this behavior.

"But he did know. He agreed with it all and ordered it all. He just didn't remember, and he never answered to the public."

Buddy was wrong. It wasn't that somebody had ripped out the last chapter. There wasn't one, just an old man going to his death not remembering what he had done, that others had been convicted of in federal court for doing, afraid even to call the crimes by their legal names, referring to them only as "activities," as if they had occurred on a school playground or, perhaps, in an arts and crafts room.

The image of the president faded and a refocused camera revealed a midwestern apartment kitchen, a Chicago newspaper on the table, a crucified Jesus affixed to the wall, looking down on a young Ronald Reagan staring out the window, alert eyes tracking trolley cars passing on the street.

Then Buddy again, as a ninety-year-old Reagan, sitting in an overstuffed chair in his home in Bel Air, California, covered by a blanket, staring out toward the back lawn, the same Jesus figure looking down at him, the old man's vision fixed and eyes unmoving.

Donnally felt his mind shoved along the path his father had created by the film and imagined the figure on the wall above Regan speaking not, *Forgive them, they know not what they do*, but *Forgive him, for he knows not what he's done.*

Then a jolt. Wasn't that what Judge McMullin was asking? *What have I done?*

Donnally slipped out as the actors rose in applause, as much in praise for the artistic aspects of the film as in relief that the story had made any sense at all.

He climbed the stairs to his mother's room where he found her sitting in a recliner talking to Dr. Pose who was taking her blood pressure. Her jittering hands screamed at him that the Parkinson's medications weren't working anymore. He kissed her on the forehead, then sat down in the chair next to her.

"Sorry," his mother said, "I should've guessed what your father was up to." She smiled the forgiving smile she always offered when she was about to excuse his father's selfish actions.

Donnally didn't express the annoyance he felt.

"Remember when he wore a special forces uniform during the shooting of *Last Man Out*." Her smile widened and brightened. "He was a fifty-five-year-old with a paunch dressed like a twenty-two-year-old marine."

Donnally looked over at Pose who was removing the cuff from his mother's arm.

"Do you really think it was an act?" Donnally asked her.

"What did you think of the film?"

"I think it's probably as good as *All the President's Men* and *The First Monday in October*."

"You mean it hangs together?"

Donnally nodded.

"Then I guess we have our answer for the time being. Maybe we should consider this a test and conclude that he passed."

"Unless it was his assistant who put the pieces together."

"It could be his behavior was nothing more than a manifestation of worry about the film that grew into full-on depression." Pose looked at Donnally's mother and then back at him. "Only time will tell."

Donnally wasn't certain time would tell. Although testing was getting more proficient and proteins had been discovered that cause Alzheimer's, there was no final and definitive diagnosis except by autopsy after death. But given that his mother's failing medications put her own death on the visible horizon, Donnally didn't say that aloud. In any case, it didn't reflect where his thoughts were headed.

"Or maybe," Donnally said, "he just needs to grow up."

CHAPTER 33

Donnally's cell phone rang as he drove up Mulholland Drive toward the Hollywood Freeway. He didn't recognize the number displayed on the screen or the man's voice or name, Alfredo Marin.

"I'm the assistant director on your father's film."

"Sorry we didn't have a chance to talk. I need to get back north."

"Do you have a couple of minutes to meet? I'd like to talk to you about your father."

"Can't we do it on the—"

"I think it would be better in person."

"Where are you now?"

"I live in the valley. I was heading home, and it wasn't until I was almost there that I gathered up the courage to call you."

Knowing how his father reacted when he'd learned that people had discussed his condition without consulting him, Donnally was certain it had taken courage on Marin's part to call.

Marin's filmmaking career might end when Don Harlan found out about it.

"Meet me at the Burbank airport," Donnally said. "I'll be in front of Terminal B."

Donnally disconnected and a half hour later he saw Marin approaching him, walking fast, his face intent, like a man late for a flight.

Marin took Donnally's extended hand and shook it, then they walked down the sidewalk toward the rental car return and stopped next to some shrubs, out of the pedestrian traffic.

"This is a little awkward," Marin said.

"Don't worry about it. I'm glad you decided to call me."

"And I don't want you to think I'm trying to take credit for your father's work."

Donnally guessed that Marin had been thinking so hard about what he wanted to say that he jumped ahead, anticipating Donnally's response to a story he'd not yet told.

"You'll need to back up a little."

Marin reddened. "Sorry. It's just that your father is—"

Donnally smiled. "I know, immortal."

Marin rocked his head side to side as if to say, *Not quite.*

"I studied him more than anyone else in film school," Marin said, "and his coming to see my work at Sundance and then calling me to help him on this project were the most astounding things that ever happened to me."

"But . . ."

"But it was the worst experience of my life. Bad enough for me to quit filmmaking altogether." Marin looked down and away, toward the shadows cast by the shrubs. "It was a dream turned to a nightmare." Then back at Donnally. "The thing was a constantly moving target. Plot, characters, story line. And what he wanted was not an assistant director, but a substitute memory, and sometimes a substitute conscience."

For a moment, Donnally felt like Marin was an actor playing

him in a movie and McMullin was playing the part of his father. He had just begun to think that memory and conscience were what McMullin wanted out of him, too.

"Meaning he was counting on you to hold the thing together and be his memory if it failed, and his artistic conscience, too."

Marin nodded.

"Except that he fought you all the way."

Marin nodded again. "Especially during editing. We'd agree on something. I'd think it was done, then he'd go back to it a few days later as though he hadn't agreed on anything. I finally had to have him sign off on each thing and keep kind of a log posted on the wall."

No wonder the film was coherent in the end, Donnally thought. It wasn't entirely his father's anymore.

"Why did he trust you?"

Marin flushed again, this time in embarrassment. "He heard good things about me in the industry."

"You mean brilliant things."

Marin reddened further.

Donnally smiled, then reached out and gripped the young man's shoulder for a moment. "You'll have to take that ego of yours down to Gold's Gym and pump it up a little if you're going to make it in the movies."

"So I've been told."

"Did you draw any conclusions about his mental state?"

"Not that so much as . . . as . . ."

"Go ahead, you can say it."

"Whatever it is, he covers it up with lies. To me, to everybody." Marin spread his hands. "And it wasn't just that he was offering rationalizations. For a while I thought it was. But he knows he's in trouble and knows he's deceiving people to conceal it, and he's worried. He kept asking, all through the filming and editing, what it must've been like for Reagan when he realized what was happening to him, the sheer terror of it."

Marin fell silent for a few seconds. "And there was something else. Even after the tens of millions that had been committed to the film and all the work he and the actors and the crew put into it, he would wonder aloud what difference it made what anyone believed about what had occurred. That what happened, happened. Nothing would change that. He once asked, since it wouldn't bring the dead back to life, what was the good of it in the end?"

It was a kind of fatalism that Donnally hadn't expected from his father, a man who he'd long been accustomed to viewing as a child in the body of an adult, that he wasn't sure what to make of it.

But of one thing Donnally was certain. At the heart of Don Harlan's thinking when he talked of bringing the dead back to life weren't the victims of Reagan's foreign policy, but his oldest son.

Instead of heading back to San Francisco, Donnally flew into San Jose and at 9:00 A.M. he was stationed along Senter Road in Little Saigon. He'd parked his rental car facing north, centered as much as he could among the stores he found listed on Rosa Gallegos's credit card statement. He hoped to spot her as she traveled from one to the other.

Donnally was certain Rosa didn't drive the sixty miles up from Salinas just to go shopping. Everything she might have wanted to buy could be found fifteen miles away in the malls of Seaside and Monterey. She had to be on a mission.

The fact that her activity was centered in a non-Hispanic district made whatever she was doing seem more deceptive and sophisticated than he'd expected.

But she hadn't impressed him as shrewd. Instead, Donnally imagined her brother-in-law directing her from where he sat in his cell up in Pelican Bay in picking up or dropping off money or delivering messages to soldiers on the street.

And then another thought. Maybe Rosa was not only making pickups and deliveries in San Jose; she could also be receiving and handing off instructions as she refilled food warmers with fried chicken or cleared the tables in the Uptown Buffet in Salinas.

While she would be the means, the methods would have been created by others. The Norteños were ingenious at communicating with their outside members using code words formed from the ancient Aztec language, Nahuatl, and using microscopic lettering written in urine, the jailhouse version of invisible ink.

An odd thought came to him, an analogy with what he was doing. He was trying to find a way to apply heat to make the invisible, visible, and to do so without burning McMullin.

From where Donnally sat, it was hard to concentrate on the six lanes of traffic at once. Not just the relative motion of the cars passing one another, but the fact that they accordioned as the distant stoplights changed and that they all moved against a disorienting background of Vietnamese strip malls, a racket of oranges, greens, and reds, of fast-food restaurants and discount outlets and vegetable markets.

Donnally had learned from Navarro that Rosa owned an old Ford Taurus, but DMV records don't indicate colors and, beyond the difficulty of spotting the license plate in moving traffic, there was no guarantee she'd even be driving it.

An hour in and he was already suffering from the surveillance officer's delusion. If you're looking for a Taurus, half the cars that pass you seem to be Tauruses, even the Camrys and Accords. And if you're looking for a Camry, at times all the passing cars look like Camrys. And if you're looking for an Accord, they all look like Accords.

The shapes seemed to merge into a generic four-door, just as Rosa became a generic Hispanic female out shopping.

Donnally watched cars pull into the driveway of Flaco Ortega Auto Repair. The drivers waited in their cars until a mechanic with a clipboard approached, then they got out gesturing toward the tires or the engine compartment or imitating a sound as the mechanic took notes. The drivers signed the estimates and then either got into the cars of those who'd come with them to give them rides back home or to work, or walked away.

At 10:15, after the morning rush was over, Rosa Gallegos appeared next to the driver's door of a blue Chevy Malibu as a tattooed, midforties Hispanic male in a mechanic's uniform walked up. Donnally snapped a photo with his cell phone and zoomed in on the picture to read his name tag. He was the owner, Flaco. His bald head rotated left, and then right as he looked up and down the road, then got into the driver's seat. Rosa walked around to the passenger side and got in.

Donnally watched Ortega open an envelope, pull out a page, and hold it against the steering wheel as he read. Rosa stared forward as though not wanting to be seen as paying attention to the contents.

Or maybe she already knew them, either had heated the page to make the writing appear or had translated the coded message into English or Spanish.

Donnally was now certain his theory was correct. She was able to live beyond the means of an Uptown Buffet waitress because she also worked as a messenger for the Norteños.

And he knew she wasn't alone in doing so. Countless women were serving time in federal penitentiaries around the country for having done the same thing, for delivering orders to move money, or execute rivals or snitches, or take over new territory. Each woman pretending she had no more moral responsibility than a cell site moving signals from one block to another, one city to another. And always the same justification. If she didn't do it, someone else would, so why not make a little money, or in Rosa's case, a lot.

Ortega swung the car around to the exit from the garage property and drove out onto Senter.

Donnally eased into traffic behind them.

They'd only traveled a half mile before Ortega pulled into the parking lot of a market advertising Mexican and Asian foods.

Donnally spotted what appeared to be the motion of Rosa handing Ortega something, then he got out of the car, leaving her where she sat. He made a pretense of wiping a smudge from the roof as he scanned the street and the parking lot, and then walked inside. He returned ten minutes later carrying a small paper bag and drove back out onto Senter.

Donnally stayed four cars back as they traveled. Ortega slowed as he approached a yellow traffic light and the cars behind him bunched up—

Then he accelerated a second before it turned red.

Donnally felt his body go rigid, straitjacketed by what he was seeing and what he knew would come next.

Ortega cut into the parking lot of a city-block-sized mall.

There was no point in trying to follow them. Donnally had no doubt but that they'd be out the other side before the light changed to green again.

When it did, he drove on, eyes forward. For all he knew there was someone watching him from behind, trying to ascertain whether anyone was tailing Ortega and his messenger.

Donnally assumed Ortega would've made a move like that whether he'd spotted someone watching him or not, for all his moves were practiced, perfected, and disciplined by the suspicion that he was always under surveillance.

While Donnally didn't know yet whether he'd been spotted, he was pretty sure when he'd find out.

Just after he was blindsided.

There were twenty thousand Norteños in California with something to keep buried in the past, and only one person, an ex-cop with a bad hip and an onrushing execution date, trying to find out what that was.

CHAPTER 35 ═══════════════

Paul Ordloff was standing behind his desk when Donnally walked into his third-floor office. His arrival had been announced by the receptionist just inside the entrance of the restored Victorian a few blocks from San Francisco City Hall.

The Frederickson Building was known in the legal community as housing indigent defense lawyers. Nearly every cop who'd worked in San Francisco knew the place since they'd all received subpoenas from one or more of the twenty who worked in the building.

"Have you found a sword I can fall on?" Ordloff said, as Donnally shook his hand.

Ordloff wasn't smiling. His eyes were bloodshot and the flesh around them dark.

Donnally pointed at the file box on his desk. "Maybe it's in there."

"That's a different sword."

At first, Donnally thought Ordloff was hungover, having extended his binge past the three days of what he'd termed the Death Festival and late into the week, but on second look, he just seemed weary.

Donnally had called from the Burbank airport and asked Ordloff to contact the federal practitioners in his building and obtain copies of the discovery materials they'd received over the years in connection with Hispanic gang cases.

The affidavits he'd read had been too cryptic, concealing and disguising specific facts that might reveal the sources of the information used to obtain the wiretaps. Donnally hoped the underlying reports, however much redacted, even with sentences and possibly whole paragraphs blacked out by the prosecutor, might disclose more.

"All these 302s and 6s came with protective orders," Ordloff said, staring down at the box.

The numbers were shorthand for the report forms used by federal law enforcement. The FBI 302 and the DEA 6.

"My friends could get disbarred for giving them to me and I could get disbarred for giving them to you."

Donnally was grateful for Ordloff's help even though he didn't trust the lawyer's motives. He knew they were focused less on resolving the issues troubling Judge McMullin than on his continuing terror of living the remainder of his life with the knowledge that one of his clients had been executed.

"I'll be careful. Did you have a chance to read through it all?"

"Not really. I figured my time was better spent organizing it for you. You're in a better position to make sense of it, and you sounded on the telephone like you knew what you were looking for."

Donnally shrugged. "I may have sounded more sure than I was," and then he described following Rosa Gallegos on the previous day and what she had told him at her house.

"An internal Norteño power struggle and not a Sureño takeover attempt?" The shock seemed to weaken Ordloff. He reached for the chair armrest behind him and sat down. "Nothing like that was even hinted at during the trial. Nothing."

"But it's probably not true. It seems like misdirection. Her playing messenger for the Norteños casts doubt on everything she told me. It would be pretty close to snitching, and she doesn't want to end up buried in an artichoke field."

As he said the words, Donnally felt his stomach tense. He remembered a line in the letter Israel Dominguez had written to Judge McMullin. It was something like, "the D.A.'s theory was wrong." He now wondered whether that was the most important sentence in the entire thing, and he'd missed it.

But if it was, why hadn't Dominguez laid it out to him during his visit to San Quentin?

The investigation into the murder of Edgar Rojo Sr. might have all been about the ID of the killer, but underlying the prosecution was the question of motive, a theory of the case.

Ordloff pointed at the box. "There's also some DVDs in there. Not for all the cases, just some. Years ago, the defense started making motions in these high-volume paper cases to get as much as they could scanned and get the wiretap data downloaded into spreadsheets. Makes it easier to search, though I suspect most of what you want, the older stuff, is probably only in hard copy."

Donnally reached down to pick it up.

"Careful. It weighs a ton. There's about five thousand pages in there."

"Five thousand?"

"You wanted everything. I got you everything."

Rosa Gallegos wasn't as much of a liar as Donnally had thought. It was true an internecine war had broken out within the prison-based Nuestra Familia and that it had been exported onto the streets in the form of oscillating shootings among rival factions of the Norteños.

Except the murder of Edgar Rojo Sr. had nothing to do with it.

All the intelligence reports and debriefings of the Norteños who'd become government informants during the years after the murder had said the same thing. It was nothing other than the Sureños trying to break the Norteño chain between the Mexican cartel and the San Francisco street corners and to become the new link.

Donnally leaned back in his chair at the kitchen table and surveyed the thousands of pages stacked in piles in front of him. It had been four hours and he'd only covered three years of the twenty. He remembered how many days it took him to read *Crime and Punishment* in college, and he was looking at the equivalent of ten of them.

The other problem was that few of the characters in the stories he was reading had names. Many just had informant numbers and those numbers had different formats than the ones in the wiretap affidavits he'd read down at the National Archives.

He had been able to match up a couple.

Informant SSF-88-V0097 in a DEA 6 debriefing report had become Informant A in the initial affidavits.

Informant SSF-90-Z0234 in an FBI 302 had become Informant B.

Names of gang members and other informants and witnesses were redacted in the intelligence and debriefing reports and on surveillance logs, blacked out to conceal their identities.

Donnally knew from his own experience that cops and agents needed to protect not only their informants and witnesses, but also continuing investigations. At the same time, prosecutors were obligated, under the U.S. Supreme Court's *Brady* decision, to turn over investigative work underlying the indictments and anything that might be viewed by the court as exculpatory.

And it was the *Brady* motion Israel Dominguez had focused on in talking to Donnally on San Quentin's death row that he said he hadn't understood at the time Ordloff filed it on his behalf.

Ultimately, it was in the hands of the prosecutor to decide what got turned over, what got withheld, and what got redacted—

Except when an agent held something back because he didn't trust the prosecutor's judgment.

Sometimes a homicide detective at SFPD kept dual investigative logs, one to keep track of his actual investigation and another one to give to the prosecutor to pass on to the defense. This second log was structured to make it appear that all trails had led to the defendant. He'd never done it himself, but understood the way in which the manipulated log prevented a defense attorney from discovering information that might lead to an argument that the wrong suspect had been arrested.

Donnally's cell phone rang. He didn't mind the interruption. He glanced at the number that showed on the screen just before he answered. It didn't mean anything to him.

"Just listen," a male said just after Donnally answered. The voice was muffled. "Say a single word and I'll hang up and you'll never hear from me again."

Donnally remained silent.

"I'm going to give you an informant code number."

The man paused, as though testing to see if Donnally would respond. He could hear the man's breathing even through the cloth he must be using to alter his voice.

Donnally wondered how the man knew he was focused on just that issue.

He decided he'd better pass the current test if he wanted a chance to find out later. He said nothing.

"Write it down if you have a pen, otherwise just hope you can remember it." The man paused again, then said, "SSF-94-X1112."

Donnally wrote the code down.

The man repeated it two more times, then said, "Figure out who it is and you're halfway to where you're trying to get." And he disconnected.

Donnally looked at his cell-phone call log. The area code was 415. The exchange 239. He ran both through a telephone search site on the Internet. It was a pay phone.

He imagined the man walking away, maybe wondering whether he'd done the right thing, maybe wondering whether Donnally would act on the information in the way he expected, or maybe just walking away, his part of whatever it was, done.

Donnally thought of the man's voice. It sounded familiar, despite the disguise.

Likely it was someone who had found out, or at least suspected, that Donnally had been to the archives.

For a moment, he wondered whether it might have been Judge McMullin. But McMullin wouldn't have access to an FBI informant number. Any state-level warrants or affidavits passing across his desk would use local police informant numbers.

Maybe it was Chen. He'd worked some joint federal-state wiretap cases targeting Hispanic gangs. He'd know the informant numbers and who they belonged to, but there was no way he'd give all that up to Donnally.

Maybe it was Grassner. Except the ex-narcotic cop wouldn't hide behind a disguised voice. He would've said it straight out, laughing, maybe in person with slap on the back and a "Fuck all them motherfuckers."

Maybe it was Ordloff, hiding his guilty knowledge, information he should've brought forward himself but didn't because he feared a new trial might reveal his incompetence; so he did it anonymously, so that it would seem to come as a surprise when it appeared in the press.

"If I'd only known . . ."

Maybe it was one of the attorneys from whom Ordloff had collected the old files, someone who'd learned something from a client, something privileged that the person wasn't supposed to reveal and didn't want to get caught disclosing.

How many attorneys had heard confessions from clients about

murders they'd committed that others were already serving life sentences for, but were forced by ethical rules to remain silent about even as the innocent lives were wasted doing someone else's time?

Providing the code number as a lead, rather than disclosing the name of the informant, might have been a compromise the attorney could live with.

There were too many possibilities, and too many dangers. It could be a diversion or a trap or even a trapdoor. In any case, or perhaps in all cases, it had to have been someone who either wanted to help Dominguez or wanted to hurt someone else.

And Donnally hoped that someone else wasn't him.

Donnally began searching through the FBI 302s and DEA 6s looking for the informant with the code letters SSF-94-X1112. A hundred pages into the five thousand, he thought of *Crime and Punishment* again. It was like trying to find every time the name Dunechka showed up.

He glanced over at the DVDs lying near the far corner of the table. Maybe . . . He grabbed the top one and slid it into the laptop drive. After clicks and whirls, a screen appeared asking whether he wanted to install the CaseLinks application. He pressed yes and followed the directions and the program activated. It invited him to do a Boolean search in a blank field, but he wasn't interested in *and*s, *or*s, or *not*s, only in the exact sequence "SSF-94-X1112," and he entered it. Fragments from the FBI and DEA reports appeared on the screen, snippets of text with the informant number highlighted.

Although he wasn't present at the time of the shooting, SSF-94-X112, later overheard a Sureño identified as . . .

SSF-94-X112 has received a total of $62,250 in informant payment since March 12 . . .

The undersigned agent received a telephone call from SSF-94-X112 stating that following the . . .

SSF-94-X112 had information about a Norteño killing of a Sureño gang member, Felix Heredia . . .

Next to each snippet was a link to activate the underlying report.

Donnally activated each one in turn and printed out the associated document. He then retrieved the remaining DVDs and did the same. He read through the stack of thirty pages he printed, turning each sheet with rising expectation—

Until falling off a cliff edge.

SSF-94-X112 had said nothing about the murder of Edgar Rojo Sr. Nothing.

There was no indication he'd even been asked about the murder.

Somebody wasn't trying to hurt him or help him, Donnally decided, only divert and delay him.

Donnally removed the final DVD from the drive and reached to close the laptop lid. His hand held there, inches away. He again got the feeling that he was missing something, something right in front of him. He folded his forearms on the desk and stared at the screen, the icons seeming to float against the desktop background image of a night sky. His eyes lost focus for a moment, then settled on a link to the *San Francisco Chronicle*, thinking he should do an archive search on the names that showed up as connected to the informant. He reached for the mouse and clicked.

A headline shot out at him.

CALIFORNIA SUPREME COURT REJECTS DOMINGUEZ FINAL APPEAL

Donnally found Junior at the outreach program at the Willie Mays Boys and Girls Club in Hunters Point. Donnally sat down next to him in the first row of the bleachers where he was supervising a basketball game.

Junior looked over. He didn't react to Donnally's presence until after he returned his gaze to the court.

"What's up?" Junior asked.

"I need some information about the Twenty-Fourth Street killing of Felix Heredia ten years ago."

It was the only incident Donnally had found in the discovery materials that Junior seemed to have a connection to.

Junior shook his head. "I told you when we first met, I ain't no snitch."

"I'm not asking you to snitch on anybody. I know all you've got is secondhand information. You couldn't testify anyway."

Donnally was lying, but he didn't feel all that bad about it. Junior's so-called outreach wasn't penance enough for the kinds of things he had done in his life.

The truth was that coconspirator statements, ones against someone's penal interest, were an exception to the hearsay rule.

"Then I ain't gonna be your domino falling on someone else."

Donnally ignored the comment and showed him a copy of a paragraph he copied from the affidavit on which he had redacted the code for the informant. Just to ensure that Junior couldn't read it by holding it up to the light, Donnally had blacked it out, then copied it and blacked it over again.

Junior read it, then held it up to toward the high gym lights. "Smooth. You don't miss nothing."

Then he read it to himself.

> . . . has information about the incident in which
> Sureño Felix Heredia was gunned down on 24th Street
> by Chico Gallegos who had come up from Salinas.

Donnally's cell phone rang. He answered. It was Judge Mc-Mullin.

"I just had—"

"Hold on."

Donnally covered the mic, then pointed at the page. "You may want to study that a little." Then he walked to the door beyond the end of the bleachers and stepped outside onto the sidewalk. "What's going on?"

"I just had a visit from Judge Madding. Calling it a visit makes it sound more pleasant than it was."

Donnally didn't like the way the judge's voice sounded, strained and exhausted. He felt protective, almost fatherly, and didn't like the feeling.

"He found out?"

"And is pissed. Grassner told Chen you said I'd asked you to look into this and then Chen told Madding."

"Chen already jammed me up outside of the Hall of Justice. Real hard and way overboard."

"So is Madding. He's saying that I should've come to him first and that the governor is about to appoint him to the court of appeals and he doesn't want to be seen in the press as being second-guessed by another judge."

"You're not second-guessing him. You're second-guessing yourself."

"That's what I told him, but he doesn't see it that way. He spent his career wanting to be seen as the crusading prosecutor, but now that a promotion is on the horizon he wants to be seen as an impartial, dispassionate agent of justice with a capital A and a capital J."

"What do you want to do?"

The judge paused. Donnally envisioned an old man, even older than McMullin really was, on the other end of the call.

Donnally knew what he would want to do. When he got pushed, he wanted to push back.

But he wasn't McMullin, or whoever McMullin was becoming.

"I don't know." His voice weakened. "I just . . . I just don't want you to be disappointed in me."

The words struck Donnally like heartbreak. The judge was a man in pain, aching under the burden he'd taken on.

"It's not about disappointment. You've shown a whole lot of courage, more than any judge I've ever known. But it may be out of our hands."

"What do you mean?"

"You see the news?" Donnally didn't wait for an answer. "The California Supreme Court turned down the Dominguez appeal."

"Which means the U.S. Supreme Court will rule in a day or two."

"Which means the Supreme Court will rule against him in a day or two and it will go to the governor."

Donnally thought of Junior sitting inside with the FBI 302 excerpt.

"Where are you going to be later?" Donnally asked.

"I don't know. I've got to get out of here . . . maybe home."

"I'll swing by when I'm done with what I'm doing."

Donnally disconnected, then walked back inside. Junior was still staring at the page, almost squinting at it like he was trying to see through it and into the events it represented. Donnally sat down next to him and pointed at it.

"You know who that is, right?"

Junior looked over. "How do you figure?"

"I saw another report. The name I'm interested in was redacted in that one too. He said you were with these guys, all set to be their alibi if they needed one."

Junior handed the paper back, then pointed at the name Donnally hadn't blacked out, Chico Gallegos.

"Ask him."

They both knew the man was dead.

"Don't play games."

"Why's it so important?"

"Remember the other thing we talked about the night we met? When you stood up, ready to go gunning for Chen."

"I didn't go gunning for anybody."

"Has your self-control improved since then?"

"It ain't no worse; otherwise, the gunning would be done."

Donnally reached into his pocket and pulled out a slip of paper with the name and telephone number of Junior's parole agent.

"Just to make sure, I'll have him yank your leash if you lose it."

Junior shrugged, then flashed a half smile. "Like I said, smooth."

"I think the guy whose name is covered up had something to do with the Israel Dominguez case."

Junior rolled his eyes. "I know that. That ain't no secret. What kind of game you playing?"

Donnally had no clue what he meant.

Junior leaned back as though to leverage himself to his feet.

Donnally grabbed his shoulder to keep him seated.

"What do you mean it wasn't a secret?"

"Benaga. It's there in black and white."

Junior leaned back and folded his arms across his chest, then his eyes widened and he jerked forward and grabbed for the paper. He stared at the redacted words.

"That ain't no name you got blacked out and that's why you didn't know. I've seen this kind of thing before. In the joint. It's an informant number."

Junior pushed himself to his feet.

"Benaga is a fucking snitch."

Donnally forearmed Junior to block him from pushing open the gym door.

The basketball stopped bouncing and the shoes stopped thumping the hardwood. All the kids were staring at Donnally and Junior.

"Get out of my way." Junior's voice was low and pit-bull mean.

Donnally shook his head.

Junior set his feet and pulled back his right fist. He feinted with a left jab. Donnally ducked it, threw up a forearm to block Junior's right, then grabbed Junior's wrist and spun him around and into an armlock.

Junior kicked backward at Donnally's legs.

Donnally pushed him into and through the door and out onto the sidewalk and kept driving him forward until they were in the street near Donnally's truck.

Instead of bending Junior over the hood, Donnally swung him down onto the pavement.

Donnally locked his hand around the back of Junior's head, pressing the side of his face hard against the blacktop.

"Chico didn't kill Heredia, man. That's a lie. It wasn't him. He wasn't nowhere near Twenty-Fourth Street. The Sureños took revenge on the wrong guy. Chico died for nothing."

Donnally heard footsteps behind him.

He glanced over.

The kids had gathered in the doorway. Silent.

He figured Junior had been a good teacher. They were staying out of it, not jumping in.

"You told me it was a war," Donnally said, leaning closer toward Junior's ear, "and it didn't make any difference who fell on the other side—or did that only apply to their people?"

Junior tried to look up at Donnally. "It ain't that, man."

"Then what is it?"

Junior twisted his shoulder, testing to see if he could scoot from under Donnally.

It didn't work. Donnally held him firm against the pavement.

"Let me up, man."

Donnally shook his head. "First you tell me what this is about."

"I told you, I ain't no snitch."

The word struck like a starter pistol.

Shoe soles thudded. The kids now yelling, "Get off him. Get off him."

Junior may have convinced the kids not to become gangsters, but snitching remained a crime in the neighborhood.

Donnally felt hands grab his shoulders and arms wrap around his legs. He held on to Junior as he fell, pulling him up off the pavement. Junior yelped as his right shoulder popped. The scream caused the hands and arms to release, and Donnally let go of Junior's wrist and rolled free, then came up with his gun pointed at the tangle of bodies.

"Get away from him."

Heads turned toward him, then most of the kids rose and backed off. Two kneeled by Junior, who lay grimacing, but silent.

Even under his jacket, by the angle of his arm Donnally could tell that Junior's shoulder was dislocated.

Donnally felt for his cell phone, surprised that it was still in his pocket, then punched in 911.

Sirens rose in the distance, angling in from north and west. The kids next to Junior stood up and trailed behind the others back into the gym.

The other thing they'd learned in the neighborhood was how not to become witnesses.

Donnally slipped his gun back into his holster just before the first patrol cars rolled up to the building and came to a stop facing each other in the middle of the near lane.

He pulled out his retirement badge as the arriving officers got out of their cars.

The older of the two glanced at the badge, nodded at Donnally, then looked down at Junior. "What happened?"

Now Junior spoke. "I fell down."

The officer rolled his eyes, then shook his head, "Yeah, right."

S tanding outside the ER, Donnally heard neither a groan nor a yelp when the doctor eased the head of Junior's upper arm bone back into its socket.

The last thing he'd heard Junior say as the orderlies guernied him inside was, "I don't want no drugs. Just jam it back in."

The swinging door opened and Junior walked out, his right arm in a sling and a scowl on his face, heading toward the exit.

Donnally stepped into his path.

Junior tried to cut around.

Donnally blocked him.

They stood facing each other in the hallway. Foot traffic and wheelchairs of the recently injured and wounded flowed around them like rough water around a boulder.

"You sure you want to do this again?" Donnally asked.

"That's up to you, man." Junior looked past Donnally toward the ER exit. "I got things to do."

Donnally grabbed the front strap of the sling. "I don't think so."

Junior lowered his voice. "Let go of me. You're in over your head. You don't got a clue what this is about."

"Then give me one."

"Let go of me."

"I'm holding on until you agree to sit down and tell me."

Donnally tilted his head toward the corner of the small waiting area. The room was nearly empty. An older couple sat huddled together along the near wall. A mother with a baby in her arms sat in the center row.

Most of the people with friends or relatives in the ER were standing in the hallway. Anticipation or hope or fear was keeping them on their feet and moving to and from the vending machines or outside to make cell-phone calls and back.

Donnally released his grip on the strap and guided Junior over to the chairs where they sat down.

"Let's have the clue," Donnally said.

"Chico died for nothing. He didn't shoot Felix Heredia."

"You already said that. Who really did it?"

"I keep telling you, man. I ain't no snitch. I'll take care of business myself."

Donnally was getting tired of the "I ain't no snitch" line and was annoyed at it and at Junior. It was starting to sound childish, like infantile posturing.

But there was no way to force Junior to rethink who he was and wanted to be, his self-understanding and his place in the world, in the few days left before Israel Dominguez's execution.

Janie had talked often about the psychotherapy she did with Iraq and Afghanistan veterans as giving them light, sometimes in flashes, sometimes in beams, to take back up the long, dark tunnel of their lives, but Dominguez's time was too short, and Junior's tunnel was too long.

The only tactic left was to try to become Junior's ally.

"You aren't taking care of anything on your own, unless you can handle a knife or a baseball bat or shoot left-handed."

Junior shrugged. "Then I'll wait. The guy ain't going nowhere."

Donnally stared at Junior. There was no way to get through to him. He needed to be an outlaw. That's who he was. For all the changes he claimed he'd been making, for all the outreach work he'd done, he couldn't leave it behind. The closest he'd ever get was the borderland, like the kids at the gym. He'd never be a snitch and he'd never be a witness.

Maybe, like Israel Dominguez, he wanted to be Rumpel-stiltskin.

I don't even exist in your world.

Except an outlaw wasn't just an outsider, he was someone who took the law into his own hands, or became a substitute for the law, and being an outlaw was the only way Junior knew of being a man.

But Benaga was different. Benaga was—

Donnally's train of thought got hijacked by an image of Benaga being debriefed by the FBI, the DEA, and by Chen and Grassner. Sitting in a hotel room smoking serial cigarettes, drinking coffee after coffee, agents taking notes, getting little adrenaline bumps as Benaga named names and described crimes, at one point getting around to talking about Twenty-Fourth Street and fingering Chico for the murder of Felix Heredia.

"Then tell me why Heredia was killed."

Junior looked over, but his eyes were dead.

"It was Benaga, wasn't it? Benaga killed Heredia and then blamed Chico and then Chico's death closed the case."

Junior didn't answer. Just stared at the blank wall across from them.

More of it organized itself in Donnally's mind. The single fact of Benaga as an informant had become the piece that made the puzzle into a picture, or revealed the picture at the heart of the puzzle.

"Chico's mother said he ran away from San Francisco to Salinas, wanting to get out of the Norteños."

Donnally saw Junior's lips move, an involuntary motion. He couldn't hear the words, but he knew what Junior had said.

Blood in, blood out.

That part wasn't snitching. That was a fact. One that in Junior's mind implicated none of them.

In Donnally's mind, it implicated every one of them.

"Benaga didn't need to do anything," Donnally said. "*La Mesa* in Pelican Bay ordered the hit to make Chico an example for anyone else who wanted out."

Donnally watched Junior's shoulders slump as he talked.

"*La Mesa* knew Benaga killed Heredia," Donnally said. "That's why the question of why Chico would kill for the gang one day and try to break free on the next didn't come up, didn't trouble them. He hadn't."

Junior took in a breath and exhaled, lowering his head, weary and resigned.

It was as though by Donnally figuring out what had happened, by possessing that information and being in a position to act on it—by taking it out of Junior's hands—he'd deprived Junior of his manhood.

And it wasn't that hard to take away, for in Junior's world it was so short. The distance between boyhood and manhood was the three-foot arc of a six-inch blade or a half-inch trigger pull.

Junior was a man because he engaged in acts of violence. And that first, original act was all it took to make the metamorphosis from boy to man, or at least for him to think he had.

But as a bystander, one who couldn't wield a knife or pull a trigger, he was no longer—could no longer be—a man.

Junior's manhood needed constant renewal, regeneration through acts of violence, otherwise he would devolve back into a child.

Donnally felt like reaching over and twisting Junior's arm out of its socket again. It was probably the only way to keep him from getting himself killed.

He thought of a Vietnam-era newsreel his father had placed near the end of *Shooting the Dawn*, a correspondent quoting a U.S. major saying, "We had to destroy the village to save it."

"You really think you have a chance against Benaga?" Donnally asked.

Junior shrugged. They both knew the answer. Junior's sense of his own manhood would require him to go after Benaga head-on, and he wouldn't survive. He'd destroy himself trying to save himself.

Donnally noticed a poster encouraging HIV testing, a photo of a woman sitting in a doctor's office, and wondered what Junior thought of women who, by definition, weren't men. But he didn't wonder for long. The answer was obvious. They were nothing but, or nothing more than, plastic Madonnas.

He asked the next question anyway. "Is this the way your grandmother wants you to live your life?"

"She got no say about it. My job is to protect her and I've done okay."

"And who's going to protect her after you're dead? You really think Benaga will keep protecting her from the Muslim Nation after he kills you?"

Junior didn't answer. The question revealed the idiocy of Junior's way of thinking, his view of the world.

Donnally shifted to a question Junior could answer.

"Why did the Norteños kill Heredia? What did he do?"

Junior shrugged again. "Nothing."

"That's not an answer."

"Then check your calendar." Junior looked over, smirking. "Don't all you gringos use them little date books?"

Junior glanced at the only other people now sitting in the waiting room, along the opposite wall, two young Hispanic men in hoodies and jeans, low-riding their chairs.

Donnally had been so intent that he hadn't noticed the elderly couple and the woman with the baby leave, and he hadn't seen the others come in. He couldn't tell whether the two were real gangsters or were just playing the part.

The two men stared at Junior but looked away when he locked his eyes on theirs. The test of wills was over in a second, and Junior, even with his arm in a sling and fresh scabs on the side of his face, had won.

"There's no such thing as being even," Junior said. "No eye for an eye. I lose one eye, you gonna lose two. I lose one tooth, I'm gonna break your jaw."

The two men rose from their seats, gave Junior what they considered a manhood-restoring glance, then walked out.

Donnally's mind flashed back on the Norteño's and Sureño's shooting at each other on the sidewalk in front of him. It happened ten years ago, two weeks before Heredia was murdered a block away. He realized that he'd fixed in his mind that the event was somehow enclosed and complete with a beginning, middle, and end.

Now he understood he was wrong.

It hadn't ended.

"Mission Street. My shooting. You mean Heredia was killed in revenge for the Norteño who died out there?"

Junior smirked again. "You just figuring that out now, Sherlock?"

Donnally turned toward him. "But I killed him, not the Sureño."

Junior shook his head, disgust on his face.

"Man, I can't believe you was ever a cop. You don't get how any of this works. If I push you into the path of a car, your people don't blame the driver, they blame me."

CHAPTER 41 ═══════════════════

Driving away after dropping Junior off at his grandmother's, Donnally realized he might not have yet grasped the logic of the crimes, but at least he understood the sequence, the mechanics.

First was the cross fire between the Norteño and the Sureño on Mission Street in which he was shot and in which he'd killed them both.

Second was Heredia's murder on Twenty-Fourth Street to avenge the death of the Norteño.

Third was Chico's murder.

The law enforcement theory was that the Heredia murder in San Francisco was the work of the Norteños and Chico's murder in Salinas was the work of the Sureños.

If Junior was right, that wasn't the truth. Chico's was the Norteños eliminating one of their own, one who no longer wanted to be one of their own.

Donnally felt a moment of vertigo as his car made the swing from Cesar Chavez Boulevard up the on-ramp to the freeway heading north, his mind pivoting too fast on the revelation of Benaga's role as an informant.

How did the police come up with the theory that the Sureños had killed Chico?

A dead gangster doesn't always mean that he was killed by an opposing gang.

Every cop knew the blood in, blood out rule.

Even more, how would the Sureños have come to believe that Chico had shot Heredia?

It wasn't like they were in the debriefing room and heard Benaga say it.

And Chico had never been arrested for it.

Even if the detectives put Chico's mug shot in a photo lineup, none of the witnesses to the Heredia shooting would've picked him out because he wasn't there.

If they had, Chico would have been in jail for the homicide, not standing in his mother's driveway in Salinas on the day he was murdered.

Donnally thought back on the wiretap affidavits written in the years after the Felix Heredia and Chico Gallegos murders. All of them contained the same paragraphs, in the same language, calcified by repetition until it seemed to have the solidity of historical fact.

What if it was all a lie?

And how could he find out?

With Chen and Grassner on the alert and maybe even desperate enough to act to bury the past and Judge Madding ready to pounce on McMullin, Donnally decided that the Hall of Justice wasn't the place to start.

Donnally exited the freeway just short of downtown.

And headed south.

CHAPTER 42

"The Chico Gallegos case was mangled from the start," homicide detective Dolores Zuniga told Donnally sitting in her Salinas police department office. "I was with the sheriff's department back then and made a lateral transfer two years afterwards." Zuniga pointed at the file on her desk. "It was already on the cold case shelf."

"Nobody was leaning on new informants to find out who did it?"

Donnally felt his heel hitting the carpet, the pressure of time vibrating through his body, and forced it to stop.

Just as he'd pulled into a parking spot in front of the police department, he'd heard on the news that the U.S. Supreme Court had rejected Dominguez's petition. Dominguez's fate was now in the hands of a governor who needed to prove to the voters, in the words of the reporter, ones that echoed McMullin's, that he wasn't afraid to stick the needle in, and victims' groups were already demonstrating in front of the Capitol to make sure he did.

Zuniga shook her head. "There was an evidentiary gap as wide as a highway. Chico's mother was a Christian Scientist. She wasn't going to let anyone cut open Chico's body to do an autopsy. That meant even if we IDed the shooter, a defense attorney would tap-dance on our proof regarding the cause of death. All he'd have to argue was that somebody smothered him in the hospital and we wouldn't have a pathologist who could testify otherwise."

That didn't make sense. No one could prevent an autopsy if there was a compelling public need, and a homicide met that standard by law.

"Back up a step," Donnally said. "How did the family—"

"While the detectives were working their way up the chain of command to force the issue, the family rolled the body onto a gurney and out of the hospital and into the back of a flatbed truck." Zuniga smiled. "The last thing anybody saw was the bottom of his feet and a cloud of burning rubber."

"Anybody isn't everybody. His mother told me they buried him in Mexico."

Zuniga nodded. "That's our understanding."

"I saw his funeral brochure in his mother's house."

Donnally paused, letting the comment hang there long enough for Zuniga to become uncomfortable.

Zuniga finally squinted at Donnally and asked, "Why's that important?"

"The services were at a church in Obregon, Sonora, called Iglesia de Nuestra Señora de Guadalupe."

She put a pretend puzzled look in her face, a way of communicating that she really didn't believe there was anything to be puzzled about.

"I still don't understand why that's important."

Donnally stared back at her. If anyone had paid any attention to the case for the last decade, even tried to ascertain whether Rosa Gallegos had heard anything that bore on her son's murder, Zuniga would know why it was important.

Who better to have heard rumors than a woman whose brother-in-law was on *La Mesa* and whose convict husband held a job in Pelican Bay prison kitchen, at the nexus of the information flow.

Once inside Rosa's house, all a detective had to do was look around at the souvenirs and family photos and funeral brochures.

"Iglesia de Nuestra Señora de Guadalupe is a Catholic church," Donnally said, "not Christian Science."

Zuniga shrugged. "Maybe his father was a Catholic or maybe there wasn't a Christian Science church in Obregon or—"

Donnally shook his head. There was only one reason he could think of for the sleight of hand. "Or maybe Chico isn't dead."

Zuniga grinned. "I thought you said the department made you retire because you were shot in the hip, not in the head."

Donnally didn't smile back. He pointed at the file. "That have a photo of Chico in there?"

Zuniga opened it and spun it around toward Donnally.

He'd seen that face before.

CHAPTER 43

There was nothing unusual in a San Francisco detective walking toward the records room at midnight. Nothing unusual in searching through old case files in an effort to use a chain of dead bodies to link the past to the present and attempt to solve a crime by connecting a present unknown to a past known. But this night was different. It was an attempt to use an unknown from the past to reveal the truth about an unknown even further in the past and thereby illuminate the present.

In that basement room were rows and rows of unknowns. Unsolved homicides and assaults and rapes and thefts to which the magic of DNA had not been applied or to which it could not be applied. Cases without witnesses or leads or ones that had been followed to dead ends, even cases detectives had recognized would go cold from the moment the still-warm victim was discovered.

It was a place of failures in which detectives had surrendered a bit of themselves, of their dignity, by handing over files to clerks and, by the act of turning away, effecting the transformation of live files into dead paper. And this night, with Donnally's and Navarro's footfalls echoing in the marble-floored hallway, then softening as they crossed the threshold onto linoleum, their heel clacks dulled into thuds by the mass of echoless paper, seeming somewhere even beyond dead.

They paused after they stepped inside the room, silent and funereal, except for the *swoosh-clunk* of a copier in a side office.

Navarro led Donnally past three rows of eight-foot-high shelves on his way to where the Felix Heredia homicide file was stored, then turned right, down toward the end, the numbered file tabs leading them on a descending trail into the past. Navarro slowed and reached up and walked his fingers along the files, then stopped. He backtracked a foot, advanced two feet, then shook his head and looked at Donnally.

"It's gone," Navarro said. "The damn thing is gone."

Donnally didn't bother asking Navarro if he was certain. He knew he was.

The noises from the adjoining office ceased at the sound of their voices, and then a crash of metal—a trashcan ricocheting or a chair overturning—and a bang of a swinging door bouncing off a wall.

Someone in flight.

Donnally pointed toward the copy room, and as Navarro ran that direction, he headed back the way they'd come. He spotted the back of a heavyset male dressed in a bulky gray sweatshirt and jeans with a cap and a hood pulled over his head running down the shadowed night-lit hallway toward the stairs, a thick file gripped like a football in his hand. Donnally chased after him, swinging around the turns, taking two, sometimes three steps at a time, his damaged hip stabbing at him.

The first-floor alarm exploded into the quiet night as the man bashed open the security door.

Wanting to make sure he wouldn't lose the file even if he lost the thief, Donnally dove through the exit and swung at the man's arm, knocking the file to the pavement, then he pushed himself to his feet and pursued him through the police parking lot, around the building, past the McDonald's restaurant across the alley, and into the street. A screaming ambulance and patrol car blocked Donnally, and by the time they'd passed, the thief had disappeared down a side street lined with bail bond offices.

When Donnally returned to recover the file, he found Navarro collecting the scattered pages. Helping him were two uniformed officers.

The alarm had been silenced.

"You get a look at him?" Navarro asked.

Donnally shook his head. "And there won't be prints. He was wearing latex gloves."

"It wasn't the copier we heard, it was the shredder." Navarro looked at the two officers. "Why don't you guys take off, I'll handle it. Anybody asks, just say someone bumped into the door by mistake and set off the alarm."

The two nodded and walked back inside.

"Are you going to do a report?" Donnally asked.

"I'll have to write something up and take it to the assistant deputy chief, but I'll try to be a little vague until we figure out what's going on."

Navarro stared out at the parking lot. A troubled and questioning expression came over his face, as though he had gone looking for his keys in a drawer and found one belonging to a car he no longer owned.

"Something doesn't feel right in all this," Navarro said. "Whoever grabbed this file had ten years to get rid of it. Why suddenly now? And what if it has nothing to do with Dominguez? What if it's just bait laid out for you, knowing you'd go after it because it was connected with you getting shot?"

What if . . .

Donnally followed Navarro's eyes into the empty night.

What if . . .

"You mean my anonymous caller is trying to get us sidelined into trying to solve the wrong homicide?"

Navarro and Donnally laid the loose pages of the Heredia case on two library-sized tables to put them back in order and to try to determine what was missing.

Navarro first collected what remained of the investigative log and handed it to Donnally.

"Why don't you skim through these, while I look through the reports."

Donnally sat down, ordered the pages by date, then flipped to the end to confirm what he had been led to believe.

The last entries read:

> D.A. declined to charge.
> Case closed.

That was preceded by handwritten, bullet-pointed notes from a telephone conversation with then-deputy D.A. Harvey Madding in which the prosecutor said that because the informant wasn't a percipient witness to the shooting of Heredia and none of the witnesses had IDed Chico in the photo lineup, and because

Chico hadn't incriminated himself when he was interviewed, no indictment would be sought.

Donnally returned to the beginning of the log, Day One, 1:00 A.M.

> Victim lying in the recessed doorway of the El Negro Bar.
>
> Two bullet entry wounds in his chest and one apparent exit wound in his back.
>
> Stippling on victim's jacket and shirt around the entry wounds, spread in a circle four inches in diameter, indicating close-range shots.
>
> Sureño gang tattoos on Heredia's neck and hands.
>
> Red bandanna in his right rear jeans pocket.
>
> Hands bagged for gunpowder residue tests.
>
> The neighborhood canvass by patrol officers turned up three witnesses who had heard male voices yelling in Spanish and three to five gunshots.
>
> Two eyewitnesses taken to the Hall of Justice for interviews.

The next page of the log contained summaries of witness statements. Both described a Hispanic male walking up to the victim saying, "What's up?" in English, followed by an exchange in Spanish, then the male pulling out a large revolver from under his leather jacket and firing. The victim then collapsing back into the bar doorway.

"Here's something," Navarro said. "A debriefing of an informant about twelve hours after the shooting. It says that they went to his place of business—"

"A body shop?"

"How'd you know?"

"Just a guess."

Navarro half smiled. "Yeah, right."

"Keep reading, you'll see."

"The informant told them he heard Chico was at a house with an unknown male earlier on the evening of the shooting. They were drinking and decided that a Sureño had to fall for a shooting two weeks earlier in which a Norteño was killed." He glanced over at Donnally. "Must be yours."

Navarro continued skimming. "They decided Chico Gallegos should do it."

"It wasn't an unknown male who was drinking at the house," Donnally said, then reached into his jacket and pulled out folded copies of the FBI 302s and DEA 6s reporting the debriefing of informant SSF-94-X1112. He located the paragraph dealing with the Heredia murder and handed it to Navarro.

"This is from a debriefing of Oscar Benaga. There were three people at the house before the shooter left, not just two."

Navarro read the paragraph. "It says that Edgar Rojo Junior was also there when the decision was made to kill Heredia."

"Now look at the first page and see the date."

Navarro flipped back a few pages, then looked up. "This debriefing is eight hours after the shooting. Not twelve hours. And not at the garage, but at the U.S. Attorney's Office."

"And who was present?"

"A couple of DEA agents . . . and Benaga's handler, Jimmie Chen." Navarro paused, staring at the page. "And that means

Chen knew about Junior being there and knew Junior saw who left to go hunt down Heredia and knew it wasn't Chico."

Donnally nodded. "How much you want to bet Junior's name doesn't show up anywhere in the homicide log?"

"What are you saying?"

"You know exactly what I'm saying. Three men were in the house. Chico Gallegos, Rojo Junior, and Oscar Benaga. The problem was that Chen would burn Benaga as an informant if they filed against Chico for the murder."

"Because Chico and Junior would figure out it had to have been Benaga who'd snitched them off."

"Exactly. And Chen used the four-hour gap to come up with a way to tell the story to hide Benaga's presence and conceal that he was an informant. Instead of telling the story as a percipient witness, he told it as secondhand, as hearsay."

Navarro leaned back in his chair, gazed up toward the ceiling, and closed his eyes. He exhaled and looked over at Donnally.

"Jeez. They let Chico walk on a homicide to protect an informant."

Donnally shook his head. "They let a murderer walk to protect their drug investigations."

"Same thing."

"Nope. The murderer was their informant."

Navarro sat up. "What?"

"Think about the sequence."

The meaning of what Donnally was saying was beginning to emerge out of the mechanics. It pulled him to his feet and got him pacing.

"I killed the Norteño, but instead of blaming me, the Norteños blamed the Sureños, that's who the war was against."

Donnally remembered Junior's analogy. He was just driving the car; it was the Sureño who pushed the Norteño in front of it. He stopped and turned toward Navarro.

"Benaga does the hit on Heredia himself. Right afterwards, Benaga discovers that Chico wants out of the Norteños, maybe, as his mother said, because he saw how senseless all the killing was."

"Then Benaga gets permission from *La Mesa* to take out Chico. Blood in, blood out."

"Norteños are sent down to kill Chico and Benaga tells the police it was the Sureños."

"It comes full circle. The whole time Benaga was Chen's informant."

Navarro stared at Donnally. "That means it had to be Chen who tried to destroy the file tonight so we wouldn't find out."

Donnally nodded. "He matches the height and weight of the guy I chased—" Then his mind caught, and he felt his muscles tense. An image of Mount Sutro came to him, the distant hill standing like a grave marker. Then a rising rage, not at Chen, but at himself for not having realized it sooner.

"Call dispatch. Send units up to the area on Mount Sutro where Manny Washington killed himself. Chen saw what I was doing as the same thing the press did to Washington."

Navarro cast Donnally a puzzled look.

"Chen told me he wasn't going to end up like Washington after he got accused of concealing evidence. But that's exactly how he plans to end up. As soon as this file hit the pavement tonight he realized we'd find out that's exactly what he did."

As Navarro reached for his cell phone, Donnally thought back on his visit to Chen's house in the foothills below Lake Shasta.

The truck with local dealer license plate frames and the sedan parked in the driveway.

"He is probably driving either a dark blue Ford step-side with a soft tonneau cover or an older Impala, maroon or burgundy."

Donnally held up his palm.

"But don't let it go out on a regular channel that the media monitors. If it breaks in the news that Chen is on the run, Benaga will take off for Mexico."

CHAPTER 45 ═══════════════

Navarro's cell phone rang even before he and Donnally had made it to the ramp onto the freeway that would take them southeast toward Mount Sutro.

"The beat officer up there found Chen's truck parked on Panorama Drive," Navarro told Donnally after he disconnected, "and neighbors heard someone walk between their houses and climb over a back fence and head into the woods."

Navarro pointed at the lights of a communications tower as it came into view. "There's a hidden memorial to Manny somewhere in there some guys in the department put up."

"Maybe Chen is thinking his way out is to wrap himself in Manny's memory."

"It sounds insane."

"But not illogical in Chen's mind. I was in his house. He's got his old service revolver in a display case, the one with the exploded grip. He deluded himself into thinking he was a hero, instead of a victim who was lucky enough to walk away."

"And that was the difference between him and Grassner. Grassner didn't twist himself up that way. It was all just a game for him, nothing personal at stake, no heroism involved, nothing to delude himself about."

"Where's the memorial?"

Navarro looped around the ramp onto the Central Freeway heading west.

"I'm not sure. Supposedly it's in a spot where you can look between the trees and see the top floors of the Hall of Justice."

Navarro scanned the contact list on his cell phone and punched send. A few seconds later he said, "It's Ramon . . . yeah, I know it's two A.M. . . . . How do I find Manny's memorial?"

Donnally wrote down the directions as Navarro repeated them.

"Keep this between us," Navarro said into his phone. "I'll explain everything in a few hours."

Navarro descended from the freeway to the rising end of Market Street and started climbing toward the mountain.

Donnally's cell phone rang. He didn't recognize the number that appeared on his screen. His first thought was it was Chen, calling to explain or justify what he'd done.

It wasn't. It was Grassner.

"I just got off work and looked at my messages. There's one from Chen, crying, saying you were gonna break him. I tried to call him, but he's not answering."

"I'm not trying to do anything to him. I'm trying to stop him from doing something to himself."

"Is this about Oscar Benaga?"

Now Donnally was certain that it had been Grassner's muffled voice on the telephone that had set him on this path by pointing him toward Benaga's DEA informant number.

There was no point in confronting Grassner about it.

"Yeah. It's about Benaga and the Heredia murder. Benaga did it and Chen knew he did it, but let him walk to protect all the other investigations where he'd used Benaga as an informant."

Donnally switched his phone to speaker so Navarro could hear.

"I knew it would come to this," Grassner said. "I told him back then that Benaga was a snake. That guy was a scumbag since he was a teenager and took over the block Rojo lived on. Anyway it wasn't . . . it wasn't . . . Never mind, it's too late now."

"Anyway it wasn't what?" Donnally said. "It's not too late to talk Chen out of what he plans to do."

"It wasn't just Chen. It was Harvey Madding, too. The DEA started thinking Benaga was double-dealing. He'd tell them something was going to happen and then it would happen and he'd rush in to collect his reward for the information. It finally banged against their heads that he might be orchestrating everything himself. The DEA wanted to put him on a polygraph. Madding had been assigned to the feds and blocked it. I've been thinking all these years that Benaga had something on both of them."

Donnally saw they were approaching Twin Peaks Boulevard. He pointed at the intersection and signaled Navarro to turn onto it.

"Wind around to Fairview Court," Donnally told Navarro. "It's quicker."

"Fairview Court?" Grassner said. "That mean Chen is up by Sutro Tower?"

"His truck is up here. I think he's headed to Manny's memorial."

Grassner blew out a breath. "I should've guessed. He's been fixated on Manny since you showed up at his house."

Donnally heard Grassner's car accelerate.

"I'm on my way," Grassner said. "It's probably too late, but I'm on my way. Be there in a few minutes."

"Wait," Donnally said. "How do we know you showing up won't make it worse? How do we know you're not in the same situation as Chen and Benaga's got something on you too?"

"You do know. You know I never cared about body counts the way those two did. Never cared about cleaning the streets. It wasn't about that. It was just—"

"I know," Donnally said, cutting him off. "It was just a hoot."

A patrol officer was waiting for them in the cul-de-sac at the end of Fairview Court, outside of the bright circle cast by the streetlight down the block. They could see Sutro Tower rising up, the thousand-foot steel trusses flaming and flashing in some places and steadily burning with red and white beacons in others, all backlit from above by low clouds illuminated by city lights.

Donnally recognized her. Kristi Bradford. They'd come out of different academies, but were of the same generation in the department.

"Does he know you're here?" Navarro asked Bradford as they walked over.

Bradford's eyes widened in surprise when she recognized Donnally, then nodded to him.

"Probably. We drove up with our overheads on." She pointed first at the hillside houses to their right and the reservoir to their left. "We pretty much lit up the place."

"Any sounds?"

"My partner snuck in there and heard Chen walking around, pacing, but he backed off." Bradford tilted her head toward a second row of houses. "He's set up by Chen's truck in case Chen changes his mind."

"Changes his mind?" Navarro asked. "Is Chen saying something?"

"No, but nobody comes up here at this time of night to pay his respects."

"Let's stay together going in," Donnally said. "If something goes sour, I don't want us shooting each other."

Bradford looked back and forth between Donnally and Navarro. "You guys wearing vests?" They shook their heads. "Then I better go first."

"That won't help," Donnally said, "he's too good of a shot. He'll get you. Anyway, I'm the one who he thinks has ruined his life, so he'll be aiming at me if he decides not to aim at himself. Let's go together, but spread out as we get close."

Bradford retrieved her shotgun from her car and then raised her chin toward a break in the trees.

CHAPTER 47 ═══════════════════════

Donnally led them up the dark incline toward the base of the tower. Despite the dry oak leaves crackling under their soles, they heard Chen before he heard them. It sounded to Donnally as though Chen was talking to himself. His footfalls were hard, less like he was pacing, and more like he was stomping in anger.

"It's too late," Chen was saying. "It's too late."

Donnally pulled out his cell phone, shielded the screen, and then navigated to the voice recorder and activated it.

Chen's voice rose in frustration and anger. "You're not listening to me, Harvey. They know everything about Heredia . . . So what if Chico's dead? Benaga'll cut a deal to cooperate against us. Why? You know why. Because that's . . . what . . . he does. That's how he came to us in the first place. And I ain't spending the rest my life in prison . . . What do you mean exaggerating? Chico is dead because of us . . . Bullshit . . . I know what a conspiracy is. You can lie to yourself, but don't lie to me . . . No, asshole. All they got you on is obstruction. What they got on me is conspiracy all the way back, all the way . . . Yeah, we put a lot of guys away. But nobody's gonna care about that now."

Listening to Chen's desperation, Donnally grasped the conclusion Harvey Madding would soon arrive at. It would be better for Madding if Chen killed himself. Chen was the link between Benaga and Madding—

That is, if Donnally understood everything, but he wasn't sure he did.

"Yeah, they got the file . . . I don't want a lawyer. What's a lawyer gonna do for me?"

Donnally heard soft footsteps coming up behind him. He looked over his shoulder, made out Grassner's figure, then raised his finger to his lips.

"Chico's dead," Chen said into his phone. "And I'm an accessory."

"Chico's not dead."

Grassner's words punched through the silence. He shouldered his way between Donnally and Navarro, then turned back and raised his palm, holding them in place, then continued forward and disappeared into the shadow enveloping Chen.

Donnally heard a snap. He hoped it was Chen closing a flip phone and not him releasing a holster strap.

"Chuck?"

"Yeah, it's me and Chico isn't dead."

Donnally heard a few more steps, then Grassner's voice. "Show me your hands."

Another snap. This time Donnally was sure it was the holster.

"Stay where you are."

"I'm staying, but listen to me. Chico is alive. I spotted him in San Jose four years ago."

"What? How?"

Grassner ignored the questions. "I need to keep you from messing up your life any worse than you already have."

"Why didn't you tell me?"

"Because Benaga owns you, that's why."

"I just wanted to scare Rojo. Nobody was supposed to get hurt. Just make him panic and think he needed his own enforcer and make Benaga that guy."

Now it made sense. Chen wanted Benaga, or someone he recruited, to shoot through the window to terrify Rojo Senior, make him feel like he and his family were under attack. All the better that the person Benaga recruited to do it was a Sureño. It would push Rojo into bringing in Benaga and raise him up from his place as a street tough guy and put him into the heart of the Norteño organization. From there Benaga could give Chen everything, all the way to the cocaine source in Mexico.

Donnally finally had most of what Judge McMullin needed. If what Chen was saying was true, it wasn't a lying-in-wait, premeditated capital murder. At worst it really was second degree. There was no premeditation, no intent to kill, just a reckless shooting into Rojo's apartment.

Israel Dominguez's attorney had made the right argument for the wrong reason. He argued implied malice not because he thought it was true, but because he was afraid what he believed was the truth would get his client a death sentence.

It was time for Grassner to back off, not push Chen into putting the gun to his head. There were gaps they needed Chen to fill.

He heard Chen pacing again.

And now Donnally understood how things happened that night.

Chen had called Senior and told him something that would bring him to the window, maybe to look down toward the gate. That's why Senior's mother said they made a space between the couch and the wall, so they could see who was ringing.

Benaga had manipulated Chen into becoming a coconspirator

in a second-degree murder, and that's what he had on Chen over all the years. And that's why Chen had to let Benaga walk on the Heredia killing.

But it was too late for Dominguez. The Supreme Court wouldn't consider new evidence. As far as it was concerned, Dominguez had his day in court. Only the governor could consider it, and no governor would block an execution over what would seem to voters to be the most trivial kind of difference between first- and second-degree murder, one that voters wouldn't understand or care about. For the public, the facts were simple. Dominguez had been lying in wait and he'd pulled the trigger.

"Jeez, man," Grassner said to Chen, "those plaques and awards really mean that much to you? Being known as the baddest cowboy on the street?"

It did and because it did, Benaga owned Chen. Chen couldn't turn in Benaga without turning in himself at the same time.

A cell phone rang.

Chen answered, then laughed, a bitter, almost hysterical laugh.

"It's our friend Harvey Madding again," Chen said to Grassner.

"Say hello for me. I'm sure he'll want to know I'm here."

Donnally cringed. Grassner's sarcasm was like a knife digging into an open wound. He felt around on the ground until he found a fist-sized rock, the only nonlethal weapon he could think of to take down Chen. And he had no doubt he was close to having to use it, for he knew the question Madding was about to ask: *How did Grassner find out Chen was up here?*

The silence lasted five seconds, then Chen said, "Donnally, come on out. I want to see your face."

Donnally gestured for Navarro to circle around to the left, but not far enough to get into a cross fire, then handed Navarro his cell phone, still recording. Donnally made a climbing motion with his hands to indicate that they should try to match their footfalls so Chen wouldn't figure out that Navarro was there.

Navarro nodded.

Chen had his handgun pointed at Grassner when Donnally stepped into the shadowed clearing. Chen stood fifteen feet away. He shifted the barrel toward Donnally's head.

"Toss your gun and show me your hands," Chen said. "Slowly."

Donnally ripped open the Velcro holster strap, then flipped the rock ten feet to his right and raised his arms.

"Shooting me won't stop anything," Donnally said. "Navarro is already at his desk printing out a warrant for Benaga and officers are on their way to pick up Chico. It's all going to come out."

"You hear that Harvey?" Chen said into his phone. "It's all going to come out."

Chen laughed again.

"You remember that old radio news show, Donnally? Paul Harvey." Chen giggled, almost childlike. "Helluva coincidence. Harvey and Harvey. At the end, the guy would always say, 'Now for the rest of the story,' then throw in a twist."

Chen listened for a few seconds, then put the phone on speaker and pointed it toward Donnally, who could hear Madding yelling, "Shut up. Shut up."

Chen lowered the phone to his side. "The twist is that Chico went in to see Harvey the day before he testified against Dominguez. He told Harvey he didn't see anything, that Benaga had threatened him into saying Dominguez did it. But Harvey needed Chico bad, real bad, claimed he didn't believe him. He didn't want to believe him because, he didn't just want a conviction, he needed it. His career depended on it. Back then nobody was moving to the top without proving they were tough, and there was no better proof than putting somebody on death row and Madding figured this could be his only shot.

"The truth was that Benaga lied on the stand. He was already a member of the Norteños and Harvey was afraid the defense would find out and get that into evidence. Harvey was positive the jury wouldn't convict a Sureño of a capital murder solely on the testimony of a Norteño. But Chico wasn't in the gang yet. I was there. In the D.A.'s office. Harvey leaning over Chico, screaming at him, 'Stick to the script, stick to the script or you're going back to the joint. Everybody knows what happens to snitches in the joint.'"

Chen held the phone up to his ear again. "I get it right, Harvey? I get it right? You tell Chico he'd be dead meat if he didn't testify the way you wanted?"

Chen snapped his phone closed and again pointed his gun at Grassner.

"Why'd you do it?" The hysterical giddiness was gone from Chen's voice. "Why'd you sell me out?"

"I didn't sell you out."

"He didn't," Donnally said. "I put it together."

"I don't believe you. Somebody put you on this trail and it had to have been Chuck."

Chen's gun barrel flashed. So stunned was Donnally he barely heard the bang.

Grassner grunted and wrapped his hands over his stomach. Donnally dropped and rolled, reaching for his gun.

Bang—bang—bang.

Dirt exploded from the earth next to Donnally's face. His back thudded against a tree. A slug punched into the bark above his shoulder. He reached out with his gun and fired at the dark shape of Chen.

More shots came from Donnally's left. Navarro.

Shotgun blasts from his right. Bradford.

Chen dropped to his knees and onto his face.

Donnally pushed himself to his feet.

A beam from Bradford's flashlight raced across the forest floor. Donnally ran over and kicked away Chen's gun, then knelt and felt for a pulse. There wasn't one.

The light moved. He turned to see Navarro bending over Grassner. Bradford ran back toward her car for her first aid kit, yelling into her radio, "Officer down," and giving their location.

Donnally walked over and kneeled down next to Grassner, the man's gasping breath the only sound in the forest. Donnally punched a number on his cell phone to light up the screen and pointed it down toward Grassner's stomach. He pulled Grassner's hands away. The bullet had entered toward the bottom of his left lung. Donnally held his palm against it to try to limit the bleeding and ease his breathing.

Grassner groaned, then looked up at Donnally, a frozen wince on his face.

"I guess . . . it . . . wasn't . . . such . . . a hoot . . . after all."

And closed his eyes.

C hen is dead," Donnally told Judge McMullin in his study at 5:30 A.M. "Grassner is in surgery, but he'll make it."

Donnally and Navarro were seated across from the judge, still dressed in his pajamas and robe. Donnally had just played the recording to him.

"And the media?" McMullin asked.

"We put out a story it was suicide by cop," Navarro said. "We gave them some speculation that Chen was distraught about his ex-wife marrying an officer from the department and he forced other officers to shoot him."

"I ripped out the little marble memorial to Manny Washington," Donnally said, "but eventually they'll make the connection. Except the symbolism doesn't really work the way Chen wanted. Manny was a victim of trial by media and Hollywood ignorance and Chen was a coconspirator in a murder."

The judge's housekeeper entered carrying a tray bearing a coffee carafe and three cups and saucers. She set it down, poured for Donnally and Navarro, then walked around the desk. Donnally noticed her slipping the judge a small plastic pill box as she poured. He wondered whether the judge had visited his doctor to obtain medication either for memory problems or for depression, or for both, to get him through these days.

They waited until she'd left the room to continue.

"There are no credible witnesses left in the Dominguez case," Donnally said. "Benaga set it up, and Chico didn't see who did it."

McMullin squinted at him. "You really think the governor would intervene based on the rantings of a suicidal ex-cop? And over a distinction between first- and second-degree murder the public won't understand?" The judge's voice ratcheted up. "And implied malice? Implied malice? Other than lawyers, there aren't a dozen people in California who could tell you what it is. Lying in wait is lying in wait. Murder is murder. Dead is dead."

"And I'll bet Madding was on the phone to the governor ten minutes after Chen hit the ground," Navarro said, "trying to discredit him."

"He may not need to discredit him," McMullin said. "All we have is hearsay from a deranged and now dead officer and no proof that Dominguez wasn't the shooter. And even if you could get over those hurdles, the only other witness is hiding in Mexico."

"San Jose," Navarro said.

"Which one? There have got to be dozens of San Jose's down there."

"No," Donnally said. "Chico is in San Jose, California. In Little Saigon. That's why we're here. If there is any new evidence to be had, it's going to come from him."

"What do you need from me?"

"Authorization to take him into custody."

"Chico was afraid to show up for his court appearances in some minor cases he had going after he was questioned in the

Heredia murder," Navarro said. "And bench warrants were issued for his arrest."

"My guess is he fled to Salinas to hide out both from the warrants and from the Heredia case," Donnally said.

"Heredia probably worried him the most," Navarro said. "The worst that happens on the others is that he would've done a couple of years."

"Heredia was a murder conspiracy," Donnally said. "Twenty-five to life. And since nobody gets paroled on murder anymore, it would be life."

"There were only three people in the house," Navarro said, "Chico, Junior, and Benaga. Talking about which Sureño to kill to get even for the death of the Norteño on Mission Street. Then Benaga left to do it."

"Benaga runs in to collect a reward by telling Chen that Chico killed Heredia," Donnally said. "Chico gets hauled in. He's wondering why. He didn't do it, so nobody could've IDed him."

"Exactly," Navarro said, "and the fact that he was a suspect at all meant that either Benaga or Junior had snitched him off."

"Nobody else knew about it."

"Then Chico ran off to Salinas to buy some time to figure things out."

"And he knew that even if he didn't pull the trigger himself," Donnally said, "he could still be convicted of conspiracy to commit murder."

Donnally realized that he and Navarro were volleying their analysis back and forth. There was something visceral about it, giving him a sense of movement. It made him miss working with Navarro and regret not fighting his forced retirement from the department.

"So that means he was hiding not only from Benaga and Junior," Judge McMullin said, "but also from Dominguez."

Navarro leaned in toward the judge. "Dominguez? Why Dominguez?"

McMullin's face flushed and he swallowed. Donnally realized the judge had confused the Rojo and Heredia murders.

McMullin looked over at Donnally. "I meant . . ."

But the judge didn't know what he'd meant, or more panicking for him, couldn't think of what he should have meant.

Donnally again felt the hurt deep in his chest. At the minimum the judge had made the kind of mistake people involved in thinking through complex facts and relationships always make. At the maximum, he'd just done a self-diagnosis.

"I think you meant to say that Chico had a lot of people to hide from," Donnally said, trying to ease the judge's embarrassment. "Chico was afraid not only of Benaga and Junior, the Norteños, but also the Sureños. The Sureños would've assumed that it was the Norteños who killed Heredia and Benaga would've put word out on the street that Chico was the particular Norteño who did it. So the Sureños would be on the hunt for Chico, too."

"With Chico running away to Salinas and hiding from everybody," Navarro said, "Benaga told *La Mesa* that Chico was trying to get out of the Norteños and got permission to have him killed."

Donnally thought of Rosa, Chico's mother, and the power her brother-in-law had over her. "And that means Chico's own uncle, Juan Gallegos, had to have been part of the decision."

McMullin's gaze fell for a moment on his undrunk coffee, his lips compressed. He shook his head. "Unbelievable that someone could do that to his own brother's son."

"The rule going in is gang first," Navarro said, "and everyone and everything else second."

"It's even worse," Donnally said. "Chico's father is also housed in Pelican Bay. Not in Ad Seg with *La Mesa*, but close by. Since he worked in the kitchen and was a link in the Norteños communication network, he might even have passed on the coded order himself without realizing it."

Then Donnally had a thought almost too horrific to think. That Chico's father had realized it and that Chico's leaving the Norteños truly would have been blood out.

"Our guess is that Chico recognized it was Norteños who'd shot him," Navarro said, "not Sureños, and told his mother when she ran outside the house after he was shot. She called the ambulance and when they got to the hospital they decided it would be better if he played dead."

"That way he'd never have to worry about Benaga or Junior, or the Norteños or the Sureños."

"But if you're hooked up to monitors, you can't play dead." Navarro snapped his fingers. "His mother must've paid off a doctor—"

"Or maybe just begged a doctor who understood the Salinas gang world, had seen enough gunshot victims—"

"To unplug him and pronounce him and later sign a death certificate. She then sent it to the public defender's office and they used it to get his cases dismissed."

"What we need now is for you to reissue the bench warrants for Chico," Donnally said, as Navarro slid a file folder across the desk to the judge. "And make them no bail. We can't take a chance he'll disappear again."

As McMullin looked over the forms, a thought struck Donnally.

Why hadn't someone ever wondered why Rosa had bothered to get the cases dismissed? Why not just let them age and get purged on their own?

It wasn't like a dead Chico would be arrested on the bench warrants or he'd apply for a top-secret security clearance in the afterlife.

The only point of doing it was to keep him from being arrested on them and brought back to San Francisco. Even if the police ran his prints, the warrants would be out of the system.

Maybe no one thought of it because there was something disquieting about leaving warrants outstanding for a dead person.

Or maybe it was simply that the dead are forgiven.

"There's also an arrest warrant for Oscar Benaga in the Heredia case in there."

McMullin looked up.

"Should I be the one to do this?" McMullin asked. "Isn't there a conflict of interest? Aren't I the beneficiary?"

Beneficiary?

The inapt word seemed to vibrate in the air. From the look on his face, Donnally guessed Navarro felt it also.

Maybe Grassner was right all along. What had been driving McMullin all along wasn't the illegitimacy of the conviction, but that *he was just a judge starting to panic when the needle starts aiming for the vein.*

McMullin's rulings in the case might be vindicated, but only Dominguez could be the beneficiary. But then Donnally realized that this couldn't be right. McMullin didn't want to be vindicated, wasn't driven by a hope of vindication, but by conscience.

Donnally heard the front door open and close, and then the soft footfalls coming along the carpet behind him. The housekeeper walked around the desk again, this time handing Judge

McMullin the morning *Chronicle*. He glanced at the front-page headline and turned the paper toward Donnally and Navarro.

GOVERNOR REJECTS DOMINGUEZ PETITION, EXECUTION SET FOR MIDNIGHT

"I guess we don't have time for a philosophical discussion about who's the beneficiary," Donnally said, and then pointed at the warrants. "We need your signature."

The judge signed both and handed them to Navarro, who headed toward the door. Donnally turned to follow him, then turned back.

"I know you're probably thinking it," Donnally said, "but I need to say it out loud."

In truth, Donnally didn't know whether the judge had figured out what Donnally had, but he needed to make sure McMullin understood where their conversation that had begun on the Smith River had now taken them.

"The jury might've gotten it right, even though they might not have understood the logic of it. It could be that Benaga decided not just to scare Rojo, but to have him killed and try to step into his place. And the best way to cover his tracks and conceal what he was doing was to set things up so a Sureño pulls the trigger. Benaga moves up in his organization and the Sureño moves up in his."

The judge took in a long breath and exhaled. "And by Sureño, you mean Dominguez."

Donnally nodded. "I mean Dominguez."

Looking out the rear side windows of an SFPD surveillance van parked on Senter Road in San Jose's Little Saigon, Donnally and Navarro watched a man in a small pickup truck pull into the shadow next to Flaco Ortega Auto Repair. As he walked into the glow of the overhead street lights and headed toward the still dark office, Donnally saw the face in the photo in the Salinas homicide file of Chico Gallegos.

Sunrise was still an hour away and the curbs were lined with delivery trucks and service vehicles waiting for their work day to begin. The Laundromat on the far side of property was still closed, as was the Vietnamese noodle café on the near side.

The intermittent growl and whoosh of the sparse commuter traffic was the only sound on the street and the headlights approaching and the taillights receding the only motion.

Having confirmed Chico's arrival, Navarro called San Jose PD and asked the dispatcher to set up a perimeter to box him in if he tried to make a run when they made their move. They hadn't wanted to use a SWAT team for fear a display of guns and raid gear would get Chico screaming for a lawyer. Since his old cases had been dismissed, he was no longer represented.

A car turned onto the property and came to a stop.

They watched the office lights come on, followed by the bay doors rolling up. Chico then walked from the office carrying a clipboard. He spoke to the driver for a moment, then moved around to the front and raised the hood. A middle-aged woman dressed in a nurse's flowered scrubs joined him in looking at the engine. Donnally heard her making a clicking sound with her tongue and then Chico laughing.

Donnally caught the motion of a head peeking around the far corner of the Laundromat. In the shadow he looked Asian or Hispanic.

Donnally pointed toward the corner. "Somebody else is watching Chico. We better move up front in case something jumps off."

Staying low, Navarro climbed forward into the driver's seat and Donnally into the passenger seat.

Another laugh from Chico and the ripping sound of him tearing the estimate from his pad.

The head ducked back. The woman took the page, then turned and walked toward a car waiting on the street in front of the Laundromat.

The head reappeared, attached to the body of a homeless man pushing a grocery cart filled with boxes of oil and filters.

"Looks like the guy burglarized an auto parts store," Navarro said.

He rolled the cart up to where Chico still stood by the woman's car.

"You Flaco?"

Chico nodded.

"My *compadre* told me you might want some of this stuff."

Chico pawed through the boxes. "Fifty for all of it."

"Once a crook, always a crook," Navarro said. "You want to grab both of them?"

Donnally shook his head. "We better let the homeless guy go and wait for SJPD to finish getting set up. We don't want to risk a fight and take a chance Chico might get away."

Chico pointed toward the interior of the bay and led the man inside where they piled everything on the workbench along the wall closest to the Laundromat. Chico pulled some bills out of his pocket, counted some out, and handed them over. The man shoved the cash into his jacket.

Donnally's body tensed when the man's hand stayed inside and began to move around, fearing he'd come out with a gun. Donnally reached for his holster with one hand and the door handle with the other, poised to jump out.

The man's hand came up. Donnally leaned toward the door.

Then he saw it was a fist, not a gun. It opened and the man displayed a handful of coins and appeared to ask if he could trade them for bills. Chico nodded and the man set the change on the workbench.

Donnally settled back.

Navarro chuckled. "Yeah, I was thinking the same—"

Shots exploded, coming from a Mustang stopped in the street. Pulling his gun, Donnally spotted the homeless man fall into Chico. More shots and they both dropped.

Donnally jumped down and using the front of the van for cover rapid-fired into the interior shadows of the Mustang, just behind the extended arms holding an AK-47. He heard Navarro firing from the driver's side.

The arms went limp and the rifle fell and rattled on the pavement.

The back of the Mustang jerked down, then lunged forward, the wheels throwing back a cloud of burning rubber. Donnally spotted cars coming into his line of sight and held his fire. It drove on for another thirty yards and slowed. The passenger door swung open and a body flopped into the street. The car accelerated again, swinging the door closed.

Navarro was now running toward the garage, yelling a description of the Mustang into his cell phone and a request for an ambulance.

Donnally ran to the body, blood pooling on the pavement. One look at the N-O-R-T-E on the back of the shooter's head told him it was Oscar Benaga, dumped by his crime partners as a delay and a diversion. He kneeled down and reached for his neck, and for the second time in eight hours, Donnally failed to find a pulse.

CHAPTER 50

Your whole life is about to pass before your eyes," Donnally told Chico in the garage office.

Chico's shirt was wet and splotched with the dead homeless man's blood. He sat in a chair, back against the wall. Donnally was propped against the desk.

Navarro waited near the street to delay the San Jose police detectives in order to give Donnally a shot at Chico unhindered by the need to Mirandize him.

"It's all in your hands how it ends."

"I didn't kill Heredia, man. I've never killed nobody."

"That's not what I want to know about."

"You ain't no cop. You can't do nothing to me."

"It won't be me." Donnally pointed at him. "You know what the penalties for perjury are?"

"Who cares. A year, two years. I can do the time."

"In the Dominguez case it's death." Donnally glanced at his watch. "The moment he gets the needle, your perjury becomes a capital crime."

Chico's fists clenched. He leaned forward to rise. Donnally pushed him back.

"I get death row and the prosecutor gets a promotion?"

"That prosecutor has gotten his last promotion, but the worst that happens to him is a little obstruction of justice charge. A hand slap. Maybe not even that. All he has to say is that he believed you when you first claimed it was Dominguez and he didn't believe you when you changed your story."

Chico looked down. "This is fucked up, man. I didn't ask to get put in the middle of all this. Twenty years ducking and hiding."

"Tell me the truth about the death of Edgar Rojo Senior."

Chico's faced turned pained and pleading. "Don't make me do this, man. Ask Chen. He knows everything I do, and a lot more."

"Chen's dead. Last night. A kind of a suicide."

"Then Madding, ask Madding." Chico threw up his hands. "Ask anybody. Everybody knows."

Donnally recognized that by everybody Chico really meant the limited group relevant to him. Benaga, his father, his uncle—and his mother. Donnally remembered her bringing him a letter when Donnally had surveilled their meeting and had tried to follow them.

"What was in the letter?"

"What letter?"

"The one your mother showed you a couple of days ago."

"How—"

Donnally waved off the question. "It doesn't make a difference how I know."

Chico reddened. "I know it don't make no difference. What I want to know is how you're gonna protect us from my uncle Juan?"

Now all the pieces gravitated together in Donnally's mind. The prowling gangsters across the street from Rosa Gallegos's house had been watching and the letter wasn't a message she was carrying from *La Mesa* to the street, but a warning from her brother-in-law to keep her mouth shut. Maybe they started tailing her to make sure she did, and she led them to her son.

And now Donnally understood for certain what it had all been about.

"You mean the killing of Edgar Rojo was part of a Norteño power struggle between your uncle's faction and Rojo's faction?"

Chico glanced around his office, his business, one that helped support his mother. His eyes focused on a photo on the desk—a woman, two small children, and him—then on another, his mother.

"You didn't answer my question," Chico said.

"Tell the truth and you'll be protected, and your wife and kids and mother. Lie, and nobody can protect you."

Chico's eyes moved on, toward a certificate of graduation from an automotive school, his state license, his desk, his file cabinet, a calendar showing a photo of Puerto Vallarta and Banderas Bay, his face taking on an expression of a man leaving his home for the last time or gazing back at a receding shoreline.

"It had nothing to do with the Sureños," Chico said, still staring at the picture, "and the Sureños had nothing to do with killing Rojo. Not Dominguez." He shook his head. "Dominguez never shot nobody. They weren't no threat back then. Benaga made up that whole Sureño takeover story and the Sureños played along because it made them look bigger than they were."

"You tell Madding?"

"Yeah. I told him. Everything. I went to see him the day before he made me testify." He finally looked up at Donnally. "How you think my uncle made it from a street captain up to *La Mesa*?"

Edgar Rojo Jr. stood in the doorway glaring into the San Francisco jail interview room. A jailor was standing behind him.

"They said my attorney was here. Not the *chingaso* who got me locked up."

As Donnally had threatened to do if Junior lost control of himself, he'd called Junior's parole agent after driving him from the hospital to his grandmother's apartment and told him Junior had made a threat to kill a government informant. The parole agent arrested him an hour later.

Donnally rose from the chair. "It was for your own good."

Junior's arm was still in a sling.

"Who's he?" Junior jutted his head toward Navarro.

"A homicide detective."

Junior smirked. "How many times you gonna go down that road before you catch on I'm not going along?"

Donnally looked over at Navarro and smiled. "Usually he just says, 'I ain't no snitch.' He's especially talkative today."

Donnally tilted his head toward the empty chair. "Have a seat. You've got a decision to make."

"The only decision I got to make is whether to kick your ass once I get out of here."

Donnally pointed at Junior's shoulder and smiled. "I guess you really will have to kick me since you can't do any punching."

"Yeah. I owe you for that too."

Navarro signaled for the jailor to close the door. They all recognized that if Junior had intended to walk out, he would've done it already.

There was too much Junior wanted to learn beyond what had been reported in the press about Judge McMullin's hand-delivered letter to the governor and the stay of execution that followed and the truth about the deaths of Chen and Benaga and of the murder of his father by Chico's uncle, Juan Gallegos.

Junior sat down, then pointed back toward the housing unit. "I saw it on the news. Is Juan Gallegos gonna get charged with killing my dad?"

Donnally shook his head. "The slug matched the gun Gallegos used in the murder six months later that put him in prison for the rest of his life, but we can't prove he pulled the trigger the night your father was killed. We've got no witnesses. Chico says he was the only person right in front of the apartment, but the shot came from behind him, from the roof of the church across the street. It was too dark for him to see who was up there."

"I thought the angle—"

"No. The theory was that your father was looking down and the shot came up. The truth is probably that he saw some motion across the street and was looking right at Juan when he fired. The trajectory would have been the same and the slug shattered the glass so there was no way to determine the direction."

Donnally knew it would've hurt Junior so he didn't describe that trajectory. An inch below his father's hairline in the front and then a horizontal path until the slug ricocheted off the back of his skull.

"Israel Dominguez was in the area," Donnally said. "He lied about that, but he couldn't have fired the shot. Chico puts him on the street half a block away with no line of sight to the apartment window."

"What about the shell casing in the driveway?"

"It was New Year's Eve and there were lots of gunshots that night," Navarro said.

"You mean Dominguez lying about not being there don't mean nothing?"

"It mostly means that his attempt to lie himself out of a frame just tied him in deeper. It made him look even guiltier of lying in wait, the special circumstance that made it a capital case."

Junior sat there, shaking his head.

"I didn't think you cared that much about lying," Donnally said, "or truth telling for that matter."

"Why you saying that?"

"Because the first words out of your mouth are always the same."

"Who you asking me to snitch on?"

"It's not about that."

"Then what's it about?"

"You already know. It's about a decision you've got to make right now about what you've done and who you've been and who you're going to be for the rest of your life."

Donnally thought of Judge McMullin. Who he would be in a few months or years was out of his control. It was a matter of physiology, not choice, and soon enough he'd be nobody, for who he had been would fade until he was just a body without a mind, without memories, without a past or a future, and then that body would fail too.

And he thought of Israel Dominguez, who grew up wanting to be nobody, a fairy-tale character who tried to disappear into the earth, and who was now condemned to bear forever the scars on his hand like a gang tattoo that couldn't be burned off.

Junior had a choice, but Donnally didn't know whether he had the courage to make it.

"How much time can I get?" Junior asked.

"Does it make a difference?"

The question answered itself in the silence that followed.

Donnally looked at Junior and realized that a junior he really was, a nine-year-old boy in a twenty-nine-year-old man's body.

"This gang outreach is just a lie, isn't it? You're deceiving the kids and you're deceiving yourself."

Junior's face flushed, but he didn't answer.

"You're not doing anything to get them out of that world. They acted it out on the street. No snitching and no witnessing. That's why they jumped in to help you."

Junior still didn't say anything.

Donnally slid a sheet of paper and a pen across the table. "It's up to you."

Junior stared at it, seeing words that weren't yet there.

Fifteen minutes later, Donnally and Navarro walked out.

Two hours later, Donnally handed Israel Dominguez Junior's confession to ordering the hit on him. They sat at the same table on death row. A stay of execution was only a stay. He'd have to remain among the condemned until the attorney general's investigation was complete and the governor's pardon came through.

Israel read it over.

"What am I supposed to do with this?"

"That's up to you." Donnally was aware that the words echoed what he'd said to Junior just before he wrote it. "It hasn't gone to the D.A. for charging yet."

"Is Junior locked up already?"

Donnally shook his head. "He was, on a parole violation, but I asked his parole agent to lift the hold and let him go. He won't be running anywhere. He's ready for whatever the court hands him."

Israel read it over again, then folded it over once, then a second time, and tore it up.

"That's good enough for me," Israel finally said. "He had to grow up his way and I had to grow up mine."

CHAPTER 52 ════════════

P eople versus Harvey Madding."

The clerk announced the arraignment without looking up from her desk as though trying to shield herself from the focused lenses of the news cameras and the peering eyes of the reporters in the courtroom.

The disproportionality of everything struck Donnally as never before, even when he was telling Chico Gallegos that his penalty if Israel Dominguez had been executed would have been death.

Judge Madding stood accused of a mere misdemeanor obstruction of justice, barely more than an infraction, but one that could have cost the life of an innocent man for a murder he hadn't committed.

All this time Donnally had thought he was investigating the worst of crimes, a capital murder, while it turned out to be the most minor of misdemeanors. But it was like a fulcrum set so light a mere touch would move a boulder.

He wondered whether Judge McMullin felt the same imbalance or even could have imagined it just two weeks earlier.

Donnally gazed up at McMullin, but his mind saw not the man sitting there before him on the bench, but the judge first standing in the Smith River, a swirl of snow in the air, and then sitting and gazing down at the translucent orange flame of a rock-ringed fire. The judge's mind struggling with his memories and working his way toward talking about the Dominguez case, starting with the law.

Murder is the unlawful killing of a human being with malice aforethought.

The judge had stared across the river, as though a generation of faces and cases had been flowing through his mind.

Then McMullin had moved on to the standard of proof to support first- and second-degree murder convictions, but Donnally didn't yet know which face and which case had come to preoccupy him, and feared that it was the judge himself.

Malice may be express or implied. It is express when there is manifested a deliberate intention unlawfully to take away the life of a fellow creature.

Malice aforethought, premeditation, and intent. Those elements had been the source of the judge's doubt over all those years.

And he was right to doubt them, but for the wrong reasons.

Judge Harvey Madding and his attorney, Robert Callahan, rose from behind the defense table.

Donnally recognized the lawyer when he entered the courtroom. He specialized in representing cops and prosecutors and was an expert at smothering the flames of public outrage. He was the master of the two-minute court appearance, never giving reporters anything new to write about.

Callahan spoke first. "We waive reading of the complaint."

McMullin looked up from the file in front of him, his face flushed as though he'd been caught daydreaming.

"Excuse me?"

Uneasiness vibrated through Donnally, fear that McMullin's mind wasn't lucid enough for the task before him, that the intermittent confusion displayed during that last meeting had returned. Surely, he must have heard and understood Callahan's words, which were as standard as entering a plea and setting a next hearing date.

"I said we'll waive reading of the complaint."

McMullin glared down at Callahan and his voice took on an edge.

"Did I ask you a question, Counsel?"

Donnally felt his fear sigh out of him. McMullin was in control of himself and of his courtroom.

Callahan drew back, surprised and embarrassed, then glanced over at the district attorney, who stared ahead.

Donnally wasn't sure whether the prosecutor was reacting to the judge's tone or ducking through silence from the obvious conflict of interest involved in the D.A.'s office prosecuting one of its former members.

"No, Your Honor. You didn't ask a question."

"Clerk, will you please read the complaint."

"On or about March 24—"

Janie sat down next to Donnally in the seat he had saved for her.

"Why go through the motions?" she whispered. "No California D.A. or ex-D.A. has ever been convicted of obstruction of justice for hiding evidence. I checked on the Internet before I drove over here."

"That doesn't mean there can't be a first. And maybe this will be it."

The clerk again, "The said defendant, Harvey Madding, in the City and County of San Francisco, State of California, did willfully, unlawfully, and with malice aforethought—"

Madding collapsed into his chair. Callahan's arms flew up. The gallery gasped as one person, smothering the clerk's words. She raised her voice against the rising disbelief. Bailiffs stepped between Madding and the gallery.

Donnally leaned forward, only catching fragments: "conspire," "Chen," "Benaga," "suborn," "perjury," "reckless disregard," and finally, "attempt to murder a human being, Israel Dominguez."

McMullin hammered his gavel, all the while looking Donnally in the eye, and both of them thinking of that day on the river.

Malice is implied when the circumstances show an abandoned and malignant heart.

Donnally felt Janie's hand grip his forearm as reporters ran past them toward the hallway. She was squinting up at him when he looked over. He answered her question before she asked it.

"Attempted second-degree murder."

No other mental state need be shown.

CHAPTER 53

Donnally stood on the pebbled bank of the Smith River watching Judge McMullin standing waist deep ten yards from shore. The current separated around his waders leaving a slick of quiet water below him. The setting sun, streaking the flat water between the rapids with shimmering yellow, orange, and gold, enveloped the judge in its glow.

The fluidity of the judge's casts first surprised Donnally, then he realized it shouldn't have. After all, it was too soon for the disease to show itself in the physical symptoms of fumbling hands and unsteady steps. But then he realized the relief the judge must feel, the liberation, not that Alzheimer's was an excuse for his confusions and failures of memory, but an explanation for them.

As the last bit of light descended in the west and twilight rose in the east, Donnally thought back on his father and the judge sitting together in the waiting room of the Stanford-VA Alzheimer's Research Center a week earlier. It was there that doctors discovered the plaque-causing proteins that cause the disease in McMullin's blood. His father had been looking for an opportunity to make up for his mistakes, to share what he'd learned about the disease during the making of his film, and Donnally had given it to him.

The two looked like old men sharing a park bench. Donnally had felt himself well up when he noticed his father had taken the judge's hand in his. His parents had always been so private in their affection, and his father had always been so self-absorbed, that Donnally hadn't expected this kind of tenderness. He wondered, even found himself hoping, that the gesture meant something more, that a time of insight into himself and sympathy for others had finally come for his father, too.

Donnally used the distraction of the nurse standing in the open door leading to the examining rooms and calling out a patient's name to turn away and wipe his eyes.

Now they teared up again, this time bitten by the chill wind sweeping up the river from the Pacific as he watched the judge cast.

The first time they had stood together in this place, the judge seemed less a fisherman than a fugitive, running away from the past, driven by fear, but at the same time drawn back to it by conscience. And Donnally still didn't think McMullin had become a fisherman. He doubted it would've have made any difference to the judge if his lure bore no hook at all.

Donnally knew the river too well to think there were any steelhead still moving upstream. The run was over. The few fish left were heading back to the sea, driven both by instinct and by a rain-fed flow that sped them home as fast as birds in flight. The judge had said he wanted to come anyway, needed to come, and not because he'd reached a time of ending, of resignation, of submission to the forces of nature and of fate, but because the river was life and light, and time and hope, even as he faced the coming of his night.

Notes and Acknowledgments ═══════

Each Harlan Donnally novel focuses on a problem in the criminal justice process. *Act of Deceit* dealt with a systemic failure relating to defendants found incompetent to stand trial. *A Criminal Defense* dealt with criminality on the part of the defense. *Night Is the Hunter* deals with criminality on the part of the prosecution.

As far as I know, this is the first crime novel based on the notion of implied malice. And for good reason. It's a complicated concept.

For those who might be interested in the underlying legal issues, the following is a standard jury instruction regarding implied malice:

1. The defendant intentionally committed an act;

2. The natural and probable consequences of the act were dangerous to human life;

3. At the time the defendant acted, the defendant knew the act was dangerous to human life; and

4. The defendant deliberately acted with conscious disregard for human life.

—*California Criminal Jury Instructions*, Judicial Council of California, 2011, Section 520.3 (paraphrased)

These elements, which are consistent from state to state, are also involved when a person engages in a provocative act that causes another to take an action dangerous to human life.

To state more formally what is shown in the story:

First, Harvey Madding, along with coconspirators, intentionally committed acts that were inherently dangerous to human life and that would have resulted in the execution of Israel Dominguez, but for Judge McMullin and Harlan Donnally's intervention.

Second, Madding engaged in a provocative act by causing the jury to convict on the crime of murder with the special circumstance of lying in wait, recommending the death sentence, and causing the judge to impose it.

Lawyers and judges, depending both on the state they live in and their views of the law, will disagree about whether a conviction for attempted second-degree murder or a conspiracy to commit second-degree murder would stand up on appeal. (Higher courts around the country have differed in their answers and legislatures have tried to resolve the issues.) But since I am a writer of crime novels and not of law review articles, I'll leave them to argue among themselves.

I ran across the Rumpelstiltskin analogy in psychiatric research into the disturbed inner logic of homicide conducted by Andrew K. Ruotolo, M.D., and reworked it for this story. The

Alzheimer's theme was prompted by my reading the wonderful novel, *Before I Forget*, by Leonard Pitts Jr. (Bolden Books, 2009).

Thanks to two fine criminal defense attorneys, Chris Cannon, who read the book in advance and offered suggestions that clarified and improved the story, and Louisa Havstad, who was kind enough to talk though some legal points early on. Thanks, as always, to Scott Sugarman; Bruce Kaplan; Julie Quater; John, Jack, and Michael Beuttler; Bobbie Chinsky; John Somerville; Diane Gore-Uecker; John Uecker; Dennis and Judy Barley; Rick and Gail Monge; Randy and Margie Schmidt; Trevor and Cassie Patterson; Glenn and Judy Pollock; and Carl and Kathy Polhemus. Thanks also to Katy Pose, PA-C, Ranjana Advani, M.D., and Alan Yuen, M.D., for fifteen extremely interesting years and to my wife, Liz, my first, last, and best reader.

Thanks also to my editor, Emily Krump, my copyeditor, Laurie McGee, and my publicist, Heidi Richter, who did such fine work in preparing and presenting this book.

About the Author

Steven Gore is a renowned private investigator turned "master-ful" writer *(Publishers Weekly)*, who combines "a command of storytelling" with "insider knowledge" *(Library Journal)*. With a unique voice honed both on the street and in the Harlan Donnally and Graham Gage novels, Gore's stories are grounded in his decades spent investigating murder; fraud; organized crime; corruption; and drug, sex, and arms trafficking throughout the Americas, Europe, and Asia. He lives in the San Francisco Bay Area.